MINDLESS PASSION

Haven took a step forward. "Such gentle pleading from a woman makes a man soft-brained; he loses concentration. My men are so distracted by attending to your needs that they fail to attend to their duty."

"Let me be certain of what you mean, sir." Gennie's hands went to her hips as temper began to override her control. "My manner with your men disturbs you, and therefore you would have me behave in an unseemly fashion. I think it is not your men who've become soft-brained. I know only one person who is dissatisfied with my actions. And that is you, Sir Addle-pate. From the day we met, you have treated me as if I were evil incarnate. You alone behave with brainless stupidity around me. If you think . . ."

"What I think is that you must needs be shown how a man behaves when a woman causes him to lose his mind."

On those words he closed his arms about her. Her feet left the ground. While she was busy trying to grasp his shoulders for balance, he kissed her. Gennie forgot to worry about having both feet in the air. She forgot to clutch at his shoulders.

Instead, she tunneled her hands into the warm, dark silk at his nape. She nearly forgot to breathe until the gentle scrape of his teeth on her lower lip caused her to open her mouth in surprise and inhale. Then his hot velvet tongue was in her mouth, succulent with his personal flavor and seeking her own. The sensation was wondrous, brilliant and dark, frightening and secure.

Susan Charnley

A True and Perfect Knight

LEISURE BOOKS NEW YORK CITY

A LEISURE BOOK®

December 2001

Published by

Dorchester Publishing Co., Inc.
276 Fifth Avenue
New York, NY 10001

ISBN 0-8439-4945-7

Visit us on the web at www.dorchesterpub.com.

To three of the four men who have inspired me in my life and in my writing: Raymond T. Romain, who is the best of sounding boards and a true friend. Dr. John Alford, who is the perfect professor and a great medievalist. Chip, who is my own True and Perfect Knight.

A True and Perfect Knight

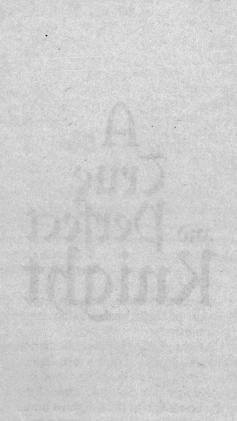

Chapter One

Yorkshire, May 1282
One league from the former Dreyford Castle

"Rumor says that the bottom of a privy is more attractive than Roger's widow." Privately, Sir Haven de Sessions wished the widow to the devil, along with the incessant rain.

"No noblewoman could be that ugly, especially one from the court in Paris," protested Soames, Haven's second-in-command.

Haven thought of the execution he had witnessed and felt his jaw clench. "If God is just, Genvieve Dreyford's face will expose every coil and stain in her black soul. 'Tis only right that the true nature of the woman who led my best friend to treason show on her face."

Soames shook his head at his commander's remarks. "Do you suppose that is her?" He slanted his head in the direction of six sodden figures huddled some distance from the byway.

Haven followed Soames's glance. "Possibly. We have come almost a league from the castle. That is the distance the bailiff claimed he had taken the widow and her entourage when the new lord threw her out. But, I doubt . . ." His words trailed off as he peered through the downpour at the figure that stepped to the front of the pitiful group.

The woman stood tall and straight, shoulders back, legs braced. She anchored herself, as if by sheer will alone she could defend the others. A young boy clung to her skirts.

Could this be the suspected traitoress who had caused the downfall of his best friend, Roger Dreyford? Haven wanted to see her face, to see if she appeared as evil as he believed her to be. Distance and the obscuring rain defeated him.

"But what, sir?"

Soames's question shook Haven from his musings. "But I doubt a woman like Roger's widow would stand out in the rain or tolerate such a humble abode."

"Are you so sure?"

"Of what? That she led Roger to treason? Or that she is proud and greedy as any of the Parisians we met on our way home from the Holy Land?"

"Either or both. Even before his marriage, Roger was ever looking for adventure. The search always landed him in trouble."

"Aye, but the trouble was harmless for the most part."

"Marriage should settle a man," Soames commented.

"He told me in his letters how unappealing he found his wife. Such a marriage is not like to settle a man of Roger's stamp."

"Odd, Roger never met a woman who didn't attract him in some way."

" 'Tis what he claimed he disliked most about her, along with her constant nagging. Her unceasing demands drove him from home."

"Of course Roger would never lie," Soames said dryly.

"We both know he loved to embellish a story," Haven said, recalling the many nights spent as squires, when only Roger's tales had relieved the loneliness.

"And never to his disadvantage."

"Aye." Haven had to admit to his friend's failings. Roger had been a charming rogue, never serious, but always dependable in a fight. What else but a woman could drive a loyal friend to betray the king?

Haven signaled his men. They turned their horses from the muddy track and came to a halt before the group crowding around a fire.

The woman bent, spoke to the child, and sent him to a stout, buxom servant near the small blaze. Then the tall woman resumed her defensive posture.

"Who are you, and what do you here?" The words danced forth on the most exotic voice Haven had ever heard. Dark and rich, it first bit the ear like the smoke in a sultan's chamber, then licked and soothed with sweet rasping strokes that somehow matched his rising pulse. He felt the tremors of that voice all the way to his groin.

"I asked, what do you here?" The woman repeated her challenge.

Haven shook his head free of her siren's call. "I seek the widow of Roger Dreyford."

She studied him.

The noisesome smoke from the peat fire made his

eyes water. Rain drizzled down his back and off his chin. The jingle of harness and creak of leather issued from his troop as it fanned out around the people on the ground. Bitter resentment toward this woman and his own part in his friend's death urged Haven to trample her into the mud. He held still, unwilling to lose control. Despite his feelings, he would keep his vow to Roger and protect his family.

"*C'est moi.* I am Lady Genvieve Dreyford."

Did that dusky voice tremble just the slightest bit? Haven looked her over and swallowed the satisfied gasp that tried to escape his throat. *Sweet Jesu, she's hideous.*

Purple-black splotches ringed her eyes. Her skin paled to chalk against dark, colorless clothing. Deformity stamped her features. Her face pushed out on one side. Odd streaks hollowed the opposite cheek. A lump decorated her forehead over one eye. As much as her appearance gratified, something about it bothered him. It was that lump, he decided. "Come closer."

She hesitated, but evidently felt that compliance was the better part of valor.

When she stood by his mount's shoulder, Haven removed one glove and grasped her chin between his thumb and forefinger. The softness of her skin shocked him. The impulse to stroke her twitched in his hand. Instead, he turned her face up to his. Astonished, he felt his eyes widen.

She was far from ugly. He had seen lumps and bruises like those that adorned her face on battle-weary men. Beneath the swelling and discoloration lay a bone structure that Aphrodite would envy. Eyes that blazed green lightning glared out at him from beneath delicately arched brows. God created wide, bow-shaped lips like hers for only one purpose.

Haven ignored the hardness forming below his waist. He glanced downward. Her shapeless, soggy robe hid any hint of her figure. For all he knew, her face was her only asset, and someone had done that serious damage.

"What happened to you?" He growled the question, angry with himself that he cared even the tiniest bit about this woman's pain.

"I was stoned," she said flatly.

At the unexpected reply, Haven's hand dropped from her face. "By whom?"

"Why, the king's good yeomen, of course. They thought to impress their new lord by stoning the widow of a traitor. But why should you care?" Her level voice struck blows at him. "You are a stranger and have no responsibility for me. You may even share the wish to destroy me simply because my parents arranged my marriage with a man who would commit treason." Her beautiful lips twisted around the ugly words.

She bent and quickly rose again. "Here." She thrust a fist-sized rock beneath his nose.

He stared at her. She couldn't know that until moments before he touched her, he'd believed hanging was too good for her. That, if given the chance, he would have cast the first stone.

More horrified by his own thoughts than her actions, he recoiled. The movement startled his mount. Haven's steed reared and threatened to kick her to Jerusalem. She neither cowered nor retreated. He steadied the horse.

"I have every responsibility for you, madame. King

Edward commands your presence. I am here to take you to him."

Her pale face went ashen beneath the bruises. She was afraid. He was certain. But of what? She was already destitute; what else had she to fear? There was more to Genvieve Dreyford than met the eye. He vowed to reveal every one of her secrets.

He watched her recover. She tilted her chin upward and squared her shoulders. A minute amount of color returned to her complexion. She broadened her stance and raised a fist across her chest, as if by that small gesture she could prevent her destiny. "Anyone may claim the king's authority. I shall remain here until you tell me who you are."

He admired her bravado, even if he considered it foolish. She lacked both weapons and the men to defy his authority, yet she did so without hesitation.

He advanced his horse, until his stirrup brushed her shoulder. He smelled the noxious muck encrusted on her clothes mixed with the unexpected scent of lavender. Still she did not yield, even when uncertainty shivered in her glance.

He leaned forward in his saddle. "Madame, I am Sir Haven de Sessions . . ."

Her breath hissed at his words.

So, she recognized his name. Then she knew he was Roger's best friend, as well as the man who had taken her husband to the king for trial and execution. Just as well. ". . . At Edward's order, I am to take you and all Dreyford's surviving family safely to Chester. There the king will adjudge your fate."

Her lip curled. "Pah. What judgment can be found with a king whose vengeance is legend? What safety with a man like you, who would betray a friend? I will not go."

Haven clenched his teeth, refusing to acknowledge the hit she scored. "If you wish, madame," he spoke with studied pleasantness. "Edward's orders are clear. You must give me your full cooperation. Your refusal will be taken as an admission of guilt, and you shall be hanged on the spot. Either way, Roger's sister, Rebecca, and his son, Thomas, are charged to my guardianship and will accompany me."

Haven watched the woman turn and call in French to the plump servant with the child. The widow bent and hugged her son before giving back his hand to the servant. Next she motioned the entire group toward the hovel of cloth and sticks, where they could stand out of the rain. When she faced him again, she folded her hands together at her waist.

"Where are carts to carry our servants and belongings?" A thread of sorrow wove through the determination he heard in her voice. That rippling, gypsy-eyed tone, so at odds with her rigid posture, nearly undid him. He shook his head and looked at his men. They seemed unaffected. *What was she doing to him?* Determined not to allow her the slightest advantage, he turned his thoughts from her voice.

Haven surveyed the messy assemblage of oiled cloth that sheltered her group, two small chests and a lute. He thought of the sorrow he had heard. No doubt it pained her to have to yield to him and admit her circumstances. "I gather you have no wish to die this day?" he remarked.

She gave a wry smile. "No day is a good day to hang. What matter if I wait a few days? Mayhap, I would like to see the face of this king who ordered my husband's death."

Haven felt his expression harden. "Roger's attempt to kill Edward justified the king's decision. Whoever led your husband into treason caused his death."

"So you say." She dismissed his angry claim with a look. "Where are the carts?"

"We will not take carts. Speed is vital. The king requires you at Chester before the end of the month."

"That cannot be done. Saint Swithin's Day shall pass before we can get that far."

"We will arrive no later than Saint Peter's Mass."

She began to protest.

Haven held up his hand. "I have no time for carts, oxen and the trouble they make. You, Rebecca and Thomas will ride pillion until we can acquire more horses in York."

"What of the servants?"

"Traitors have no need of servants."

"Surely you do not think that a child and a girl are traitors, simply because they share the name of one?"

"What I think matters not. The king did not order servants, hence I need not bring them."

Her mouth twisted. She dared to smirk at him!

"Sir knight, I doubt that your men will wish to replace Marie as nursemaid to Thomas, nor Therese, who is handmaiden to Rebecca."

Haven ground his teeth. The widow had a point. His troop was small, and he could ill afford to use his men as servants. "Well enough," he conceded. "Your servants also will ride pillion, but that is all. What you cannot carry on your person you must abandon."

Haven's hard glance slid away before the heat in her battered face.

16

"Then I fear Sir Haven that you must hang me after all, for I will not leave without the remnants of my son's heritage."

Angry at the flash of guilt he felt, Haven glared at the woman. "It would be best if the boy had nothing from a treasonous father."

"An oilcloth to shelter us from the rain. The clothing we need to shield our bodies, some food, a few tapestries and a lute? Oh, *vraiment*, sir knight, these are certain to teach Thomas his father's treasonous folly."

Haven ground his teeth. Despite her derision, she did not deserve his anger. Traitor or not, she had survived much. He should have asked what baggage she had. He shouted, "Soames."

"Aye, sir." His second-in-command rode forward.

"Go to the keep. Ask for pack mules. Offer this." Haven tossed the man a pouch full of coins. "If they hesitate, insist in the king's name and mine. Do not come back without at least two mules."

"Aye, sir."

They waited there, in the rain, Haven, the widow, her servants and family, and his troop of armed men, until Soames returned leading two mules with pack saddles on their backs.

"Madame," Haven ordered, "make your preparations."

Except for a slight shaking of her body, she did not move from her spot an arm's length beyond his mount. Her hands gripped her cloak, and she appeared to choke back something. More honeyed words with which to wound him? he wondered.

"Sir Haven, we have little skill at loading packs. I beg you, ask your men to assist us."

Why was he not happy to hear her beg his aid? "Ber-

17

gen, Lindel, Sutherland, help the servants load the animals," Haven snarled, impatient with the added delay. "Soames, assign one man each to ride with Rebecca Dreyford and the servants. You there"—Haven pointed toward the plump woman who held the boy's hand. "Give the boy to my squire."

As the servant made to pass by, the widow stepped to the side and grabbed the plump woman's arm.

"*Non,* my son should ride with me."

Haven calmly walked his mount forward, forcing the widow to lose her hold. He looked to the servant and the boy. "Do as I have bid."

The boy's eyes were wide.

The serving woman nodded and hurried off with the child.

Haven turned to the widow.

"Do you see an extra horse, madame?"

"*Non,* but I will not allow . . ."

"I cannot constantly explain myself to you, madame." He reached his hand down. "Be so good as to mount behind me."

The widow looked up at him, then down at her skirts and up again. She threw instructions over her shoulder, and the small group dispersed among his men. She grasped his hand and lifted her hem to her knees. She placed a rag-covered foot atop his booted one and pulled herself onto the horse's rump.

The horse sidled, and Haven had no time to think about the shape of her limbs.

Genvieve grabbed at the knight's cloak and the mail shirt beneath. When the horse settled, she shifted her grip to the knight's belt.

"Are you comfortable, madame?"

"I am ready." She choked out a toneless whisper.

Speak loud and clear, Gennie chastised herself, lest the lout recognize your fear.

He raised his arm. Several shouts came from the mounted men assuring him that all were in place and ready. De Sessions lowered his arm. The horse started forward at a bone-breaking trot. She grasped the man's waist tighter to steady herself.

Still she was cold and had much difficulty keeping her seat. Winds whipped around her, and she struggled closer to de Sessions's broad back, seeking what little shelter she could find there. She cast caution to those winds along with her voice and shouted, "If you continue at this pace, my son shall fall from your squire's horse."

"Be at ease, madame. My squire will have every care of your son."

By afternoon, her arms ached with the strain of riding pillion for hours on end. What would become of them? Gennie did not worry for herself. Life had dealt her such blows that hanging might be welcome, even if she did not deserve it. But that would leave her son with his aunt as his only family.

Rebecca was barely fifteen. Old enough to bear children, yes. But the girl was too flighty and self-occupied yet to be a good mother, or even a good guardian for Thomas. Gennie shivered as the cold of worry settled over her. Unable to see her way through the terrifying situation, she sought guidance and comfort from the only source she knew would give ear to her desperate and silent plea.

Hail Mary full of grace protect my son and succor us all. Beseech our Holy Father to forgive my resentment at being married to Roger Dreyford. Thank the Lord God for

*never allowing Thomas to realize his father had been a
drunken sot, whose lust for excitement put his son at risk.
Give me strength to keep my son safe. To raise him as a
brave, honest and noble man, like the knights of the Holy
Grail. Please help me learn to accept my fate, for I do not
know how to protect my son, if I am dead or worse. Grant
the king a merciful heart that for Thomas's sake Edward
will spare my life. I pray this in your son's name, Amen.*

Weak with hunger and exposure, Gennie leaned
against the mail-clad man before her.

The worst moment of her life had occurred when the
new owners tossed her from her home. Or so she had
thought until now. At least when she had been beg-
gared, then stoned by peasants trying to impress their
new lord, she had known what was happening to her.
She had known what to do.

Now, despite her prayers, her helplessness rankled.
The man she clung to was hard and big enough to
shield her from the wind. But no warmth came through
the cloak and steel mesh that covered his solid frame.
Nor had she seen any warmth when she'd first looked
into his well-armored brown eyes. His assessing gaze
had calculated her value as a female and a human being and dismissed her. To him, like all the others who
knew of her husband's treason, she was worth less than
the effort it took to grind her beneath his heel. She trembled with cold and worry. The constant drizzle had
soaked her clothing through. Her stomach grumbled.
Her life could not get much worse.

She had done her best to defend and provide for her
small band. That morning, she had given her portion
of their scant supplies to Thomas for his breakfast. Days
ago, when Rebecca lost her shoes, Gennie had given
over her own hand-sewn slippers. The constant rain

and chill winds had taken their toll. Her head ached. She still felt every rock thrown at her. But until she assured Thomas's safety, she refused to coddle herself.

The only certainties she could cling to were this saddle and the harsh man who carried her to the king. Life, in the shape of Sir Haven de Sessions, rushed away with her. Where would it take her?

Chapter Two

A watery glimmer of sunlight seeped under the clouds at the western horizon's edge. The small cavalcade wound its way through the countryside. De Sessions brought his horse to a stop and raised his left hand. Behind him, the entire column halted.

He turned to Soames, "We'll stay the night here."

"But sir, we've stopped so often this day that we've barely traveled four leagues."

"Dark will come soon. I want the widow and her party well rested so that tomorrow we may make up the distance they caused us to lose today."

Too tired to take umbrage at de Sessions's comments, Genvieve looked about her. No keep or abbey broke the tree line, not even a farmstead. *What in the name of* le Bon Dieu *was the man thinking?* "Sir, what shelter do you plan to offer us in this place?"

De Sessions twisted his body, peering at the widow through the damp mist. Had the swelling in her face

22

lessened? he wondered. Her rain-drenched hair still hid most of her countenance, so he could not tell. With one sweep of his arm he grasped her around the waist.

"Unhand me."

Before the words fully left her mouth, she found herself placed on the ground, her eyes on level with his knee. His arm left her. Her angry gaze traveled up his long, muscular thigh, past his broad, mailed chest to his clear, brown eyes. She felt her own eyelids widen at the strong emotion she saw there. An eternity passed in the instant before he blinked. Exhaustion threatened to overwhelm her. She reached out to steady herself against the horse.

De Sessions dismounted.

The action brought that disturbing breadth of chest within a quill's length of her nose.

He fisted his hands onto his hips and leaned forward, crowding her.

She refused to yield.

"Had you used the sight God gave you, madame, you would see that He gave us yon bluff to block the wind and rain. Water to drink runs just beyond that spit of sand. These trees"—he pointed to the encircling copse—"provide firewood, bedding and food."

He spoke to the top of her head. His breath passed her ear. She shivered again.

Unable to see anything through the broad chest in front of her, she backed one step from his arrogant barrage of words and locked her gaze with his. She lifted her chin at what she hoped was a haughty angle and surveyed him top to toe and back. "I see quite well, sir, as perhaps you do not. For I see before me one of *le Bon Dieu's* less modest creations."

Several male chuckles sounded, and de Sessions's

23

brows lowered. He looked as if he could not decide whether to be flattered or insulted. His wide mouth thinned. He tilted his shoulders forward, crowding her once more. The open clearing shrank to the small patch of earth that separated her from him. Her heartbeat quickened. Heat wrapped around her. She forced herself to breathe. The smell of damp leather and male musk filled the air.

"Madame, I have no time for nonsensical banter." He pointed to a nearby fallen log. "Sit you, while I instruct my men. Then, madame, I will have answers from you about treason." Turning away, he stomped off, shouting for Soames.

De Sessions's behavior reminded her of Roger, who turned aggressive when he was confused. Her jaw tightened against the pain that thoughts of Roger brought. She set her mind to the present. *A bien.* If the noble lout is confused, so much the better. As for treason, she had nothing to tell him. She lifted her hem, ignored the log, and walked toward the pack mules at the back of the cavalcade, calling for her servants.

"Marie, Therese, Rene, *attendez moi.*"

The three came running. Thomas and Rebecca approached at a slower pace.

"Madame," huffed Rene, her skinny cook. "What is it you desire?"

"That man says we must make camp in this place. I will have decent food for us all. Rene, I know we have little. Can you manage?"

"Aye, milady."

"But milady . . ." Rebecca's maid, Therese, protested.

"No buts. We are in difficult circumstances. However, we all know our duty and shall not lower our standards simply because our surroundings are unusual. I have confidence that you can manage. Rene, build the fire and prepare the meal. Therese may assist you."

"Madame, I cannot . . ."

"Do not be foolish, Therese. Of course you can."

"But I am a lady's maid."

"And a very good one. Yet Rebecca shall have to do without your skills, as she has done these past weeks. Rene needs you more." Before Therese could object further, Genvieve turned to her son's nurse. "Marie."

"Aye, milady." A smile beamed from the plump woman's countenance, soothing Gennie's sorely tried temper.

"Take Rebecca and gather what wood you can from those trees over there."

"Aye, Lady Genvieve." Marie turned to her task with a speed belied by her size and shape.

Rebecca lingered, a mulish look on her face.

"What is it, sister?"

"Why do I have to gather wood? I am no servant."

Two weeks living as a beggar and the girl still failed to understand their situation. Studying her sister-in-law, Gennie could imagine the younger woman's feelings. The pampered child of doting parents, Rebecca had been second in their affection only to her wayward brother. As a mere in-law, Gennie presented no threat to Rebecca's status. However, when Thomas's birth eclipsed his aunt's place with her parents, the girl had become jealous.

Rebecca doted on her nephew but turned sullen resentment on his mother. Anything that needed to be done was deferred to Gennie. Then the elder Dreyfords had died, followed less than a year later by Roger's execution. Rebecca had become even more difficult.

So much loss hurt unbearably. Gennie knew that from the loss of her own parents.

Instead of chastising Rebecca, as Gennie might have a fosterling or a servant, she drew the young woman into her arms for a hug. She stroked the girl's back.

When she felt her sister-in-law relax, Gennie pushed herself away. She looked Rebecca squarely in the eye. "You have been a great help to me these last weeks," she lied encouragingly. "I do not know what I would have done without you to support me and help Marie with Thomas. We're on our way to the king. You will not have to labor like this for much longer. Please, hurry to help Marie find the wood. The fire we build with it will warm you all the faster."

Gennie took her son's hand and watched Rebecca depart. No sooner had the girl left than Rebecca's maid approached.

"What is it, Therese?"

"Madame, you must see that staying here is impossible."

"Impossible or not, we shall remain here for the night. Best get on with your duties, before you find yourself unable to share our meager food and shelter."

Therese's mouth snapped shut. "*Oui,* madame."

Gennie watched her stomp off. With a shiver of cold, she bent to her son. That Thomas appeared warm and no worse for his ride with the squire pleased her. "Shall we go walk among the trees a bit? We might find some eggs to give Rene for our dinner."

Thomas nodded, light shining in his eyes, eager for the adventure she offered.

Gennie took his small hand in hers. "Good. I must speak with some of Sir de Sessions's men; then we will go hunt for eggs."

*   *   *

With Soames and half of the men sent off to hunt, Haven told those remaining to picket the horses, build a fire, and erect a shelter. He tethered his mount. Deciding to wash the mud from his person before he questioned the widow, Haven headed for the river, with Watley, his squire, in tow. As they walked, Haven observed the other side of the clearing, where the widow directed her small retinue. What was the woman up to?

She had ignored his order to rest on the log, when other women would have complained about the lack of a cushion. His mother would have commandeered half of his men to see to her comfort and that of her family. The widow Dreyford neither complained nor added to his men's work.

She marched off and spoke quietly to her family and servants. She sought no assistance from him or his men. She took on a difficult task for a noble lady, two children and three servants, none of whom were trained to survive out of doors for very long. But she had, he reminded himself, survived for weeks, when circumstances forced her to it.

His thoughts still on the widow, Haven proceeded to the stream. He found her appearance and demeanor . . . unexpected. She did not seem the type of woman to incite a man to treason either for greed or power. Her attention to her son, her sister-in-law, even her servants bespoke a sober woman, who cared too much for the well-being of others. Such a woman did not fit with the picture of the scheming temptress that he and the king believed her to be.

With Watley's help, Haven removed his mail, tunic and breeches, and then plunged his body into the stream. The rushing water loosened the aches of several hard days' ride. The tension resulting from the woman's hands on his belt washed downstream.

Oh, it was not the widow's fault, he assured himself. Place any woman's hands at any man's waist and he would suffer similar consequences. He felt again the surprising jolt of desire that consumed him at the sound of the widow's voice, and heat flushed through him.

He scrambled for mental control before the water would boil and steam around him. He should not feel such heat for his best friend's widow. This is ridiculous, he told himself. She's much too independent and probably not as pretty under those bruises as I imagine. He stood, allowing the evening air to shiver away what the water could not.

Watley handed him a cloth. Haven stepped from the stream. He dried himself and then donned the dry clothing that the squire held ready.

Could the widow truly possess such an alluring voice and not own a body to go with it? Mayhap he had misjudged her. Who could tell what lay beneath that shapeless, sodden exterior? Nor should her shape matter to him. She was a traitoress. Who was behind this conspiracy to kill the king? What did she know about her husband's activities? As he rubbed water from his own countenance, he promised himself that he would ask those questions and more of her when he returned to camp.

The widow was nowhere in sight. But what Haven saw at the campsite stopped him in his tracks. The men went busily about their preparations. However, nothing was as he had expected.

The fire blazed on the opposite side of the camp from where it belonged. The horses were tethered too close to the trees and thus vulnerable to attack from wild animals. The low profile and poor location of the shelter showed all too clearly the inexperience of the new men in his troop. Edward had ordered Haven to take every able-bodied man he encountered into service against the Welsh. Since the best warriors were already with Edward's army, most of the men Haven found were green youths or ham-handed slackards.

Haven stalked to where a fellow named Bergen put the finishing touches on the shelter. "Did I not tell you to set the tent nearer to the bluff?"

Bergen jolted upright. "Aye, sir."

"What then is it doing here?"

"The widow, sir, she said you would be displeased if your tent were too far from the water."

Haven held his temper. It was not *his* tent, but Bergen could not know that.

"She is wrong. The oilcloth will provide greater shelter for more people if it is attached to that rock overhang on the bluff, thus giving at least one solid wall and a roof, as well as providing some dry ground on which to sleep.

Bergen darted an anxious glance across the camp.

"Did the widow say anything else, Bergen?"

"N-nay, Sir Haven."

Precious time would be lost correcting the widow's mistake. *She should have consulted me.* He nodded to Bergen. "Move the tent, then continue with your work." Haven walked off to solve the problem of the fire while he contemplated what to do with the horses.

"Cook." Haven eyed the thin man who tended a pot suspended over the fire. "What is your name?"

"Rene, sir." He stirred the pot's contents.

"Did you order the fire built here, Rene?"

29

The cook cast a quick glance at Haven. "Nay, sir."

"Who did?"

"Milady Genvieve wanted the cook fire placed where the wind would not blow smoke and sparks back toward your shelter."

Haven felt his temper jab at him again. Why did the widow seem to think he would let her sleep in the cold and wet while he stayed warm and dry? Still he bit his tongue on the sharp words that pushed to be said. Rene had no knowledge of his intentions.

Rene continued, "When she saw your men also building a fire but in a different place, milady suggested they stop. One fire is enough for the whole camp and will conserve wood."

Haven could not fault the widow's intent to help. Yet, in trying to save wood and effort, she had created a problem. The horses could not be moved closer to the river until the fire was moved elsewhere. More wasted time and effort. All because the widow chose to give orders without asking him. Just who did she think was in charge?

"The tent will be placed against the bluff. I want that fire moved across the clearing before my men return with meat. When they do, you will take a fair share for your lady and allow my man to cook for us. I will not have my needs or those of my men increase your work."

Rene raised his eyebrows. "Aye, Sir Haven."

Haven stalked away. Why should the cook be surprised that he be shown consideration? *I have every right to be as thoughtful of others' needs as the widow.* More than a little cross at the widow's misguided intentions and failure to ask his permission, Haven approached the men tending the horses. None of this would have happened if the men had been seasoned warriors. Warriors who knew that women, especially women suspected of treason, did not give orders in camp.

"Sutherland, Lindel, why did you not picket the horses nearer the river?"

"Sir." The two dropped their curry brushes and snapped to attention.

"Well?"

The men looked at each other, then faced Haven and spoke in a rush.

"It was the widow . . ."

"The widow Dreyford, sir . . ."

"Wait." Haven held up one hand, palm outward. "One at a time. Lindel, you first."

"The widow, sir. She told us that you would be unhappy if the horses were placed above the level of your tent. She said they would make an unappealing mess and might interfere with your sleep."

Haven's mouth thinned. By the Rood. As soon as he finished here, he would find the widow. He would inform her that he was in charge. That he was not a selfish, overbearing ogre who left women and children to sleep in the rain when shelter was to be had. She would sleep safe and cozy inside that tent if he had to sit on her to make her do it.

In that instant the memory of her slender arms wrapped around his waist popped into his mind. Again he felt the softness of her skin as he touched her face. What if she was just as soft all over? His body hardened. What would it feel like to *sit* upon that pillowy form? Haven groaned. Why must he think of such things now? He did not want to ease the tightness in his groin on the widow. He absolutely did not.

"Sir, sir, your face is red. Are you ill?" Lindel shook

31

Haven's shoulder. "Sutherland, run. Find Lady Genvieve. A woman will know how to soothe Sir Haven's pain."

"Nay!" Haven's tone knocked away Lindel's grasp and halted Sutherland in his tracks.

'Twas the last thing he wanted to think of—having the traitorous woman soothe what ailed him. She was his best friend's widow and a suspected traitor. "Nay, I am not ill." He gritted his teeth against the need surging through him. "As wise as the widow is in ordering the horses down slope from the tent, they are much too close to the forest. Move them."

Haven pointed to a flat grassy area a few paces from the running water. "That spot is flat enough, and the horses will be neither too close to the fire nor the woods. Do you understand?"

"Aye, sir," Lindel agreed.

Sutherland nodded.

"Good. When you have done with the horses, get Bergen and post yourselves at guard. Sutherland, I want you on the bluff. Lindel, patrol the perimeter at twenty paces out. Bergen can patrol the edge of the clearing. Is that understood?"

The men nodded. Haven set off to find the widow. As before, she was nowhere in camp.

He asked his men if they had seen her.

Bergen answered. "I thought I saw her take the boy into the trees earlier, sir."

"What direction?"

"Over there, by that fallen log."

Haven's jaw tightened on his thanks. "You mean they left alone?"

"Nay, sir. They left together."

Perhaps I should just slit my own throat and save Ed-

ward the trouble. Not only must I bring the king a pack of bumbling fools to add to his army, but also the widow must endanger herself and her son by wandering about a strange wood, alone. Frustrated beyond patience, Haven plunged into the trees and cursed his oath to protect Roger Dreyford's family.

Chapter Three

Gennie limped a bit as she and Thomas stepped out from among the trees opposite the side of the camp from which they had left. She held the hem of her kirtle lifted in both hands and cradled two dozen or more quail eggs within the fold. Thomas too had formed a sack from the folded-up hem of his tunic and carried a load of berries. Juice stained his little mouth red. Gennie had pretended not to see him sneaking the plump tidbits. The two laughed as they approached Rene, and Gennie called out, "Sir cook, we bring you eggs and berries. We'll have a fine dinner tonight."

"My thanks, milady." He took the eggs from her.

"Thomas, will you help Rene to put the eggs and berries away?"

"*Oui,* Mama."

Gennie looked out over the camp and saw the horses had been moved once again. She nodded, approving the change to her instructions. Her feet felt numb and cold, and as she saw no work that needed to be done, she headed for the fallen log. She was in the midst of dragging the log closer to the fire when Marie ran into the clearing.

"Milady, milady. Come quickly. Rebecca has slipped and fallen in the muck. She's having a terrible fit. I cannot calm her enough to see if she's hurt."

Marie tugged at her arm. Gennie dropped the log and clasped the nurse's hand.

"Just a moment, Marie. I must see that Thomas is taken care of before I can go to Rebecca."

"I will stay with the boy."

"*Non.* You must lead me to Rebecca. Give me a few moments. I will have all settled. In the meantime, calm yourself."

Gennie looked about the camp for Therese, but the maid had disappeared. Rene was busy preparing supper. De Sessions and his squire were gone, like most of his men. All that she saw were Rene at the fire and Bergen, walking along the tree line. As quickly as her sore feet would allow, she marched up to the man. "Bergen, I am in need of your aid."

The warrior looked warily from her to where he walked his post and back. "I cannot leave my post, milady."

"I see. I do not ask you to cease your guard duty, only to add my son to it."

Bergen's brow wrinkled.

"I must aid my sister-in-law. Thomas is too tired to come with me. Please watch over him while I am gone."

"I must watch outside the camp, lady."

"*Oui.* Could you not carry Thomas on your shoulders? He would think it great fun, and you could teach him how to be a proper guard."

35

Bergen nodded and stuck out his chest. "Aye, milady. I can do that."

"Thank you, Bergen. I will be back very soon." With Thomas settled happily on Bergen's shoulders, Gennie followed Marie into the woods.

Once more Haven pushed his way into the forest. After a fruitless search, he had returned to camp, to find that the widow had come and gone in his absence. She had much to answer for, and he began to think she eluded him apurpose. During the short time he spent looking for her, she managed to turn Bergen from a guard into a nursemaid. The big man had been rolling on the ground, tickling Thomas, instead of guarding the camp.

When Haven demanded an explanation, the boy cowered behind Bergen, while the man stammered that it was an emergency. The lady, he explained, said she would only be gone a few moments, and that he should teach Thomas how to be a proper guard. Haven almost inquired when tickling had become part of a proper guard's duties, but he changed his mind. Instead he asked the lackwit which way the widow had gone.

Heading off in the direction of the man's pointing finger, Haven found two pair of mushy footprints near the riverbank. The prints turned, and Haven followed them along the river, then into the wood. Before long he heard the sound of Rebecca's sobbing.

Wondering what caused such caterwauling, Haven went to see. He stopped just short of a little vale beyond the tree line. No one noticed him, for the girl's wails drowned all sound of his approach.

Rebecca lay in a heap of sticks, dirt and leaves near the riverbank. Mud covered her from head to toe. She shook. Whether from cold or fright, Haven could not tell. The widow sat on the ground, her arms around her sister-in-law. Rebecca rested her head on the woman's shoulder and wailed louder. The widow let her cry. Soon enough, the tears ran dry, and Rebecca's breathing evened out. "What happened?" the older woman asked.

Uncertain if he would be needed or not, Haven watched from behind the trees. He desired no entanglement with womanish tears if he could avoid it.

With her face still pressed to the widow's shoulder, Rebecca told her tale. "I reached for one of those horrid sticks that Marie said we needed for kindling, and I swear it moved."

The widow looked past Rebecca to where Marie stood shaking her head, arms folded across her ample chest.

"You think you saw a snake?"

"I did, Gennie. I truly did see a snake. I feared it so that I tried to run backward. But my arms were full of sticks. I could not lift my hem. I tripped and fell. My foot is stuck. The snake will bite me. Gennie, I am so scared." Rebecca's voice rose, and she started crying again.

How had Roger survived such a fountain for a sister? Haven wondered.

The widow waited patiently, rubbing Rebecca's back and murmuring the same kind of sounds that Haven's mother had murmured to calm him when, as a child, he had woken afraid in the night.

Soon Rebecca calmed once more.

"The snake is gone, sister."

"It is?" The girl looked fearfully about her.

"*Oui.* Marie chased it off before she came to get me."

Beyond Rebecca's huddled form, Marie's mouth rounded in surprise.

The widow was a good liar, Haven thought. He prayed that Marie would know better than to reveal the truth.

"Now you must help us get you out of here."

"Me? How can I help? I am trapped here until a tree falls on top of me or lightning strikes me dead."

"You can be a great help. Just lie back and let Marie and me take a look at your foot."

"But I will get all muddy."

"Rebecca," the widow smiled and said with gentle firmness, "you are already all muddy."

"Oh."

"Now lie back. Marie and I will take care of everything." She slipped from behind Rebecca, and the young woman lay down.

Next, the widow examined the root's hold on Rebecca.

Even from his tree-screened vantage, Haven could tell that when the girl fell, her foot had pushed the mud and stones temporarily out from underneath the root. The foot had slid under the root, and then stones and mud flowed back, wedging the appendage firmly in place. They would have to scoop the stones away to loosen Rebecca's foot. The difficulty would lie in removing sufficient stones long enough for Rebecca to work herself free. The mud would make the stones slippery, complicating the effort.

The widow and the nurse dug for a while and threw great handfuls of stony muck toward the river. But with each throw, more rocks and mud would slide beneath the root, keeping Rebecca trapped.

Finally the widow sacrificed part of her kirtle to make

a temporary dam by wrapping the scrap of cloth around some sticks that Marie broke to the right size. Marie dug like mad, and Gennie jammed the makeshift barrier in place. "Now, Rebecca," the widow shouted.

The girl tugged, wiggled and pushed. Soon she was free of the root's grasp. The widow sat back. Her bottom met a mud puddle, giving a great squish. Rebecca covered her mouth and made a choked sound. Marie sagged onto a tree, trying to hide her face in the bark. The widow rolled her eyes and gave in to the laughter that Haven knew the other women shared. In a trice they all hawed hysterically. When the laughter subsided into giggles and snickers, Marie helped the widow and Rebecca to stand.

"Are you all right, Rebecca?" the widow asked.

Rebecca moved a couple of steps to test her legs and feet. "Yes."

The widow took her sister-in-law's arm. *"Merci, le Bon Dieu.* The dirt will wash off. An injury would not."

As Marie and Rebecca began walking toward camp, the widow stayed behind.

"Are you not coming with us, Gennie?"

"I need a moment or two alone, Rebecca. I will be there soon. Would you see to Thomas for me? He is with Bergen."

"Yes, sister. Marie and I will watch Thomas."

Haven did not want the women to know they had been observed. They were close enough to camp to be safe without his protective eye watching them every step of the way. He faded back into the forest, uncomfortable with the picture he had just been given of the widow Dreyford. Her patience, generosity and good humor did not fit the image of a greedy, power-hungry traitor that he had carried in his mind for so long. Deep in thought, he made his solitary way back to camp.

When the other women disappeared from view, Gennie let her head drop and her shoulders slump. She was so very tired. Only one clean gown remained in the small chests that she had rescued from her belongings at the Dreyford keep. Rebecca would have the clean clothing. Gennie did not know if she had the strength to wash her own long tunic. Even if she did, it would be damp on the morrow. Of course, she had been rain-soaked for days; what would a little dampness matter?

The thought occurred to her to walk into the stream with her clothes on and let the rushing water do the work. But the water was cold, and Gennie was relatively warm beneath her coating of muck.

She would ask Therese to clean the gown. The maid would complain, of course, but that was nothing Gennie had not put up with before. Therese would do the work, and tomorrow, Gennie would be damp but clean. The arrogant Sir Haven de Sessions would not have to soil his cloak when he took her pillion again.

Gennie turned away from the river and limped toward camp. What she would not give for a bath and a long, hot soak for her maltreated feet.

Haven watched Rebecca and the nurse return to camp muddy and laughing as if they had not a care in the world. They took Thomas from Bergen and disappeared into the relocated shelter without a word.

He paused near the fire, undecided as to whether he should still confront the widow over her tendency to forget that he was in charge. Since she was not available, Haven started for the bluff to check on the guard there, when a flash of movement caught the corner of his eye. It approached from the direction of the river. As Haven turned to investigate, he realized it was the widow hobbling into the clearing.

What was wrong with her? Whatever had happened, she was clearly in pain. Deciding to get the details later, when he questioned her about Roger, Haven strode forward, grasped the woman about the waist and hoisted her into his arms. Her body was sodden, cold and covered with mud. Part of her kirtle had been torn away. Had someone attacked her? Haven felt anger chase fear through his belly, until he remembered that she had sacrificed her own clothing to rescue Rebecca.

"Put me down."

"No."

"Why, you . . . you . . . you pompous, arrogant goat."

The fist she smacked onto his chest hurt less than a fleabite. He ignored her outrage and shouted for Watley, who had been feeding the horses.

The squire came at a run. "Aye, sir?"

With a jerk of his head, Haven indicated a nearby log. "Drag that log close to the fire. Then go and get my woolen cloak."

Haven waited. When the log was in place, he set the widow down gently. Now he would have answers.

As her feet touched the ground, Haven heard pain whimper from her cold lips. He saw agony shudder through her thin frame. She raised her knees toward her chest and wrapped her rag-covered toes in the remnants of her skirt.

Toes! Haven remembered the quick flash of long limbs as she had pulled herself onto his horse that morning. He hunkered down beside her and grasped her hand. Firmly, he pried her fingers from around her

41

feet. The skirt fell away. Her feet lay revealed in his hands. Frayed, mud-stained strips of cloth wrapped her from ankle to toe. He pulled his knife from his belt, intent on cutting away the offensive rags.

"Non." She tried to snatch her legs from his grip.

"Aye." He clamped her ankle beneath his arm and split the cloth with a deft stroke. Fury welled inside him at the sight of her bare feet. "How long have you been without shoes?"

"It is not important."

"Pride is a sin. You are hurt. You will tell me the whole of it."

She looked at him. Her face reddened. "And then what, oh great and wonderful knight? You'll use your renowned strength and your reputation to fix the problem? Will you order my feet not to freeze or cause me pain and you undue inconvenience?" Anger roared out at him from those green eyes. Her words hissed at him with the speed of a drawn blade.

Impatient with her stubbornness, Haven bent to examine her injuries.

His gasp of shock echoed her gasp of pain at his gentle touch.

On top, where not covered by dirt or bruises, long, slim bones arched beneath translucent skin that was nearly blue with cold. On the bottoms, hard calluses decorated the pads of her toes, and blisters seeped and boiled over heel and ball. Elsewhere, skin that should have been baby soft was toughened through misuse. Scratches ringed her delicate ankles. One of them oozed bright red droplets onto his broad fingers.

"Why did you not tell me?" Anger and sympathy shook his voice.

"When had I the chance?" she challenged.

Haven felt his mouth thin. The woman was correct. He had not given her any chance for discussion. He had erred because he preferred to ignore her. She reminded him too much of his own part in Roger Dreyford's death. Unfortunately ignoring her was less than easy.

He shook his head. Right now, her health must concern him more than his error in judgment. Injury was serious business, even when one had a roof and walls for shelter. He gathered her in his arms and felt her shudder. "You are cold and wet too."

She opened her mouth. In the time it took for her to protest against his touch, Watley appeared. Haven took a large, fur-trimmed cloak from the squire and wrapped it round her twice.

"Sir Soames has returned and asks to speak with you," Watley announced.

"Stop pushing me about. I must . . ."

Haven placed a finger against her surprisingly soft lips. "No. You must sit and get warm."

She glared at him.

He glared back. "Watley," he bellowed.

The squire, who stood right next to him, jumped.

"Fetch the salve I keep in my saddlebags. Then tell that cook to prepare a healing posset."

"Aye, Sir Haven." The squire took two steps.

"Tell Bergen to gather more wood for this fire."

"Yes." Watley started to depart.

"And bring bandages from the pack mules."

"Yes, Sir Haven." Watley took another step.

"Tell Soames, I will be with him shortly."

The young man halted once more. "Aye, sir." Again, the squire made as if to leave.

"When you return, bring your spare boots for ma-

43

dame. See that she stays warm and drinks the brew."

"Aye," the squire waited.

"What are you waiting for?" Haven shouted. "Cannot you see that madame shivers with cold and ague?"

"Yea, sir." Watley ran off.

Haven focused on the widow. "When that posset is ready, you shall drink every drop."

Genvieve emitted a raspy chuckle. "Oh, *certainment,* Sir Haven."

Haven eyed her askance. What ailed everyone? The woman was too stubborn and prideful to inform him that she was in pain. She turned a warrior from a guard into a nursemaid. His squire suddenly had to have orders explained in detail, then be told to go about those orders. Did the widow have some form of contagion that caused thick-headedness?

The woman huddled into his cloak and leaned closer to the fire. She shuddered less. Her face appeared less pinched. He could not press her for answers now. His questions would have to wait.

When Watley returned, Haven surveyed the camp. Soames and the rest of the men not on guard sat as near the fire as they could get without disturbing their leader. Haven rose, walking over to where Soames sat. "You wanted to speak with me?"

Soames opened his mouth to answer and a terrified screech rent the air.

All heads turned in the direction of the bluff.

Haven jolted into motion, with his men close behind. Breathing hard, he crested the top of the bluff and could not believe his eyes. "What in Judas's name . . . ?"

Chapter Four

"Lower that weapon," Haven ordered.

The blade clattered to the ground, and the nurse heaved a great sigh. " 'Tis a blasted heavy thing, and glad I am not to have to hold it longer."

Haven ignored her. "Sutherland. Get off that woman. Straighten your hose and stand at attention. Therese, cover yourself." Haven turned around, hoping he could block the worst of Sutherland's folly from the rest of the men. "Soames, get those men back down to the clearing. When Sutherland joins you, send someone up here to take his post."

"Aye, sir."

Haven waited until the last man, grumbling because he had missed the fun, ran down the hill at Soames's command. When Haven turned around, Sutherland stood at attention, fully dressed. Therese still sat on the ground, hiding her face in her skirts.

"Marie," he spoke very quietly, trying to keep a rein

on his temper. "Give me that sword. Then take Therese to the tent. She is to remain there until your mistress decides the maid's fate."

"Aye, sir." The nurse handed him the blade, hilt first.

He took it and waited, again, until the sounds of the women's progress down the hill faded.

Haven approached his man-at-arms and placed the point of the sword under his chin. "Is this your sword, Sutherland?"

The man's eyes shifted in a downward glance. The rest of his body remained motionless. "Aye, sir."

"You were on guard duty, were you not?"

"Aye, sir."

"Then why was your sword in someone else's hand and pointed at your back?"

"Because I deserted my post."

"I will give you one chance to explain why you were fornicating with that woman instead of standing guard. If I do not like what I hear, I will slit your throat on the spot."

Sutherland's chin trembled so much that the sword point pricked his skin and blood trickled in a thin, hot line down his throat. "Th . . . there is no explanation, sir."

"I am glad you realize that. Because you just saved your own neck." Haven lowered the sword. "There will not be a next time, will there, Sutherland?"

"No, Sir Haven."

"Good. As a punishment for neglecting your duty, you will cook dinner for myself and the rest of the men."

"Nay, sir. Anything but that. The men. They will kill me."

"Aye, none shall be happy that you do the cooking.

We all know you need more practice. And if the men remember why you practice your cooking this eve, they shall also remember to see to it that you do not place your cock higher than your duty ever again. You will not forget either, will you Sutherland?"

The man hung his head. "Nay, sir. I will not let a pretty wench lead me astray again."

"Excellent. Now get back to camp and start cooking. Tell Soames to send up your relief."

"Aye, sir." Sutherland dragged his feet to the hill and started downward."

"And walk like a warrior," Haven shouted after him.

Before he disappeared from view, Haven saw the man's head come up and his shoulders straighten.

Much better. Haven turned the sword in his hand, examining the blade for nicks and scratches. He found none.

The condition of the sword told him that Sutherland cared for his equipment. Haven thought back over the weeks that the Yorkshire man had served with him. Sutherland was a good man. No doubt it was Therese who lay at the bottom of all this. The woman caused nearly as much trouble as the girl, Rebecca.

Were the maid and the girl truly annoying, he wondered, or did the widow encourage them to keep suspicion from herself? Haven shook his head, confused as much by the widow's actions as by his own fascination with her. He could not get to Chester and be rid of her soon enough.

The guard arrived, and Haven descended to the camp. Satisfied that for the time being, peace and calm would reign, he sought out his second-in-command. When he found Soames, they walked a little away from the fire, talking quietly.

"Did the men have a successful hunt?"

"Aye, Sir Haven, five plump partridges and four hares."

"And has Sutherland taken the food for cooking?"

"Aye. Must you have Sutherland cook, sir? The men will not thank you."

"They need not thank me. It is Sutherland, and his neglect of duty, to whom they should show their gratitude. Make sure they know that."

"I will, sir."

"Did you tell Sutherland to give some of the meat to the widow's cook?"

"I did."

"Good. I like it not that she is so thin."

Soames remained silent.

"What else have you to tell me, besides of a successful hunt?"

"We found no evidence of any other riders nearby. We should be safe enough with a minimal guard for the night."

Haven nodded. For a few more moments he discussed the safety of the camp with Soames and assigned the necessary duties and watches.

That done, he turned his attention to where the widow sat under Watley's watchful eye.

As Haven approached he saw the squire hand her a cup. She took it in both hands and blew steam from the rim, then sipped cautiously. Her eyes squeezed shut and her mouth formed a frown around clenched teeth.

Haven knew the brew he had ordered had a bitter flavor, but it was not that awful. Despite the pleasing odors wafting from that direction of the camp, perhaps her cook did not know his craft.

"Allow me, madame." He held out his hand for her cup.

She stared at him for a moment, as if uncertain what he wanted. Then she shook herself. *"Oui,"* she whispered and placed the cup in his grasp. Her hand dropped away. The thin shoulders slumped, and her chin sank to her chest.

Haven lifted the vessel to his lips and tasted the brew. From that single sip, bitterness filled his mouth and parched his throat. He turned and spit the vile stuff toward the fire, "Pah." He looked back at the widow. She seemed to fade and waver before his eyes. "Watley, fetch some cool water and get mint from that cook. If he has none, take some from my saddle's pack."

"Aye, sir."

Haven hunkered down to study the widow's face. Unable to force himself to look at her, he took up her hand instead. That fragile assemblage of long bones and delicate skin bore signs of unaccustomed work. Blisters and bruises dotted her palm, reminding him of her feet. She trembled slightly in his grip. Her small hurts inspired an odd ache in his chest. He thrust the cup back at her, as if the action could thrust away the unaccustomed feelings. "Does your cook not possess the skill to brew a healing posset?"

The widow raised her head, and her hair fell forward curtaining her visage. "I had your squire prepare the drink."

"Watley is not in the habit of taking orders from anyone but me. Pray, how did you manage to convince him to disobey me?" Haven spoke with a politeness he was far from feeling.

" 'Twasn't difficult. He's a squire, with the usual aspirations to be a knight. I simply pointed out that you would be displeased if he did not behave in a knightly fashion and honor a lady's request." She looked across the camp to where Watley searched among Haven's gear.

Haven allowed his glance to follow hers. To prevent his anger from blasting her, he chewed the inside of his cheek. "Did it occur to you, madame, that having my orders obeyed pleases me?"

She snapped her head back. "Of course not. Why would you prefer that the hungry people in this camp wait upon my posset?"

As she continued, Haven frowned at the ground. He didn't like the storm he felt brewing within himself.

"Your squire must be taught how to prepare such things. Rene is very busy. Watley had nothing to do. I knew you would be angry if I did not get the potion. I did not believe that you would care about the manner of it."

Frustrated beyond measure, Haven clutched a fistful of his own hair and tugged. The gesture caused his eyes to water, but he held his temper. "I don't care if you dance naked with the king of the fairies in order to get the posset. I do care that the tent is put up where I order it put, so that *you,* madame, may sleep in comfort. I care that the horses remain where I order them. I care that the fire is built where I order it built. And I much prefer that you cease giving orders to any of my men without my express permission. Is that clear?"

Behind damp strings of hair, she stared at him, open-mouthed, then turned her focus to the ground. "Quite. I am sorry, sir, if I caused any problems with my instructions to your men. Such was not my intention."

That small speech seemed to exhaust her. Haven felt a queer pang at her humble words. *What care I if the widow's pride is hurt? 'Tis better she know her place.* He gave himself a mental shake and turned his attention to her feet.

Noticing the bowl, salve, rags, and shoes that sat by the widow's side, Haven tested the water. Finding it sufficiently warm, he grasped one of the widow's feet and set to cleaning the sole.

"Please. You must not." Her voice sounded high-pitched, robbing the protest of any real force.

He continued to soothe her foot. "Should I do less than sweet Jesu did for his disciples?"

From the corner of his eye he saw her shake her head.

"Good." He spread salve on her foot, top, bottom and ankle. Then he swaddled the entire appendage in clean strips torn from more of the rags. He slipped one of Watley's spare shoes over her bandaged foot and placed it gently on the ground before he picked up her other foot and repeated the action.

Watley returned as Haven finished. He removed the cup from Gennie's slackened grip and dumped half the cup's contents on the ground. He took the water from Watley and diluted the remainder of the posset. Then he crumbled some of the mint his squire gave him and sampled the brew. "There." He returned the cup to the widow's clasp. "You should be able to drink that without frightening the camp with your grimace."

Genvieve drank.

Watley departed.

Haven sat on a nearby stone and watched. "We must talk of Rebecca's maid, Therese," he said.

The widow nodded. "Marie brought her here and told me what happened. Therese admits that it was her fault. She was bored and angry with me for turning her

51

into a scullery wench. She understands now that such was not my intention."

"You are too softhearted. Even was it your intention to so demote Therese, as a servant, she must accept your decisions in good grace. She must be punished for her impudence and thoughtlessness."

"You mistake me, sir. Therese has been punished for her behavior."

"How so, madame? I hear no weeping and wailing."

"Precisely so. Therese loves to talk and does not hesitate to make her opinions known. I have made her swear an oath not to speak for the next se'enight. I gave her one exception for tomorrow morning, when she shall apologize to you and your men."

Haven smiled. "You are an evil woman, madame."

A small answering smile flickered across her mouth—as if she were too weary even to bend her lips upward. "I have my moments."

He watched as she raised the cup and drained it.

When she had done, she handed him the vessel. "My thanks, sir." She rose and crossed the camp, spoke to her servants, then retired to the shelter.

Haven stared morosely after her.

All the while, aromas from Rene's cookfire assailed his nose, making his belly rumble in concert with the empty stomachs of his men. Dark had fallen by the time Sutherland placed half of a burnt and bleeding partridge carcass in front of Haven. He was hungry enough to swallow the unappetizing meal whole.

He stared at the blood-encrusted, semi-charred mass and reminded himself that he had eaten worse many times before. Haven swallowed a lump of revulsion. "One of your best efforts, Sutherland," he uttered the false praise without a qualm. None of his men would say a word false or true. Haven knew that Sutherland needed encouragement before the man would ever achieve an edible meal.

"Thankee, Sir Haven." Sutherland stood waiting for Haven to try the bird.

Haven looked up. All his men waited, expecting him to lead the way in this as in all things. So be it. He lifted the poultry to his lips and tore off a huge bite. The meat came away from the bone, dripping bright red juices. "Mmmm," he managed to mumble as he chewed and chewed.

Sutherland sat down at the opposite side of the fire, and the men began to eat. Before Haven could swallow the first stringy bite, Marie entered the circle of light. In her arms she carried a stack of flat bread. Behind her, Therese struggled into sight lugging a huge pot. A ladle hung from her belt and banged against her leg as she walked.

The contents of the pot smelled like heaven.

The women stopped in front of Haven. "Our lady wishes to share with you all the bounty that you and your men have provided." Marie beamed the words and leaned forward, offering a round of flat bread.

Haven nearly choked on his lumpy mouthful. What could he say? *I hate food cooked in the French style. I prefer poorly cooked partridge to rabbit stew that smells fit for the saints.* If he refused, his men would have to refuse. He looked around the fire. He had seen sterner looks on the faces of orphaned babes. Silently he reached out and took the bread.

Marie curtsied and moved on to the next man. Therese approached. She set the pot down, dipped her ladle, and then held it ready over the pot.

Haven thrust the bread forward with both hands. He

watched thick brown sauce, great lumps of root vegetables and juicy cubes of meat drip from the ladle onto
the bread. Therese dipped the ladle a second time and
offered again. But Haven shook his head. He had already folded the bread around the stew and taken his
first bite.

It was delicious and totally unexpected.

After Edward's crusade to the Holy Lands, Haven had
spent a month traveling to Paris and back on the king's
business. At every stop the food had been highly spiced
and overcooked. Not burnt, just mushy. Nothing that a
strong man could sink his teeth into.

This stew was nothing like any French food Haven
had experienced. Delicate herbs mixed into the bread
accented the flavors of meat and vegetables alike. He
wondered if Rene could be hired away from the widow.
Mayhap it was time to change his policy about who did
the cooking. Potatoes, other roots, even the onions
were crisp. His tongue wanted to dance. The only other
time he felt like this was in the early stages of bed play.
He laughed aloud at the thought.

Several of the men nearby jumped up, reaching for
their weapons. Others swiveled their heads in his direction. Startled looks adorned their gravy-stained faces.

"What's the matter? May a man not laugh at a passing
thought?"

His men sat and looked away, all but Soames.

"Why did they start so at my laughter?"

Soames looked at his feet, then back up at Haven.
"Sir, it's just that . . . well, you have not . . . that is . . ."

"Just what is it that I have not and is . . . ?" Haven
bellowed, suspecting what Soames feared to say.

"You have not laughed, Sir Haven," the man blurted.
"Not since Roger Dreyford was convicted of treason."

"Enough." Haven held up his hand, neither wanting nor needing the reminder. Roger was ever present in Haven's thoughts. Silently he cursed the marriage that had changed his friend from loyal subject to traitor. "Finish your dinner and set the guard. I am going to sleep."

He turned his back on his men. Wrapping himself in the cloak that Watley had retrieved from the widow, Haven lay down. He prayed to God for guidance and forgiveness. Then, pushing guilt and regret aside, he forced himself to sleep.

He woke to a morning filled with fog. He could barely see his hand when he lifted it at arm's length from his face. He called out to the guard and received an answer. Seeking Soames or Watley, Haven moved carefully around the camp, shaking bodies awake as he encountered them. By the time all his men were roused, the fog began to clear. The clang of pots sounded from the direction of the cook's fire.

Haven could make out the glow and several figures moving near it. Good; the widow's party was awake. Now he would set down the law with her. This was the only morning they would dawdle over a meal.

He passed Marie and Therese carrying bread and cheese to where his men sat. With one hand, Haven snagged a piece of bread from Marie. He shoved it into his mouth, chewed and strode toward the tent.

He tucked his gloves into his belt and moved through the opening.

Behind him the tent flap muffled Marie's, "No, no, Sir Haven, you must not."

But it was the widow who made him halt.

Chapter Five

A worn white sleeping robe draped the widow's body. A subtle scent, like lavender and cream, tangled in his head, and he stopped, chained in place by the sight before him.

She stood at a right angle to him, her head turned away as she lit a branch of candles. Could this be the same woman? Certainly the form outlined against the translucent cloth was tall and slim, but this woman had curves. Rounded hips swayed beneath a tiny waist. Above that, as she raised her arms, a gentle swell hinted at delicate breasts. Haven's whole body tightened. And that hair. No dark sodden mass this, but a wild tumble of curls that cascaded like sabled fire over the fine, pale column of her neck—a neck that swans would envy. He should leave, but he knew he would not.

"*Une moment*, Marie . . ."

At the sound of her sultry, sloe-eyed voice, lust jolted through him, hard and hot. Visions of twined bodies,

56

limned in fireglow, hazed his head. He felt dizzy, as if a thousand feathers had stroked his skin from top to toe and lingered on the straining flesh between his . . . This is Roger's wife his conscience screamed at him. A thought which prompted him to offer up a prayer, for God help him, he seemed unable to stop the need she inspired in him.

". . . I am almost ready for the salve."

She dropped the robe from her shoulders, and fury choked the words that would have announced his presence.

Her shape was everything her silhouette had promised. But the skin that should have glowed with good health bore ugly purple-green splotches. The injuries looked so painful that he almost failed to notice that her ribs stood out against her skin, bespeaking long-endured hunger.

He grasped her shoulder with the anger-hard fingers of one hand and spun her round to face him. "How did this happen?"

She screamed once, and then stared at him, her body rigid, her eyes wide with some emotion—surprise, fear, anger or pride. He could not say which. She uttered a small gasp and moved to cover herself with her hands.

He looked into her eyes. He had seen too much of her already. More than enough to know that bruises like those on her back covered her front and legs too, just as they covered her face. Yesterday, rain, mist and bias—yes, bias, he admitted to himself—had obscured his vision. Then he had thought her face, beaten though it was, her only claim to beauty. Now he knew better. *Did she feel so much guilt over what she had done to Roger that she hurt herself in penance?*

"How did this happen?" He repeated through teeth clenched against anger.

From behind him came the sharp whisper of steel. He shot out his free arm from the shoulder in a backward motion. At the same moment that a blade's tip stung his neck, he grasped the wrist of his attacker with an iron hand. Cold fury threatened his reason. His gaze remained on the widow's face.

"Get your hands off Milady Genvieve. Else I will sheath this dirk in your neck." Marie's cheerful voice had become a defensive growl. Despite his grip on her wrist, the blade never wavered.

Haven dropped his hand from the widow so quickly that she stumbled backward. Yet he stared at her, still. The wounded beauty of the widow was a greater lure than the unsheathed metal behind him.

Curtained by that stunning hair, the widow bent and retrieved her robe. She raised wary eyes to him, then scrambled toward the bedding, the robe shielding her body.

"Now, Sir Haven, please leave me to tend to milady."

"Put away your dagger, Nurse. You need it not."

"Aye. Ye're right at that, sir."

He heard the knife slide home in its sheath. What was wrong with him? He had not heard the nurse enter the tent and barely noticed when she drew her blade. He had even let that blade remain drawn at his exposed back, rather than tear his gaze from the widow. Never before had his reaction to a woman's body made him stupid. So this could not be simple lust—but it had to be. No other explanation was possible.

What was it about the widow that dulled his brain and made him lose all good sense? Was she a witch? Was that how she led Roger astray? Did she now work her wiles on him? He shifted sideways, pulling the nurse into his line of vision, but he kept his focus on the widow. "You will explain."

She gave him gaze for gaze. "I have already told you of the stoning. Besides, you have no authority to demand explanations."

"I have the king's authority over your person and all you own. That alone gives me the right. And stones do not cause thinness such as yours."

He could see defiance build in her narrowed eyes and tightened jaw.

If the widow wanted a battle, so be it. He set his hands on his hips and leaned forward in challenge.

A figure in brown wool filled his vision. "Go break your fast, sir. Milady will fight with you soon enough," Marie interrupted with all the bluster of a sergeant-at-arms.

Haven allowed the nurse to place her hands on his shoulders and turned him about. She gave his back a shove, propelling him out of the tent.

Behind him he heard the nurse mutter, "Good, milady. If you must butt heads with a mailed knight, do it after you are dressed."

His lips formed a smile. Laughter grew in his chest and then cut off abruptly when he saw young Thomas barreling toward him.

"What . . . ?"

The boy ignored the question. He stopped half a stride short of impact with Haven. A rapid series of blows to his knees and lower thighs followed, accompanied by several kicks to his shins.

"Do not hurt Mama. *Je vais te tuer!*"

Haven ignored the threat of death at five-year-old hands and looked down at his assailant. He grabbed the boy, pinning his flailing arms to his sides, then raised the child to eye level.

"Would you kill your king's loyal servant, boy?"

"Vraiment, que tu et bête."

"Perhaps, but Edward Plantagenet does not share your opinion. Thus stupidity alone is not cause for murder of one of his knights."

The child's lip trembled, and Haven saw fear widen the boy's eyes.

"Ne t'approche pas de ma mere, ou je te tue," the boy muttered.

"So you will kill me if I come near your mother?" Haven admired the boy's courage, a trait shared by both the child's parents, as well as a tendency to take on more than he could handle. At least the widow had not made a coward of her son. But like his mother, the boy lacked discretion. "Will you now? And what makes you think you've need to kill me?"

The boy glared silent hatred at Haven.

"Answer me, young sir." He stood the boy back on the ground. Haven loosened his hold and squatted to maintain eye contact. Still the boy had to look upward.

"The bad men, they hurt Mama when we went to live outside. I heard her scream at them. I wanted to kill them, Mama said I should not, and the men went away. Mama screamed at you. You are a bad man."

"No. I am not a bad man."

The child shrugged out of Haven's grip, doubt drawn in the boy's raised eyebrows and the mouth that had ceased trembling.

Despite the rage that poured through Haven at the thought of the woman's pain, he kept his voice calm. He did not want to frighten the boy.

"What did these bad men do?"

"They stole our food. When Mama tried to chase them away, they threw stones at us and kicked her."

"Did I throw stones or kick your mama?"

The boy crinkled his brow. "No. But she screamed at you."

"Women scream for many reasons."

"Not Mama." Thomas's expression twisted into a determined pout.

"Mayhap not. But you have my word that I did not harm your mama."

"I do not believe you." Thomas thrust his arms out and shoved with surprising strength for one so young.

Unprepared for this new assault, Haven swayed before bracing himself with his hands, then rose to his full height.

The boy ran in the opposite direction. "Stay away from Mama," trailed behind him.

Haven stood, amazed that anyone, even a child of Thomas's inexperience, would question his word.

Footsteps approached from the direction of the tent.

"Do you now bully children as well as defenseless women, Sir Haven?"

Haven felt anger tighten his neck and shoulders. Who was this sultry-voiced witch to think she could call him a bully? In one swift movement, he turned to face her.

"No, madame, I do not threaten children, or defenseless women. By all rights I should have killed your nurse for drawing a weapon on me. But I tolerate even that out of concern for your person."

Incredibly she gave a snort of disbelief.

He had to put her in her place. "Do not imagine, madame, that your meager charms bewitch me." Haven leaned forward and spoke softly, his face a quill's breadth from hers. "I do not like you, Madame Genvieve Elise des Jardins Dreyford. I do not like your manners. I despise the treason you inspired in my good friend, your husband."

He grabbed his gloves from his belt and saw her cringe. Did she imagine he would strike her?

"You are entirely too independent for your own good and will bring disaster on us all unless you learn how to take orders. Had I the choice, I would see you burn at the stake like the witch you are. But I do not have that choice. King Edward orders that I bring you to him. Bring you to him I will, and no one will be able to say you suffered harm in my charge."

"How dare you, sir."

He ignored her outrage. "Even more important to me, I swore an oath to your husband to guard his family. I will perform my duty to the king, and I will keep you safe until I bring you to him, with or without your cooperation. Even if I must protect you from yourself. Do you understand me?"

Genvieve tucked her chin in toward her neck and nodded, too furious to speak.

"Good. Now wait here. We will leave as soon as I am mounted." He strode away casually, slapping his gloves against his thigh.

Gennie goggled at his retreating backside. Her hands fisted at her sides. Her feelings seethed in rank confusion and boiled unchecked out of her mouth. "You bullheaded ox. How dare you accuse me of fostering treason, when you yourself betrayed your best friend to the hangman's noose."

She saw de Sessions's shoulders tighten and his stride hesitate, but he walked on, ignoring her verbal stab.

Just who did the high-and-mighty Haven de Sessions think he was to say she was too independent? If what he claimed was true, she wanted the same thing he did, safety for Thomas and his family. Of course, men rarely meant what they said. Roger and his broken marriage vows were proof of that.

Gennie shook her head slowly. She had no intention of learning how to take orders from a lout like Sir Haven de Sessions. Imagine calling her a witch and insulting her manners, as if his own unmannered display did not prove how little he knew of courtesy.

How could he claim that she inspired Roger to treason? If anyone had betrayed her husband, it was Sir Haven de Sessions, Roger's supposed best friend. De Sessions, and none other, had brought Roger to the king and certain death. If she had any alternative, she would be damned before she trusted herself and her family to his protection. Hah! Roger's good friend indeed.

Yet the men seemed to respect de Sessions, and some had been with the knight for years. Behind her, she heard the sounds of men dismantling the shelter. Soames's orders rose above the general noise. It might be worth her while to know what de Sessions's own man thought of him. She turned to Soames, determined to discover all that she could about Haven de Sessions.

"Sir Haven is a man of strong opinions."

"Aye." Soames eyed her suspiciously but did not move away.

"I am surprised a man with such strong opinions remains in favor with the king."

"Mayhap you are, milady."

Soames's reticence was less than encouraging. Nonetheless, Gennie pressed on. "I gather the knight is a man of some repute."

"Aye, true and perfect is what many say of him."

"My experience of him would not lead me to say so."

"Begging your pardon, milady, but I will risk saying that your experience of Sir Haven is limited."

"True," Gennie conceded to the gentle censure. "Still, 'tis my belief the man is misnamed."

"How so, milady?"

"Sir Haven is not my idea of any sort of haven."

"Is he not?" Soames chuckled.

"Non."

"Maybe you would prefer to be scrabbling and starving in the rain as you were yesterday instead of warm and safe, with a full belly, as you are today."

"I would have managed." Gennie sniffed, unprepared to admit that she hadn't known how to feed or care for herself and her family.

"As you say, milady. But is that what you want for your son?"

Gennie looked up at the older man's face and saw the understanding there. *"Non,"* she said quietly and looked away.

When she looked at Soames again, she found his kind gaze still on her. "You give me much to think on, Soames."

"You don't seem to me to be an unreasonable woman, milady, so here's somewhat more to think on. Sir Haven suffered greatly because of Roger Dreyford's death."

Gennie's brows rose. "Really?" She shifted to watch the men disassembling the tent.

Soames moved with her.

"Indeed, milady. Sir Haven and your husband were squires on Edward's journey to Acre. They were blooded in battle together and became fast friends. When the king ordered Sir Haven to bring Dreyford to court, my master struggled mightily with his conscience."

"He seems lacking in conscience to me."

"That comment is unworthy, milady. You do not know Sir Haven as I do."

She flushed. "You are right. I do not know de Sessions as well as you. Please tell me more of this struggle."

"As I said, he and Dreyford were fast friends. They would joke about the marriage of their children, when neither had a child. Often they spoke of Sir Haven acquiring lands near the Dreyford holdings, when Sir Haven's service to the king was done. There was troth between them, as only could be for men who saved each other's lives. So much so that they felt no need for the vows that usually bind men in friendship."

"Given such a friendship, Sir Haven's course should have been clear when the king gave his orders about Roger."

"Sir Haven's course was clear. That was the problem."

"Soames, you speak in riddles."

"It is no riddle to honor a vow of fealty, even at the cost of friendship. You know as well as I, milady, that to break a vow is to risk the loss of one's soul to eternal damnation."

"I also know that one may be released from any vow by the church."

"Perhaps, but breaking one's oath to a king, especially a king like Longshanks, warrants the axeman's blade. Unlike your husband, Sir Haven has no death wish."

"My husband did not want to die."

"No? Perhaps he was only foolish."

Roger had been foolish in the extreme, but Gennie was not about to share that with de Sessions's loyal warrior. If Soames wanted absolution for his lord's foul acts, let him seek it elsewhere. "My husband is not at

65

issue here. He has already suffered for his misdeeds."

"And you still think that Sir Haven has not?"

"I know not what to think, Soames."

"I am more than willing to be at your service, should you wish to pursue this matter further."

"And what matter is that, Soames?" Sir Haven's stern voice issued from behind.

Gennie jumped. She turned to him with Soames. She felt very small with de Sessions glaring at her from the back of his horse.

"Lady Genvieve only wished to reassure herself of her son's safety, sir."

Gennie wondered at Soames's vague, if true, response.

Stone-faced, Sir Haven looked at her. "You may come to me with your questions, madame. You need not bother my men." He put his hand out to help her mount.

Faced with the choice of taking his hand or blistering his ears, Gennie spoke. "Sir, you . . ."

"Please you, madame, mount the horse."

She shivered at the coldness in his expression; now was not the time to chastise him for his rudeness. She took his hand and mounted, wondering just how much more she would take from de Sessions before she killed him in a fit of temper.

Unfortunately, at the moment, he was all that stood between herself and a fate similar to her careless husband's. She would find a way out of this, she just did not know when or how.

Chapter Six

Haven frowned. They should have arrived in York yesterday. Now another dawn would pass before they saw the outskirts of that city.

The delay was the widow's fault entirely. A league back, he had paused so that she might eat. He had heard her stomach rumbling. And since the stubborn woman would not ask, he had kindly offered her some dried meat from his pouch. Of course the first thing she had done was pass the simple fare to her son. He would have let her go hungry, but the nearly constant sounds from her stomach annoyed him. So they had stopped and eaten.

He watched her tend her son and see her sister-in-law and servants fed. When she turned to serve his men, he had had enough. He took her by the arm, marched her to a fallen tree and, with a hand on her shoulder, forced her to sit. Grabbing the bread and cheese from her hands, he gave her a portion, then called Bergen to distribute the remainder. He ordered her to eat and watched to make sure she did not once more give her food away to Thomas, who came scampering up to his mother with a plea for sweets.

The display of hugs and teasing words between mother and son nearly turned Haven's stomach, but the boy was obviously hungry for her attention.

The widow sent the boy off to her cook. Haven waited as patiently as he could for her to finish eating. When the last crumb vanished, he ordered the party to mount. Too much time had been wasted in coddling this woman.

Now, because the boy had a bellyache, they were stopped for the fourth time since morning. Shortly after midday, Thomas had begun to whine. Whimpering from the child had prompted Soames to request a halt. The severity of the boy's condition concerned the older man.

Before they had reached an appropriate clearing, the whimpers had become cries. Haven had ground his teeth at the interruption, swallowed his curses and, at the first clearing, ordered the party to stop. And while the widow and her women tended the child, the cries had turned to howls.

Haven had left. A cowardly action, but one he excused because he knew nothing of childish bellies and how to fix one that ached. He had grabbed the water skins and stomped off to fill them at the nearby creek.

Now he had returned and found the boy sleeping in the sun with the nurse and Rebecca watching over him. Haven surveyed the edge of the clearing. Not a guard in sight.

He looked for the widow and found her, accompanied by her maid and surrounded by his men. What does she do, he wondered, that turns my men to mindless dolts? Whatever it is, it will cease now.

From now on he would brook no further delays. Edward wanted them in Chester. By all that was holy, he would perform the task his king set for him, even if he must take the widow ahead by himself. His men could keep Thomas and his aunt safe and come on to Chester at a slower pace. The plan was good. Yes, if they did not cover more than forty leagues beyond York in the next three days, that was what he would do.

Determined, he strode from the tree line into camp. He heard laughter rumble from the men circled about the widow.

"Soames! Get these people mounted and ready to ride."

His lieutenant gave him a startled look, then snapped to attention. "Yes, sir." He bellowed orders at the men.

The knot of men surrounding the widow scattered. She glared up at Haven, as if an ill wind had tattered her carefully spun web.

No doubt she tried to plant seeds of insurrection among the warriors. Too bad she did not know his men as well as he did. Some were inexperienced, but all were blooded. She would find poor soil for her schemes among loyalties forged in battle. Satisfaction turned up the corners of Haven's mouth, and he was able to bank the anger the widow ignited in him.

He grasped her elbow and urged her toward his horse. "Do not think to charm my men into foolishness as you did your husband."

She shook off his hand.

He heard her outraged gasp at the same time that he felt pain shoot up his leg from where she kicked his shin. Grasping the injured limb, he hopped toward his horse. "I curse the day I ordered Watley to give you those boots.

69

What ails you, woman, that you must kick me?"

"What ails you, Sir Numbskull, that you accuse me of such a loathsome action as leading my husband to treason?" She crossed her arms over her chest.

Haven opened his mouth, then closed it, for she had thrust her face within a hand span of his. The scent of lavender filled his head. He lost track of his words.

"You threaten me with death," she spoke with surprising calm. "I have no choice but to come with you. Then you insult my servants and me at every turn. I refuse to suffer your rudeness any longer."

Even uttered in her houri's voice, her tirade raised his hackles. Haven narrowed his glance and lowered his mal-treated leg, wincing as the abused limb took his weight. "Tell me, madame, how you will end this so-called suffering?"

"Simple, Sir Bully; I will pray." With that, she turned abruptly and walked to his horse where she waited for him to assist her.

Haven eyed her suspiciously, uncertain how prayer would relieve her suffering. He mounted his horse, then lifted her up behind him. Pray as she might, he would show her no more courtesy than any other suspected traitor.

Three days later, despite acquiring more horses, they had made less than thirty leagues beyond York. Haven did some praying of his own. The party was stopped once again, and taking the widow to Chester by himself was now the only option, if he wished to arrive on time. He prayed for patience and for deliverance. He had had no idea that one woman not in holy orders had so many prayers stored up inside. And if he had to listen to one more supplication to *le Bon Dieu* for the softening of his heart and the saving of his soul, Haven was certain he would strangle the widow.

After a mere league of constant prayer, he had ordered her to ride farther back, with one or another of his men. Haven savored a blessed silence until he had seen how his men behaved. Each and every one of them became simpering, mooning idiots.

After York she had ridden next to Sutherland at the back of the party, and the warrior had become so distracted by her that he had let their horses wander from the trail. Once the disappearance had been discovered, precious time had been lost retrieving the two stragglers.

In the process of rejoining the party, Sutherland's horse had thrown a shoe. Haven sent Bergen off to find the nearest village with a smithy and get the horse reshod. Trouble followed the widow, and Haven began to believe she existed just to aggravate him.

Is it possible, he asked himself, that the widow somehow loosened the horse's shoe unobserved? He shook his head at the ridiculous image. *She's driving you mad, de Sessions. No doubt that's how she sent Roger to treason. She drove him mad. Do not allow her to do the same to you.*

Haven resigned himself to the necessity of traveling alone with the widow to Chester. That moment when he had seen her bruises and more, he had proven to himself that he was immune to her wiles, despite his strong physical reaction to her. It seemed he was the only one of his men to resist. Even Soames had come under the widow's influence. Haven recalled his second-in-command's disturbing offer of service to the widow.

Haven surveyed the grassy bank where his men waited. Some time would pass before Bergen came back and they could turn their steps again toward Chester. Perhaps he should speak to Soames about the widow. As if conjured by thought, Soames approached.

"Please you, sir, I would have private speech with you."

Haven nodded, checking to see that they would not be overheard.

"Lindel reports finding tracks to the north."

"What direction are they traveling?"

"The tracks parallel ours."

"How many men?"

"Fifteen."

"Did you have a man backtrack this trail?"

"Aye, I sent Lindel to follow the trail forward and Sutherland to backtrack."

"Why Sutherland?"

"He needed reminding where his duty lay."

"Good. The widow has charmed too many of my men into forgetting their duty.

"Sir, I think the problem lies elsewhere."

Haven paused. The last time Soames had contradicted him was before the battle where Haven and Roger had saved the day and won their spurs. But the cost had been great. Afterward, Soames, who had been his mentor to that point, had praised Haven's prowess and fighting skill, then told him how foolish he had been. The criticism had hurt at the time, but he had never again rushed blindly into battle.

"I value your counsel, Soames. Tell me where you think the problem lies."

Soames shifted and looked at the ground, then off into the distance, before looking squarely at Haven. "Sir, you know that nearly all Edward's court calls you his most true and perfect knight."

Haven felt heat rise on his neck. "Aye. It's a silly,

womanish notion that a man as unsaintly as I might be perfect."

"You got that reputation for perfection because of your pleasing bed manner with the women. They gave it you. And the men, seeing your success with the women, agreed."

" 'Tis no less silly."

"Lady Genvieve might agree with you. But your men hold you in high regard nonetheless. They have noticed that, with Milady Genvieve, your manner is less than gentle."

"And this is cause for acting like fools around her?"

"They are proud of their service with a man of your repute. They think you are still overcome by grief at Dreyford's death. They want the widow to believe about you as they do."

"They should not. The woman led her husband to treason."

"So you and our king believe. Have you proof of her perfidy?"

Haven gave a quiet snarl. "Look you what became of Roger Dreyford."

"Despite your love for him, Dreyford had a passion for stories and danger. He would have come to a bad end regardless."

"His wife should have influenced him to remain loyal to his king and satisfied his passions at home."

"Are you so certain she did not try?"

"On the scaffold, Roger said he could not trust his wife."

"And on the basis of Roger's word, you treat Lady Genvieve as if she were Lucifer's daughter, rather than a gentle dame whose husband's lust for danger put her and her son at risk."

Haven felt grief and guilt surge sourly in his stomach. "Roger may have been careless, but he was not mean. He would not falsely accuse his wife."

"Did he accuse her? You said he could not trust her. That does not sound like an accusation of treason to me."

"You did not see him as he said the words. He was my best friend. He could mean nothing else."

"As you say, sir, I was not there. But you might talk to Lady Genvieve and discover if she loved Dreyford."

Haven bit his tongue on a sharp response. To discuss the more intimate aspects of Roger's marriage with his widow seemed completely inappropriate, yet the idea pricked at him. Dark emotions stirred him. At their source stood the widow Dreyford. "I agree, Soames. I shall speak with her before we leave this place."

Soames gave him a long look. "I pray you and Lady Genvieve will come to a better understanding." Then he turned and left.

"So do I, Soames. So do I," Haven whispered to the air as memory overtook him.

Roger had stood at the foot of the scaffold, his wrists bound behind his back. The executioner motioned him forward. Roger set his foot upon the stair, but looked back at his friend. "My son is barely five, Haven. He cannot protect himself, and I cannot trust my wife. Swear to me that you will guard his life in my stead."

Haven hesitated, feeling the pull of his friend's request like a noose. "Roger, I cannot . . ."

Roger gave a dry laugh. "You would deny me your oath, when you are the one who brought me to my death?"

"Nay," the word crawled from Haven's throat. "I did not bring you to this. For all that I love you as the brother

74

I never had, you brought death upon yourself, when you drew a blade upon the king."

"The king is a curse upon England, with threats to tax the clergy and his defiance of the Pope."

"That is folly, and you know it. The king seeks only the funds he needs to protect that same clergy who without that protection would fall prey to every thief and vandal."

Roger spit on the ground. "That for the king. He matters not to me now. What matters is that e're this, you and I were friends. Sworn to each other in battle, the only oath that cannot be broken."

"I have never sworn to you, nor you to me."

"You would deny it." Roger's widened eyes and jutting chin dared Haven to oppose him.

Haven's eyes slid away. He could not look Roger in the eye and say him nay. "Not in words. I never swore to you in words."

Roger sneered. "Pah. We needed no words. How many times have you and I saved each other's lives? How many times did we speak of the marriage of our children? When your family died of sickness, did my father not take you in and give you a home? How can you not promise to care for my son as my father cared for you?"

Haven felt heat flush his face. To refuse an oath to a confessed traitor was not wrong. So why did he feel guilty? Why did Roger remain defiant? Haven set his jaw. He had always done what was right, not just what was easy. Why else would he bring his own friend to the hangman, if it were not the right thing to do? 'Twas surely not the easy thing to do. Before Roger had been a traitor, he had been Haven's friend. And the right thing to do was to safeguard an innocent child's life.

"Please, Haven. Swear to protect Thomas."

The priest who stood behind them silently urged Roger

up the stairs, and the space between the two friends grew.

Haven gave a curt nod. "Aye." He reached out and grasped the cross that hung from the prelate's neck. "I swear to protect your son and all his family."

The priest's movements up the stairway pulled the cross from Haven's hand.

"Tell me one last thing, Roger." Haven's voice broke.

His friend looked to him from atop the scaffold. The executioner gripped one of Roger's arms in a meaty hand.

"Ask quickly, Haven. I have little time left."

"Who wants the king dead? Who talked you into trying to kill Edward?"

The executioner pulled Roger forward. As the noose was placed 'round his throat, he twisted his head and called out. "I don't know them all, but Gennie knows the man who convinced me that England is better off without Edward Plantagenet on the throne."

The snap of the rope going taut did not hide the crack of Roger's neck breaking.

Haven swallowed the bile that rose in his throat and watched his friend's body dangle in the gentle breeze.

"A clean death, sir." The executioner's face swam into Haven's view, obscuring what was left of Roger Dreyford. "D'ye want to dispose of the body yerself?"

"Aye." Haven reached in his pouch for silver to pay the man. A clean death was not usually given to traitors such as Roger. "I have a cart for transporting him."

"Very good, sir. Bring it 'round, and I'll load the body on fer ye."

"Indeed," Haven murmured to himself. "I should certainly have a talk with the widow. For it is not my manner that leads my men to foolishness, but the widow's serpentine charm. She needs to understand just what the bounds of her behavior are."

Determined to set the widow straight about her behavior with his men, Haven walked to where she sat with her son.

The sun gleamed in her hair as her laughter rippled forth at the boy's pranks. Still too slim, the gaunt, dry look of hunger had disappeared. The bruises had faded, no longer hiding the fine slant of her cheekbones. Contentment shimmered in her green eyes, and her full mouth smiled berry bright. Did those lips taste as ripe as they looked?

Her creamy lavender scent struck him hard. Haven shook his head. She did not affect him. Now that she was clean and healing, she was an attractive woman. Any man would wonder about the feel of her in his arms. But he knew what lay beneath the pretty surface of Genvieve Dreyford. He would not fall victim to her seductive glamour and betray Roger with his wife, no matter how tempting she might be.

So when he stopped before mother and son, he spoke more sternly than he intended to the boy. "Thomas, attend your aunt. I must speak with your mother."

Thomas looked up at him. The boy's lower lip trembled, but he stood up straight. "Aye, Sir Haven."

"It's all right, Thom. I will only be a little while. When Sir Haven and I are finished, I will join you and Rebecca, and we'll have some of Rene's good bread."

The boy looked at her.

"Go on."

"All right."

He left, peering over his shoulder every three steps, as if he feared she would disappear.

*   *   *

Gennie studied de Sessions as he watched her son run off. The sun gleamed on the man's mail shirt, surrounding him in a golden haze, much like the angels shown in the windows of the chapels in France. The mail-covered shoulders and chest could have been forged by God's own smithy. His golden-brown eyes looked on her with the kind of blazing light that bards gave to fairie kings.

But this was no magical being, she reminded herself. Sir Haven de Sessions was solid and real. His broad forehead, straight nose and unsmiling mouth seemed chiseled in marble. She knew that beneath his hose, his rock-hewn thighs were supple enough to guide a horse without the aid of reins and hands. And those hands. She had come near to swooning the day he had tended her feet, running his strong fingers over her, smoothing lotion into her pain-ridden soles, then binding each foot with a gentleness belied by his strength.

The man was a danger to any woman who did not know he owned a heart of stone. *'Tis a good thing I know how pigheaded he is, or I might be tempted by all that manliness.*

"What is it you would say to me, that my son may not hear?"

"Walk with me." He grasped her by the elbow, giving her no opportunity to protest. He marched toward the riverbank and the screen of trees there.

She sighed at his abrupt manner and doubled her strides to match his long ones. She had been on her best behavior since he had refused to ride with her. She had hoped that he might notice how cooperative and uncomplaining she had been with all his men. She had asked each man for aid or advice when she needed none. She had no desire to put the party at risk as Sir

Haven claimed she would if she did not curb her independence.

"You must stop trying to enchant my men." He halted to hold back a branch so she could pass to where the bank broadened again.

Upset by this unjust accusation, Gennie brushed past him, hoping he would not notice the flush of fury in her face. "Wh . . . why . . . yo . . ." She stuttered, trying to remain composed. She would not let his idiotic stubbornness make her lose her temper again.

"Surely you must see why?"

His words brought her to a halt. He thought she wanted an explanation of his request. In order to do so she would have to have tried to *enchant his men*. Her eyes crossed, and her breath choked in her throat.

How could the man be so wrongheaded? Charming his men, any man, was the last thing Gennie wanted. Being married to Roger had taught her that men were generally more trouble than they were worth. Why could not de Sessions see that all she wanted was a safe haven for her son? "You are mistaken, Sir Haven."

"So you do understand; good. We can ill afford more accidents like the one that befell Sutherland's horse."

Gennie gritted her teeth, pursed her lips and turned to face him. She held a stiff rein on the temper that threatened to run rampant at his words. "No, sir. I do not understand at all. What causes you to believe that I attempt to enchant your men? Have I not curbed my independent ways, as you requested? Have I not sought out your men to speed our making and breaking of camp each day? Have I not kept my eyes downcast, my words gentle and my manner seemly?"

"That is just what you have done." He took a step forward. "Such gentle pleading from a woman makes a man soft-brained; he loses concentration. My men are so distracted by attending to your needs that they fail to attend to their duty."

"Let me be certain of what you mean, sir." Her hands went to her hips as temper began to override her control. "My manner with your men disturbs you, and therefore you would have me behave in an unseemly fashion."

"Yes." His brow wrinkled. "No. That is, uh . . ."

"I think it is not your men who've become soft-brained. Your men have been thoughtful of the needs of my family and servants. They have shown naught but respect and kind consideration for my son and my sister-in-law. I know only one person who is dissatisfied with my actions. And that is you, Sir Addlelpate. From the day we met, you have treated me as if I were evil incarnate. And despite some small consideration for my person, you alone behave with brainless stupidity around me. If you think for one minute that I . . ."

"What I think is that you must needs be shown how a man behaves when a woman causes him to lose his mind."

On those words he closed his arms about her. Her feet left the ground. While she was busy trying to grasp his shoulders for balance, he kissed her. Gennie forgot to worry about having both feet in the air, so unexpected was the soft press of his lips against hers. She forgot to clutch at his shoulders.

Instead, she tunneled her hands into the warm, dark silk at his nape. She nearly forgot to breathe until the gentle scrape of his teeth on her lower lip caused her to open her mouth in surprise and inhale. Then his hot velvet tongue was in her mouth, succulent with his per-

sonal flavor and seeking her own, until he teased her
into response.

A rapid beat filled her ears. Her entire body vibrated
to that elemental rhythm. She inhaled more deeply. His
masculine scent intensified her need. She pressed herself against him and felt his arms tighten about her. The
sensation was wondrous, brilliant and dark, frightening
and secure.

She hung suspended at the boundary of a heaven
created solely for her. At the very edge of her senses, a
rustling disturbed the need that rose in her. She felt a
change in the strength that held her safe. A tiny mewl
of protest escaped her.

But Haven set her on her feet, his arms already leaving her. The need to remain in his embrace confused
her, especially when she looked into his face and saw
not a gentle lover but a hunter.

His head was up. His eyes searched the glade. His
nostrils flared, as if scenting his prey.

"Wait here." And he was gone as swiftly as a hawk
that sights a hare.

Genvieve shivered but felt no cold. She put her hands
to her cheeks. Her fingers warmed with the flush of heat
on her skin. She could not be yielding to the horrid
man, could she? When Roger had gone whoring, Gennie had vowed never to allow a man to dominate her
again. But if she held to that vow, then what were these
strange feelings that de Sessions inspired? Even in the
first days of her marriage, Roger had never kissed her
breathless. "*Sacre bleu*, what is happening to me?"

Before she could answer her own question, Haven
returned.

He continued to scan the clearing as he spoke. "Whoever was in those bushes is small and fast, or I would

have caught him. Come." He held out his hand to her. "We've been too far from my men for too long."

Gennie looked at him as if he had grown three new heads.

"Well." He finally looked at her, and thrust his hand closer when she did not take it.

Gennie shook her head and sidled out of reach.

"What is wrong with you? We must return to camp now." The words rushed at her like arrows.

Her daze broke at the sound. She darted around him and out of the clearing.

Haven watched her flee, since she was headed back to the rest of their party. But for several moments he stood gazing after her. *I kissed her speechless.* He smiled at the thought. He savored the remembered flavors of her mouth, the lavender-cream scent of her and the texture of her trembling body's response to his.

Still, the kiss was a mistake that he would not make again. He had lost all control and placed them both in danger. If he ever again kissed Genvieve Dreyford he would be certain they were safe and secure from all interruption. Of course, another chance to kiss the widow was unlikely at best, given the way Edward felt about traitors.

Even worse, she was Roger's widow. To dally with her would be to dishonor his friendship with Roger, and that Haven would never do. Nor would he break the oath he gave to that condemned friend to protect the man's family. What kind of protection would it be to bed his friend's wife? No, touching the woman again was out of the question.

Chapter Seven

Haven stepped out of the woods and saw Gennie standing on the opposite side of the clearing. She spoke with Therese, her gestures sharp and impatient. The widow was still flustered. Obviously he had a strong affect on her. The thought pleased him and broadened his smile. Therese departed, throwing a glare at Haven as she did so. He considered going to the widow, but before he could decide, Soames approached with Lindel in tow. So Haven turned his grin on his second-in-command.

"What ho, Soames?"

"Sir, Lindel has news of those riders to the north."

Haven's grin became a thin line with the speed of a Welsh arrow. He gestured for the two men to accompany him into the trees sheltering the edge of the clearing. "Tell me."

"Sir," Lindel spoke quietly, "I followed the tracks, as Soames ordered. Since the day after we left York, fifteen armed men have ridden the same course as ours about a league to the north. Sometimes one or two of them break off to come south and watch our party. Yesterday, when we crossed the river, they remained on the other side."

"Have any forded the river to continue their watch on us?"

"Nay, sir. The far bank is higher ground, so they need not approach to keep eyes on our progress."

A muscle twitched in Haven's cheek. He rubbed the spot, reminded of another day when trouble had loomed. A day when he battled back-to-back with Roger Dreyford over an ever-growing pile of bodies. "The river runs faster now than before. I doubt they'll find good fords nearby. What think you, Soames?"

"I think three things. First, they may do as we do, guarding their backs by watching other travelers closely. Second, they may simply be stupid vandals. Third, they may be extremely clever, especially if they know more about this area than we."

"Aye." Haven continued to soothe his cheek, which now cramped most painfully, just as it had in the Holy Lands. "'Tis that third possibility that concerns me most."

"We could attack them, sir." Lindel's eyes gleamed with the suggestion of a fight.

"Nay, we could not bring our full force against theirs, for someone would have to guard the widow and her charges. That would leave us outnumbered."

Soames frowned. "As yet they do not know we watch them. Let us leave the less-experienced men to guard the widow. The rest of us are among Edward's best fighting men and have been outnumbered many times before. Do you doubt we could use surprise to our advantage?"

"I am confident in our abilities, as ever. And surprise, as you say, would be an advantage. But not, I think, sufficient advantage to overcome the difference in numbers and the fact that they hold the higher ground. No, attacking them now would be a foolish waste and could leave us prey to others. As long as we are prepared to defend ourselves and they remain on the opposite side of the river, we need do nothing more than keep careful watch."

"Aye, sir." The two men echoed their understanding.

"Lindel, go get you some food from the cook. Then, continue to keep watch on those men across the river."

The warrior nodded and walked away.

Haven turned to his second-in-command. "Soames, we are making better progress since York, but we will still fail to reach Edward in Chester at our current pace."

"I doubt the boy and his aunt can go much faster, sir."

"I agree. That is why I have decided to go on ahead with the widow. We can be in Chester within a few days' hard riding. I can wait for you there, once I have discharged my duty to Edward."

"Should you not take more men with you for protection?"

"Mayhap, I should. But I do not intend to fight. Should I come across any trouble, I intend to avoid it. A third rider might make that more difficult to do."

"Another man could delay an attack long enough for you and Lady Genvieve to escape."

" 'Tis a good point. I will think on it."

"Think you that the lady can keep up?"

"I will make sure of it."

Soames nodded. "As you say, sir."

"Good. Have Watley prepare my steed and the gray mare. They are the fastest and strongest. When they are ready, the widow and I will leave. You must follow with all possible speed."

"Aye, sir."

"And Soames . . ."

"Sir?"

"Have a care for the boy. I doubt it much that Thomas has ever been separated from his mother before."

"Aye, Sir Haven."

"I will go inform the widow of our change in plans."

Across the clearing, Gennie rubbed her upper arms. The heat of de Sessions's embrace lingered there. She still tingled from top to toe, as if the wings of a thousand butterflies beat against her skin from the inside. The feel of his lips on hers remained. Even Therese's sour complaints had not lessened the remembered sweetness of Haven's touch. How, Gennie wondered, could she find pleasure in the arms of the man who had betrayed his friend—her husband? She must be mad.

Therese had departed after spilling her venom about the discomforts de Sessions imposed upon them. *Merci Dieu.* Gennie had not even had the energy to scold the maid for breaking her vow of silence. Gennie needed to be alone, to consider what and how she felt about that terrifying kiss and the man who had given it to her. A man she knew could not be trusted.

Look how he undermined her confidence and made her doubt her own sanity. Conflicting feelings raced through her. E'er she could gather her thoughts, de Sessions approached and stole what little calm she had been able to gather.

"Madame, we have very little time to get to Chester."

"I told you, sir, that the journey could not be done in less than fourteen days."

"So you did, but I have never failed in my duty to my king, and I will not do so now. You and I will stand before the king in Chester before the next se'enight is out."

"Just how do you plan to work such a miracle?"

"We will leave my men and your party behind and ride posthaste to Chester."

Gennie felt her heart leap to her throat. "Thomas?"

"Will be quite safe with Soames and my men to guard him. He'll have his nurse and his aunt for comfort."

Gennie nodded, only somewhat reassured, for she might never see her son again. She swallowed, realizing that this decision was out of her hands. "How . . . ?"

"Since we obtained extra horses in York, you and I no longer need to keep to the slower pace of your son and his aunt. We will take the two fastest mounts and proceed with all speed to Chester. We will stop for naught but to rest the horses. Is that clear?"

She nodded again, unwilling to voice her fears at the too fast approach of her fate.

"Then make what preparations you can and say your farewells. We leave as soon as our mounts are ready."

Gennie went in search of her sister-in-law. Before saying good-bye to Thomas, Gennie wanted to inform Rebecca of the change in plans and advise her how best to help Thomas through a difficult time.

She found the girl with Marie. Marie was shouting at Rebecca, who cringed and twisted her hands in the face of the nurse's ire. While Marie did not normally hesitate to speak her mind, she rarely unleashed such fury. Something was very wrong.

"Marie." Gennie voiced all the authority she possessed to halt the nurse's verbal barrage.

"Milady." The woman's tone dropped to a respectful tone.

Rebecca uttered a sound that was half whimper, half gasp, before covering her face with her hands.

"What goes on here?"

Marie eyed Rebecca critically. "Rebecca should tell you, milady."

The girl shook her head. "I cannot," muffled out from behind her hands.

Impatient with her sister-in-law's hysterics, Gennie asked. "What must Rebecca tell me?"

"That Thomas is missing, Lady Genvieve."

Gennie's vision grayed and her world tilted. She felt someone's arms support her. Through the buzzing in her ears she heard Marie shout. "Rebecca, go fetch Sir Haven this instant."

When Gennie's vision cleared and the buzzing stopped, she found herself seated on a rock, her face and hands gently patted by Marie. Still, Gennie could not seem to find breath with which to speak either question or worry.

From somewhere behind her, de Sessions's voice prodded her out of panic.

"Rebecca, fetch a drink for your sister-in-law. While you are about that, tell Soames to have all the horses saddled, and when he has done so to gather the men and attend me."

The order snapped across the air. His calm question followed. "Are you well, madame?"

"Well?" The words strangled out of her as fear and anger battled within. "Of course I am well. It is my son who is far from well. And if you think I will leave without seeing him safe in Soames's care, you are more of a fool than I thought possible."

"Nay." His face came into her line of vision as Haven knelt before her. He took her hands from Marie. "We will not leave until Thomas is safe. No doubt the boy just followed a rabbit too far into the wood."

Heat from his hands seeped through her fingers and up her arms. She had not realized how cold she was. She looked into his brown eyes and saw compassion there. It nearly undid her. "Please, find my son."

"He will be found with all possible speed."

Haven looked up as Rebecca returned. He took the cup from her and placed it in the widow's hands; then he stood.

"Nurse, who was last to see Thomas?"

"I do not know, sir. I left the child with his aunt and stepped into the woods for a moment of privacy." Marie looked accusingly at Rebecca.

The girl trembled slightly, but she held her arms folded before her. A mulish pout decorated her mouth.

Haven pierced her with a glance. She dropped her arms. "When did you last see him, mistress?"

"A few moments after Marie departed."

"How long ago was that?"

"I am not certain. I know you and Lady Genvieve had not yet left the clearing together."

Haven thought back, estimating the amount of time that had passed since his encounter with the widow, and found himself appalled. "You left a child unattended that long?"

"Marie said she would return quickly. I waited. When Watley came by, I told Thomas to wait right here, since I wished private speech with Watley."

"I see." Haven spoke in his most forbidding tone. No

doubt the desired speech with his squire was nothing more than a flirtation.

"Nurse, how long were you gone?"

"Not long at all, sir. Yet when I returned, neither Thomas nor Rebecca was here."

"Did you go looking for them?"

"I searched the entire area. Until I found Mistress Rebecca dallying with your squire."

Haven made a mental note to lecture his squire on his proper place and the dangers of girlish flirtations. "Is that when you discovered that Thomas was gone?"

"Not quite, sir. First I boxed that squire's ears, begging your pardon. Then I gave Mistress Rebecca a sorely needed lesson about young men. Only when Mistress Rebecca tried to excuse her behavior did I realize that she had no more idea of Thomas's whereabouts than I."

At that moment Soames arrived. "You asked for me, sir?"

"Aye, Soames. Thomas is missing."

The man paled and shot a quick glance toward the river and the suspected location of the unidentified men who had been traveling a similar course to their own. "How . . . ?"

"We do not know," Haven cut in. "He may have followed a rabbit too deeply into the wood." Haven shared Soames's concern about the armed men from across the river, but he did not want to add abduction to the widow's worries.

"What are your orders?"

"We'll stay the night here. Even if we find Thomas quickly, his mother will want to spend some time with him before we have to travel again. Choose three men to remain with the widow as guards and to set up camp.

I want everyone else searching for that boy. We start at the river's edge and sweep the area forward past this clearing to one league."

"Aye, sir."

"Send one man upstream and one man down. Tell them to search both banks for any sign of Thomas, but not to leave the riverside except to return here. I will take the reports of all men when we return to the clearing. Any questions?"

"Nay, sir."

"Then assemble the men. I will follow."

Soames left, and Haven turned his attention to the widow. She no longer trembled, but she was pale and tense.

"Madame, I promise you, I will not rest until I have Thomas safe."

"Thank you."

The barely audible whisper squeezed his heart. She showed remarkable courage. He had expected her to demand that she accompany them in the search. Instead, she accepted his orders. With extraordinary calm, the widow placed her son's life in the hands of a man she claimed not to trust with her own.

"Marie, keep your mistress well. Thomas will need her when he returns."

"Aye, sir."

Haven left swiftly. If he lingered, he feared he might gather the widow into his arms.

Chapter Eight

Haven studied the faces of Soames and the rest of the men. All save two had returned, and each face told the same story. He felt a similar despair written on his own visage. He dismissed the men, telling them to get some rest. When they had all dispersed about the camp, Soames remained.

"You wished to speak with me, Soames?"

"Aye, sir. I am somewhat worried about Lindel and Bergen. They should have returned from searching the riverbanks by now."

Haven felt his mouth settle into a grim line. "I know, but as long as they remain away, there is still some hope that Thomas will be found. I do not relish the duty of telling the widow her son is stolen or drowned. Let us be certain first."

" 'Tis the stolen part that has me worried."

"Did you warn the men not to leave the riverbank except to return here?"

"So I did, but both men are fond of the boy. I think either man would pursue a trail if he found one. Were that the case and should the trail lead to those armed men, mayhap our man too is now prisoner or dead."

"That would be unfortunate, for then we would have to fight them, and Edward would be upset should we lose."

"Why should we lose? We have an almost equal number of men and surely the battle prowess of our men would measure up to, if not surpass, our opponents."

"Aye, but you yourself taught me that there is more to winning in battle than simple numbers. And I suspect that men who can steal a boy from under our noses have the kind of cleverness needed to sway the numbers in their favor. No." Haven rubbed his twitching cheek. "A battle is not my best choice."

"You would not fight just to get Thomas back?"

"If Thomas is with these men, I would steal him back. But if I were them, I would suspect that and be extra vigilant until I had put more distance between us."

Soames nodded sagely. "Then what will you do, sir? What will you say to Lady Genvieve?"

"Indeed, Sir Haven, what will you tell my brother's widow has happened to Thomas? What excuse will you give her for the convenient loss of a reminder that together you and the king murdered Roger Dreyford?"

Surprised, Haven turned together with Soames to look at Rebecca. Rage distorted the pretty girl's features into a hideous mask. The expression shocked Haven, for up to this point the girl had been obedient, if rather sullen and silent. Could she have overheard his refusal to attack the men on the opposite side of the river? He had deliberately not told the women and servants about the fifteen men, to avoid just such a confrontation as he was having now. Or was her outburst the result of a guilty conscience?

Regardless, her hysteria had to be stopped now. He had neither the time nor the inclination to indulge the girl's temper. "Quiet yourself." He used the same tone that he employed on the battlefield to shake sense back into green warriors who panicked at the first charge. "You know naught of what you speak." He continued in a softer voice. Unfortunately his words fell on deaf ears.

The fury in Rebecca's face fled, rapidly replaced by tears and sobs. "You great hulking bully," she wailed. "You kill your friends and abandon small boys to the wilderness. What will you do next, sir? Will you rape my sister-in-law and me, then sell our servants for slaves? You are more cruel than the king . . ."

Haven watched in horror as the girl ranted on, drawing the attention of all in the camp. Never in his entire career in the king's service had his command failed to restore order. Appalled at the effect of his words, Haven hesitated, uncertain for once in his life of what action to take.

From the corner of his eye, he saw the widow running toward them. She had lifted her skirts, revealing flashes of slender white calves above the boots he had given her. Her feet had barely begun to heal. She would hurt herself moving like that. Rebecca was the cause of this. "Stop that caterwauling. Now," he bellowed at the girl.

The young woman's eyes widened and her wails ceased with a loud gulp followed by a choking sound.

Haven ground his teeth. He might finally have stopped Rebecca's outburst, but he had been unable to save the widow pain, for she skidded to a halt, hugging Rebecca to her side.

"Rebecca, dearest sister, what is the meaning of all these tears?"

"Madame . . ." Haven spoke sternly but softly. He had no desire to provoke another outburst, but he wanted to explain what had happened.

The widow completely ignored him.

Rebecca's tears began afresh, and she turned her head into the widow's shoulder. "That awful man is going to abandon Thomas to the wood, after which we shall be raped and our servants sold."

The woman patted the girl's back. "Nonsense. He promised me before witnesses that we would not leave this place until Thomas is found."

Rebecca raised her head. "Lies to fool us into cooperating with him." The girl no longer shrieked, and her tears began to dry.

The widow placed one hand on Rebecca's shoulder. With the other, she raised the girl's chin until they stood eye to eye. "In all the days since we left Yorkshire, Sir Haven has never lied to us. He is an honorable knight, dedicated to his king's service. He has never failed in his duty nor in the performance of any oath. Is this not so, Soames?" As she sought confirmation of her claims, the older woman's gaze remained on Rebecca.

"Aye, milady. Sir Haven is Edward's most true and perfect knight in all things."

"Truly?" Rebecca hiccoughed and looked from the widow to Soames and back.

"Truly." The widow nodded. "Now calm yourself and tell me where you got such foolish notions."

The girl swallowed. "I would prefer not to say."

"Rebecca," the widow urged. "If someone is telling

lies of Sir Haven, he has the right to know who and to confront the man."

"It was not lies. Watley would never lie about Sir Haven."

An audible gasp poured from the group crowded around them and nearly drowned out her words.

Haven's eyes narrowed at her ridiculous statement. "Do you say that my squire accuses me of murder, rape and slavery?"

"Nay, sir, he accuses you not." Within the shelter of the widow's arms, Rebecca trembled. "He . . . he but told me tales of things that you and others did on the crusade. He never said you did those things, but others did, and you were with them. . . ."

Her voice quailed and wavered before the ire Haven took no trouble to hide.

Haven opened his mouth, but the widow spoke first.

"Foolish child." The older woman stroked the girl's face, making an endearment of her words. "You dishonor Sir Haven and his squire by drawing such groundless conclusions from stories no doubt exaggerated to impress the ignorant."

"No, I meant no such . . ."

"Hush now. No matter what you meant, you still insulted two good men. You know what must be done."

Rebecca nodded. She straightened her shoulders and stepped away from the widow. "Please, Sir Haven, forgive my rash and foolish behavior. You have been all that is kind to us, and I have offered you undeserved insult in return. How may I make amends?" She looked Haven straight in the eye as she spoke.

Haven studied the girl, looked briefly to the widow, who raised her eyebrows at him, then returned to the girl's steadfast gaze. "I accept your apology. You may

make amends by seeking more information before you
jump to conclusions, and by taking better care of your
nephew when he returns. The time before you will be
difficult, and you may find that you need Thomas as
much as he will need you. Now find a seat by the fire
and contemplate what has happened here."

Rebecca left, and the gathered men dispersed, leaving Haven alone with the widow. "Thank you, sir, for
dealing so evenly with a young woman's pride."

He gave the widow a level look. "Did you mean those
things you said of me, or were you lying to keep the
peace?"

"I . . . uh . . . I . . ." Gennie could not explain her
words to herself. How could she defend his honor when
Roger's death spoke so plainly that de Sessions had
none? He could not be trusted. She must remember
that, always. So why had she defended him?

Whatever she might have said was lost at the guard's
shout announcing the return of the last two men.

Haven scrambled up the far riverbank after Lindel. At
the top the two men separated and moved silently into
the forest, keeping each other in view at all times. Behind them lay the stones that they believed Thomas had
used to cross the river. Why the boy had done so would
have to wait until they could ask him.

Haven recalled the widow's reaction when Lindel
had returned to camp with a scrap of blue cloth and
news of footprints on the far side of the river. She confirmed that the cloth came from Thomas's shirt. Then
she had turned to Haven and calmly begged the safe
return of her son. The combination of fear and hope
that dawned in her eyes filled Haven with fierce determination to see Thomas found with all possible speed.

Time crept, as Haven and Lindel searched for further signs of Thomas's passing, but they found nothing until they crossed the tracks of the fifteen mounted men. There, barely visible on one side of the track, a small, damp bootprint overlay the crusted impression of a horseshoe in the soggy earth. A tiny amount of tension left Haven's shoulders. The mounted troop had passed this way before Thomas. The chances that the boy not only lived, but roamed free, had just increased.

"I see more of the boy's footprints on t'other side of this track, sir," Lindel whispered.

"Aye." Haven checked the angle of the sun, noting that dark would fall soon. "Go you back to camp and report to Soames. I will continue in search of Thomas." Haven issued his orders in a hush.

"But, sir . . ."

"Nay, we have no time for discussion. You will barely make it across the river before dark. This track is fresh. No doubt I will find Thomas soon and arrive in camp before dinner is past."

Lindel nodded and eased himself back toward the river, dragging a branch behind him to hide signs of their passage.

Haven stepped across the tracks. He turned to obscure the evidence that he and Thomas had been there, then proceeded along the same path as the faint prints. When he heard hoofbeats crashing toward him through the forest, he went to ground behind a fallen log. But the sounds veered off, leaving him alone and undiscovered. He waited the space of a hundred breaths and then a hundred more. When he again rose to follow the trail dusk had fallen, and Thomas's tracks faded to nothing in the dim evening light.

Haven continued forward, searching for softer

ground where a stray print might still linger. Nothing. Where had the boy gone? Haven raised his eyes to the trees. None had branches low enough for a small boy to grab on to and pull himself into that leafy safety.

The light continued to fade. Haven remained still and quiet, listening. Blundering forth in the dark would serve no purpose but to alert the mounted force that a fool had crossed the river. *Dear Lord give me aid to find Thomas so that I might keep him safe this night.*

The silent prayer no sooner left his thought than a tiny, distant sob answered Haven's desperate plea. He moved toward the sound and was rewarded with a second, louder hiccough, followed by a small rustling noise. There. Had that bush moved?

"Thomas." Haven projected the whisper with as much strength as he dared without alerting the entire wood to his presence.

"Sir Haven?" A sniffle sufficient to rouse an army followed the question.

"Sssh. Where are you?"

"Here, sir." Thomas's small dark form rose from the vegetation.

"Come to me, boy, but be quiet."

In a twinkling, Haven felt Thomas's childish arms stretched round his legs. He bent to grasp the child around the waist, lifting him into a hug.

"I am glad you found me. I could not find my way back to the river, and I heard noises, so I hid, and it got dark, and I was scared. I did not want to be scared. I wanted to be brave, like you and Father."

The boy paused for breath.

Haven closed his eyes tight on the memory of Roger's courage, despite the perfidy that ended his life. Thomas would never know his father.

Haven placed a hand over the child's mouth. "Hush now. You are safe with me." Haven lifted his hand. "As soon as I stop walking, you may talk all you like, but right now we must be quiet."

"Why?"

"Sssh. All good warriors are quiet when they move. You can be a good warrior, can you not?"

Thomas opened his mouth.

Haven placed a finger against the boy's lips.

Thomas closed his mouth and nodded his understanding.

Haven gave him a gentle squeeze of approval, then started walking at a right angle to his former track. His direction led him through heavy growth that made soundless travel nearly impossible. He prayed that he made no more noise than any other animal that prowled the night.

After he had traveled an estimated half a league, Haven stopped at the first clearing. His muscles ached from carrying Thomas, who had fallen asleep once Haven had settled into a steady pace. The sudden cessation of movement woke the boy. His stomach grumbled in concert with Haven's empty belly.

"I am hungry. Can we have rabbit stew? I like rabbit stew best of all the things Rene makes, except for honeyed oat cakes."

Haven put Thomas on the ground and took his hand, leading him across the clearing to a large oak tree. "I like rabbit stew also, Thomas, but we cannot build a fire for cooking tonight, nor do I have a rabbit to make stew from. We must be warriors tonight and eat warrior's food."

He studied the arrangement of branches in the old tree. While he might be able to climb the tree and haul

Thomas up with him, none of the branches was thick enough to provide a bed for a man his size without danger of falling. He doubted that he could get Thomas to sleep in the tree without him. Haven resigned himself to a night spent on the damp ground. The tree would guard his back. God would have to guard the rest as he saw fit.

He felt Thomas tug on his hand. "Did you hear me?" The boy sounded worried.

Haven knelt. "I am sorry. I do not think I heard your question."

"I asked if we are going to stay here."

"Yes, we are."

"Where are the beds and linens? Mama says sleeping without linens is uncil . . . unci . . . uncibilied."

Haven smiled inwardly. The boy put up a good front. But Haven could feel the child tremble. "Your mama is correct. However, warriors do many uncivilized things."

"Why?"

"Because at the time those things are necessary, and civilized things might get in the way of a warrior doing his duty."

"When will we eat the warrior food?"

"As soon as we make ourselves a bed to sleep on."

"How will we do that?"

"Do you see those pine trees over there?"

"Aye."

"Help me gather as many fallen branches as you can. We'll pile them here in the notch between these two large roots. When we have a pile as wide as you are tall and half again as long as I am, we'll eat our warrior's dinner."

"C'est bon." Thomas scampered off to the pine trees. Haven searched his chosen spot for hidden burrows.

He had no desire to be awakened in the early hours by an angry animal trying to get out of its home. Finding nothing, he joined Thomas in the search for good branches from which to make their bed. Soon they settled on a springy mound of pine boughs. Haven sat with his back to the huge oak, placing his drawn sword ready to hand by his side. Thomas placed himself squarely between Haven's legs and held out his hands.

"I suppose you want your warrior's food now."

"Please you, Sir Haven. I've been a good warrior. I was quiet, and I helped to make our bed as you bid me."

"And a good warrior deserves his meal. Here you are." Haven placed several slivers of dried meat into Thomas's hand. "Have you ever eaten dried meat before?"

"No, sir."

"Well then, do not bite the meat. Put one end in your mouth until it gets soft. Then bite off the soft part and chew it up. When you've done that, do it again until all the meat is gone. Do you understand?"

"Yes, sir."

Thomas fell silent while he worked at eating the hard food.

Haven watched the clearing. As the moon rose, its light cast sharp shadows over the grassy space between the oak and the trees on the clearing's opposite edge. But nothing took on the shape of a man, and nothing moved.

Eventually, Haven became aware that Thomas slept. He shifted the boy to a more comfortable position. Then Haven resumed his vigilance. He offered a prayer to God for Thomas's safety and waited, watching all the while.

Haven feared the time when weariness would overtake him and he too would sleep, leaving them both defenseless. He would do everything in his power to delay that moment as long as possible, but he knew it would come.

Chapter Nine

Haven's hand leapt to his sword before the noise of several horses completely woke him.

"I would not, if I were you," came a lazy warning.

Haven heard the rasp of more than a dozen blades, and he dropped his hand from his weapon. He turned his head to see who spoke, but sudden movement from Thomas distracted him.

"Owain," the boy shouted, as if he had just been crowned King of the May.

Haven grabbed Thomas before the child could scramble away and go running into the circle of armed and mounted men who cut off all possible escape. "Hush, Thomas, these are enemies."

"No." Thomas now stood on Haven's thighs looking toward the men. "That's Owain, my father's sergeant-at-arms. He cannot be an enemy. On my birthday, Owain swore to my father that he would protect me," Thomas explained, his face now nose-to-nose with Haven's.

Too many thoughts raced through Haven's mind. *Now is not the time to remind Thomas that his father is dead. If Owain was Roger's man, then Thomas is in little danger, but I may be as dead as Roger. Is Owain the leader of these men? If not, who is, and what is their connection to Owain? How do I get Thomas to stay silent so I can handle this, and if I am lucky, save both our skins?*

"Thomas," Haven spoke with the same gentle firmness he used when training Watley, "are you a warrior, and am I your commander?"

Thomas nodded.

"Then get behind me, while I talk with Owain."

Thomas's face scrunched into a concerned pout. "Owain's my special, good friend. Promise you will not hurt him."

Haven smiled at the boy's drastic misreading of who might hurt whom. "Thomas, a warrior does not question or put conditions upon his commander's orders."

"Aye, Sir Haven." The boy climbed off Haven's legs and squeezed himself between Haven and the tree.

When Thomas had settled himself, that lazy voice came past Haven's shoulder once more. "You are wise to retain the only advantage you have. Turn the boy over to us now, and we will let you go unharmed as soon as we have all of Roger Dreyford's family in safekeeping."

"I cannot do that."

"Are you certain?"

"Show yourself. Only cowards negotiate from hiding."

A mailed man rode into the center of the circle. "A cautious man knows when to let the enemy believe him a coward."

So this was the Owain of Roger's letters. Dreyford had described his sergeant-at-arms as one of the most skillful, but unorthodox fighters he had ever seen. According to Roger, Owain employed a fighting style that combined animal cunning with cold logic and an overriding passion for bloodletting. Roger had been very glad not to be on the wrong end of any weapon Owain held. Now it looked to Haven as if he were in that unenviable position.

"I will tell you once again, de Sessions. Surrender Thomas peacefully."

That Owain recognized Haven's insignia was no surprise. Any good sergeant-at-arms should know the symbol of every man—friend or foe—that his master knew. "I cannot. The king charged me to bring him Dreyford's family. I shall do so or die in the attempt."

"Then I suppose we'll have to kill you, but have care for Thomas. He seems fond of you, and it might distress him to see you gutted."

Behind him, Haven heard Thomas gasp.

Haven felt like groaning in despair. He grinned instead. "Fear not Thomas, Owain is not going to gut me. In fact, he will not hurt me at all."

"Whoa ho." Owain laughed. "Is Edward's true and perfect knight also a fool?"

"Hardly," Haven snorted. "What's more, I think you know how little a fool I am."

"Since you seem to think that I am blessed with foreknowledge of your plans, why not explain to my friends here how you'll manage to escape in one piece with Thomas when fifteen armed men surround you."

"I will not escape. You and your friends will escort me back to my camp and there swear fealty to me and my overlord, King Edward of England."

"Do you also believe that boars have teats?"

The men in the circle laughed, adding crude jests of their own about Haven's lack of reasoning skills.

"Nay. I do believe you know that the moment news of my death at your hands reaches Edward he will hunt you to the ends of the earth. I do not think an outlaw life is what you or your men want. In fact, I am certain of it, because Roger wrote that you shared with him your dreams to gain a holding. I would wager others of your band have similar dreams."

The laughing men fell silent. So he had hit home. Roger had written no such thing. Haven had gambled on what he knew to be true of most men in service to another man.

"Bah," Owain snorted. "As the loyal retainers of a traitor we are already condemned and outlawed. What difference does it make if we kill you or not?"

"If that's what you believe, very little. But have you seen the order outlawing any or all of you? I doubt that Edward wrote such a thing. He's more interested in finding the source of Roger's treason than in the men who followed him because they vowed to do him service."

"Just because I have not seen it does not mean such an order does not exist."

"True, but what if you could prove that you were not vassals to a dead traitor but to a living, trusted servant of the king?"

"Are you offering us places in your retinue?"

"I am."

"Why?"

"Many reasons. Most chief among them is that I do not believe Roger would accept fealty from men who would betray their overlord, no matter who he was.

That means you are trustworthy. Second, Edward needs experienced men to fight against the Welsh." Haven decided not to mention as a reason the guilt he felt for his own part in their former lord's death.

"A moment, Sir Haven, I would confer with the others." Owain turned his mount to face the circle of men. "Each man must make his own decision to accept or reject this knight's offer. Each man must agree to abide by the majority decision. Consider carefully; tell your yeas or nays to Blacksund. He will state the tally after each man has had his say."

Owain then turned his mount about again. "I will watch you while the men make their decision."

They waited, Owain with unparalleled patience, Haven with barely leashed worry.

Shortly Blacksund came forward and whispered in Owain's ear. The knight gave a shout of laughter and slapped his thigh. "You just might get what you want, sir."

Haven smiled and started to rise. "I knew you and your men could recognize the wiser course."

"But first I get what I want."

Haven straightened. Keeping Thomas well behind him, he focused on Owain. "What do you mean?"

"The men are split evenly, seven for and seven against. They want the matter decided by combat. You and I will fight. If you win, we all swear fealty to you. If I win, Thomas comes with us, and you . . . well, you'll probably be dead."

Haven kept his face carefully blank. He did not want Owain to know how much he wanted this fight. The man deserved a drubbing for his conceit, if naught else. Haven prayed he could beat the man.

"What's the matter?" Owain taunted. "Afraid you'll

discover how true and perfect you are not?"

"Nay." Haven bent and spoke quietly to Thomas. "I will fight you. But only under terms."

"Terms. You think to offer terms when we could kill you and not suffer a blow?"

"I doubt it would be that easy, but yes, I offer terms. Thomas will sit in this oak tree where I put him. No man will touch him until I breathe my last or Owain yields to me. Agreed?" Suiting action to word, Haven placed Thomas securely in the tree.

Every man, Owain included, nodded his agreement.

Haven picked up his sword, flexed his arms and shoulders to loosen his muscles, and saluted Owain. "Shall we begin, my friend?"

Chapter Ten

The sun had already marked midmorning before Gennie heard a shout rise up from the guards posted near the river. The noise swelled, was picked up and echoed at each guard post between the ford and the camp. Gennie had not realized that so few men could make so much noise.

They did not. If she had been able to see Thomas in the throng, she might have found relief in the fact that the noise came from a crowd numbering closer to thirty than ten. But neither Thomas nor de Sessions was visible among the mass of mounted warriors who spilled over the rise and into camp. Nor could she tell for certain if the shouts were of gladness or alarm.

One hand at her throat, Gennie ran forward to where Bergen stood guard opposite the fire. She arrived at the warrior's side in the same moment as Rebecca and the servants. Knowing how foolish it would be to search for Thomas between the milling men and horses still crowding into camp, she fisted her hands in the folds of her skirt in order to keep herself from doing just that.

"They've come back, milady." Bergen beamed his broad smile her way.

Relieved that the news must be good, Gennie gave a short nod. "So I see." The dry words forced themselves past her lips. She would not rejoice until she held Thomas safe.

At that moment, the mounted men split. Thomas sat grinning on the shoulders of a bloody and bruised de Sessions. Fear warred with relief at the sight. Gennie felt a tug on her arm pull her backward. She had not even realized she had started forward.

"Nay, milady. 'Tis better you wait for Sir Haven to bring the boy to you." Bergen's gruff tones reminded Gennie of her earlier thoughts.

"Yes," she whispered as de Sessions left the throng of men and carried Thomas to her. A slight hitch marred de Sessions's stride. Blood still seeped from a nasty gash on his lip, and red splotches adorned his mail. Yet when Gennie turned her attention from Haven to Thomas she found nothing but a dirty, smiling boy.

"Mama, it was wonderful."

Gennie took Thomas from Haven and hugged her son to her.

Finding himself safely in his mother's arms, Thomas's story spilled out unchecked. "I wanted to talk to you, but you were busy kissing Sir Haven."

Gennie felt her cheeks flame as all eyes turned on her. Rot Haven, she had not sought his kisses. Now all would think she bartered herself for de Sessions's favor. She glared at the man. He lifted a brow in silent challenge, as Thomas's tale took centerstage once more.

"So, I went looking for more quail eggs and got lost.

But I was only a little scared. When I heard all those noises I hid. But Sir Haven said the noises were only . . ."

Gennie's heart twisted. Public knowledge of de Sessions's kiss was a small price to pay for Thomas's safety. Over her son's shoulder she met Haven's gaze. "Thank you, sir." She could think of naught else to say and felt herself blush again. She clutched Thomas tighter and hid her face in his neck.

". . . said I was a good warrior. Mama, you are squeezing me too tight . . ."

Gennie set Thomas on the ground and eased her arms away. Kneeling beside him, she placed her hands in his hair and ran them slowly up and down his small frame, searching for injuries.

". . . and then I woke up, because Owain was there with Father's guard. They looked very angry, and they wanted to kill Haven. I wanted to go to Owain and explain, but Haven said I must not. So Haven and Owain had a fight."

"Sir Haven," Gennie corrected. Assured that Thomas remained uninjured, she listened in appalled silence to her son's account of the events since his disappearance.

". . . and I was in the tree. And Owain thrust his sword at Sir Haven, but he pushed it away. And then they both walked around in a circle and made snarly noises. And they ran at each other, and Sir Haven tried to hit Owain with his sword, and Owain did the same, and they did it over and over. Then Owain slashed at Sir Haven. But Sir Haven jumped back and twirled around like my spinning toy. Then Sir Haven gave a mighty chop, and Owain's sword went twisting away like a seed in the wind."

Gennie turned a worried look on de Sessions.

"He was in no danger, madame." The words rumbled from de Sessions's split lips.

Thomas tugged at her sleeve, and she gave him her attention once more. "Sir Haven won, Mama, but you know what he told me? He said that Father had taught him how to make that mighty chop with a sword."

Gennie felt her throat close with tears of confusion. What kind of man betrayed the memory of a dead friend by kissing his widow, then praised that dead and traitorous father to a frightened little boy?

"Then Owain and the other men wanted to bend their knees right there in all the blood and make their vows to Haven. But Haven said we should wait."

She felt herself grow more pale with each gruesome revelation. Thomas was too young to witness such violence. Too young to be abandoned by an irresponsible father's lust for excitement. Too young to be left alone when his mother was hanged for the sin of being married to a traitor.

"Mama, why are you crying?"

"Because I am so happy to see you safe."

"I do not cry when I am happy."

"No sweetling, you do not."

"Now that I am a warrior, I will never cry, even if I am sad."

She looked past Thomas to where de Sessions stood talking to his squire and several other men. He paused in his speech, turned his head to observe her, and then nodded. For a moment she thought she saw kindness in his bruised face. Yet something steely remained beneath that chiseled visage.

"I missed you, Mama."

Gennie returned her gaze to her son and saw the

worry beneath his excitement. She hugged him to her once more and planted a smacking kiss on his ear, then set him at arm's length so he could see she was not angry with him. "I missed you too, sweetling."

"Eeiuw." Thomas rubbed at his ear. "Did you have to kiss me? Now I have to wash my ear."

Gennie felt her heart clutch. Never before had Thomas objected to a kiss from his mother. Her boy was changing, growing up. She smiled to hide the small hurt. "*Oui*, off with you. See that you wash a few other places besides your ear."

"I will melt," he protested.

"*Non*, you shall not," she sniffed loudly. "You might rot if you do not remove that grievous stench from your person. But first promise me that you will never go off alone again."

Thomas bowed his head and scuffed at the dirt with his foot.

Gennie placed a hand under his chin and lifted his gaze to hers. "Promise me."

"I promise." The words dragged out of him.

"Good." Gennie laughed and slapped a gentle swat on his behind, raising a small cloud of dust. "Now thank Sir Haven for his care of you and be off."

The boy turned. "Thank you, sir."

Haven nodded. "You are most welcome, Thomas."

In a wink, her son disappeared toward the river, with Marie in close pursuit. Gennie watched him go. She forced herself not to follow. It seemed too soon to let him out of her sight, even though she knew he was safe under Marie's watchful eye.

To keep herself busy, she approached de Sessions. "I thank you for my son's safe return, and I am sorry that you were hurt. Please allow me to tend your wounds."

Haven took in her stiff posture and conciliatory words. He could not allow her to touch him. No doubt she was both angry at him and grateful. Angry over that kiss. Grateful for the return of her son.

He had felt the strangest mixture of relief and emptiness at the widow's tender reunion with her son. As he watched the two embrace, that emptiness rapidly filled with what remained of battle-spawned lust. If he allowed her to touch him, he would spread her legs and thrust himself deep inside her before she could so much as gather breath to protest.

He recognized the feeling as irrational. The woman was a traitor and Roger's wife to boot, Haven reminded himself. Better not to risk being near enough for her to touch.

"Nay," he said. "I am not ungrateful for your offer, but Watley will tend to me while I confer with Soames and Owain."

She had forgotten Owain in her concern for Thomas. "Surely Owain has injuries that need tending."

Haven gritted his teeth. He would not let her touch his own person. As certain as Hades, he would not allow her hands on anyone else. "Watley will see to Owain as well. You and I will leave as soon after as possible. Go, make your preparations, so that you are ready when I send for you." Haven turned as if to leave. He forbade himself to act on the desire that seared him whenever she was near. What matter if the witch sought another man's caress? The possible answers were so ridiculous that he rejected them. It was enough that she was in his charge. He did not want her to touch other men, so she would not.

115

Gennie goggled at him. "You cannot mean to leave now."

Haven swung back to face her, determination in the set of his jaw. "Without fail, madame. I mean to have you thirty leagues closer to Chester 'er we stop this day."

"But I have only just regained my son. He needs me."

"Thomas will survive without you, and the king demands your presence."

"But . . ."

"This is not a matter for argument. Will you, nil you, we depart anon. Best say your farewells."

Shoulders back and fists clenched before her, Gennie watched him stride away, for all the world as if he did not have a pain in his leg that caused him to limp.

Gennie turned in the opposite direction. She let her fists fall and her shoulders slump. He was right; she would have to say her farewells to Thomas. But how could she? How could she say she loved him and then leave him with only Marie and Rebecca to care for him? Gennie shook her head as she walked through the trees toward the riverside and the sound of Thomas's laughter.

Much though she wanted things otherwise, she had no choice but to bid Thomas good-bye and ride posthaste to the king. She prayed that God might forgive her sins and allow her to see her son once more before she died. She knew King Edward would not.

Haven knew when she had left the clearing. That subtle perfume of lavender and woman was gone. The very air felt somehow flat and stagnant without her presence to stir it to life. He shook his head. What foolishness was this, imagining that the widow made breathing easier? Owain's lucky blow must have done more damage than Haven had originally thought.

He stood before the tent and moved his jaw from side to side. It still pained him. His whole body hurt. But he knew Owain hurt more. The memory of the man-at-arms sprawled in the dirt rose before Haven. He smiled, then winced. The smile resplit Haven's barely healed lip. He swiped at the trickle of blood and entered the tent, bellowing for Watley.

The squire jumped, spilling soapy water down the front of Owain's jerkin. Watley hurried to rise from where he bent over the man-at-arms and managed to slam the now empty bowl into the older man's chin.

"Ow." Owain threw Watley a hostile look.

In the opposite corner, Soames hid a chuckle under a cough.

Haven remembered not to smile and sat himself on a pile of bedding.

Watley left to get clean water and rags.

"Sir Haven, I almost feel sorry for you with such a clumsy squire."

Haven ignored Owain's dig.

"Can you ride as you mend?"

"Aye, sir."

"I've very little time. Will your men accept your oath to me as surety for themselves as well?"

"Aye, sir."

"Soames, call two of the men who were with Owain this morning to stand witness to his oath. On your way back fetch me quill, ink and parchment."

"Aye, sir."

His second-in-command left. Haven studied Owain for several moments, wondering how much faith to put in his new vassal. "You and the men with you pursued

117

Dreyford's family out of loyalty to Roger?"

"Out of loyalty to the Dreyford family, sir. Roger was a changed man since he returned from the crusade."

"Not since his marriage?"

"He grew wilder after marrying Lady Genvieve, but the changes began before he wed."

"So you did not follow him into treason?"

"We did not betray our king."

"Why were you not at the Dreyford holding when the new owners arrived?"

Owain looked away. His throat worked before he spoke. "I had tried to keep Sir Roger from his treasonous companions on other occasions. This time, I was given false information that took me far from Dreyford lands. By the time I learned of the deception and returned, Sir Roger was dead, and you had taken Lady Genvieve and her son with you."

Haven watched the man as he told his halting tale. Did Owain's difficulty speaking his story come from grief and regret over his own failure or from an innate difficulty with lies? "Who gave you this false information?"

Owain's face took on a stricken aspect. "Lady Genvieve," he said quietly.

"Could she have been misinformed herself?"

Soames returned, forestalling further discussion. Haven took the parchment, ink and quill. He wrote as he instructed the men in their duty as witnesses. "Do you understand what you are to do?"

"Aye, sir, we're t'watch Owain swear fealty to you and make our mark on the paper after he does."

"Good."

Owain knelt before Haven, his hands raised in front

of him as if in prayer. Haven placed his hands around Owain's.

> I, Owain Langdon, banneret and knight of Yorkshire, do pledge my fealty to Sir Haven de Sessions and his overlord King Edward of England and acknowledge that I owe homage and service to you both as the troth between us commands. This I swear in the presence of these witnesses, on this day anno domine MCCLXXXII.

Watley entered as Owain and the other two men exited.

"Soames, have the horses made ready," Haven ordered.

Watley dabbed at Haven's face with a damp cloth.

"Ow." Haven grabbed the cloth from Watley's hands. "You've the touch of a goat. I will do this myself. Go and practice your swordplay. When you are able to slice an onion with a single stroke of your blade and the halves remain standing as if whole, then you may tend my person again."

Watley flushed. "I try to please your lordship in all things," he said backing out of the tent.

The squire's hero worship put Haven on edge. Good thing Watley would have to stay behind with Thomas. Haven could use a few days' respite from the young man's nervous care. In fact, this whole business with the widow made Haven short-tempered. He would be glad to have the journey over and the widow off his hands.

Alone, finished with the water and rags, Haven let out a groan as he stood. Owain could fight well. Haven prayed that he was right to trust the man.

* * *

Gennie sat on the riverbank watching Thomas play in the shallows. She had said her farewells and given Rebecca, as well as the servants, instructions for Thomas's care.

"He is a good boy."

De Sessions's words struck her from behind her. Her body jerked. It was time to leave. "Yes, sir, he is," she said, rising. Worries for Thomas's future shook her voice, and she turned around.

"He needs a man's influence."

"Oui."

"Do not fear for him, madame."

Had de Sessions heard the tremor in her voice when she thought of Thomas's life? "And why should I not fear for him? He is the child of a traitor. However innocent Thomas is, his father's crime will follow him all of his days. What surety is there for such a child?"

"There is little surety for any child. He is young, strong and resourceful."

"Mayhap too young."

"Nay, he is not. You have taught him right from wrong, and to recognize when he needs help. That will sustain him while he learns his place in the world."

"I fear 'twill not be enough."

"Tell me, can you do aught to change his circumstances?"

"Non. I pray daily for a safe place where Thomas may grow into the kind, good man I know he can be. But, of myself, I have nothing to offer him."

"Then leave be and turn your mind to your own future."

"That too is out of my hands."

Chapter Eleven

Gennie held her weary head up and stumbled through the crowded hallways of the royal castle at Chester. She could do aught else, since de Sessions had her by the arm and paced at full stride past wide-eyed stares and hand-shielded whispers. Days of hurried travel had taken their toll on the only clothing she owned. Despite the modest, but new, clothes she had been given, she knew the stares and whispers focused on her, for she had heard snippets of "traitor . . . killed her husband . . . temptress," even "witch."

Haven slowed as he approached the anterooms to the king's chambers. Genvieve recalled that she had more serious problems than castle gossip and bleary eyes to worry about. De Sessions knocked, and the door opened. Gennie found herself in a room lined with benches, and those benches filled with men.

Few of the men dressed in the fine linens and furs of nobles. The long, nubby wool coats of clerks attired the majority. Others wore the distinctive habits of monks and ordained priests. Beneath the only window, a clutch of drab, ragged, mendicant friars frowned at their more richly appointed brothers from abbey and church. Many of the men used small traveling desks. Their quills hummed a scratchy descant to the chorus of murmurs from the various groups.

A quiet buzz followed Gennie's progress behind Haven to the opposite side of the room. The murmurs gradually ceased. The quills halted. By the time she reached the opposite door full silence reigned, and Gennie found herself the object of curious clerical study.

Haven's knock echoed around the large antechamber. Gennie watched him peruse the room, noting that he seemed to take no pleasure in the company of clerks. He frowned at the group of friars, who stared openly at Gennie. Many people disliked the traveling clerics, whose vows of poverty and humility served as visible chastisement to noble and industrious commoner alike. Gennie did not mind the friars, for they brought news along with their begging. She simply wished that some of them bathed more often.

"What? Have you not seen a gentlewoman before this day?"

Haven's reproach boomed into Gennie's thoughts, and she jumped as she felt his hand slide from her arm to her shoulder.

The men stopped staring.

She turned her gaze to where Haven's touch burned her, and from there to his face.

"Do not let them concern you. They are only intrigued. Edward rarely summons women to his council chamber."

If de Sessions meant to reassure, he failed. She did not blame the clerks for their curiosity. It was the audience with Edward that dried her mouth with dread. "I am fine."

"Good," he grunted. The door opened behind him, and he pushed her onto a bench. "Sit here. I will be back to get you soon."

He disappeared into the next room. Gennie twisted her fingers into a tight clasp and watched the door as if her life depended upon the wooden portal with its leather bindings. And indeed, she thought, my life does *hang* upon that door and what goes on behind it. A corner of her mouth twisted at the gruesome humor of her own thoughts.

Determined not to brood over what she could not change, she turned to observe the room and found herself staring into the blazing eyes of a friar from the group beneath the window. What was *he* doing here?

The door closed behind Haven. He stood, waiting for Edward to call him forward. A wine-laden table stood in the near corner of the large room. The king bent over a second, bigger table in the center of the room. His councillors too focused on what Haven took to be a map. The conversation murmured on for several minutes. Despite the sense of urgency that pervaded the chamber, Haven could tell that Edward was pleased. The smallest of smiles quirked one corner of the wide royal mouth, and Edward's eyes sparkled in a way that told those closest to him, he was about to spring a trap.

The conversation ended, and with much head nodding the councillors moved en masse toward the wine. Edward reached for a goblet near his left hand and

123

drank. He drained the cup, then wiped his mouth and bent to study the map once more.

Has he forgotten I am here? To keep from worrying about his audience with the king, Haven studied the room. There was not much to look at. The fireplace was cold. The walls were bare. Even the cushions had been removed in preparation for the king's departure. Haven looked for patterns in the rushes on the floor, anything to ignore the sweat that had begun to trickle down his back.

"You are late." Edward's voice boomed into the chilly silence.

Chuckles came from the council's corner.

Haven suppressed the startled urge to jump in response. Instead, he bowed his head and went down on one knee to honor his king. "Aye."

"I've lost half a day waiting for you and Dreyford's widow."

Haven raised his head. "The widow's party slowed us down, so I left my men with them and brought her here posthaste. But you need not have stayed. We would have caught up with you."

For a moment, the king studied Haven. "Aye, you would. Get up then. I delayed to share news with you, and privacy is difficult for a king to find."

Haven watched the councillors turn their backs and crowd closer around the wine table. Then he rose and approached Edward. "Does this news concern your plans for the Welsh and Llewellyn ap Gryffudd?"

"Aye." Edward turned toward the map. Haven turned with him. "We believe that Gryffudd is at his seat in Gwynedd, here." The king pointed to a flag painted onto the middle of the mountains of northern Wales. "I've ordered the Cinque Port fleet to deliver half my army here, on the upper west coast, then to blockade the Welsh ports. The fleet will also assist in maintaining the bridge of boats that supply us from Anglesey. I do not want Llewellyn getting supplies from Anglesey or anywhere else. The Marcher Earls will secure the mountain passes to the east and then press westward. My brother Edmund will lead a loyal force from the south. The main army will leave from Chester.

"I will pin Llewellyn inside Gwynedd and strip him of everything. When I am done with him, his title as Prince of Wales will be all he has left." Edward's fist smacked down onto the painted flag. "Five years ago, I was much too generous. I will crush this viper and all the Welsh as a lesson to any other vassals who would break their vows and betray England."

Haven nodded his approval and studied the map that spread out from Edward's fist. " 'Tis a sound plan. You can trust the Marcher lords now. But where is Llwellyn's brother, wild Daffydd?"

"That is the news I have. Until yesterday, I could not carry out this plan, for fear that Daffydd remained outside the circle of armies with which I intend to squeeze Llewellyn."

"And you now know where he is."

"Aye, he is marching on Two Hills Keep, here." Edward's hand moved to a spot in mid Wales near the coastal plain. "Approximately four days' ride from Twynn."

Haven's brow crinkled. "But that is outside the area in which you have Llewellyn pinned. Will not Daffydd come to his brother's aid?"

"Mayhap. Who can tell what wild Daffydd will do? He and his brother do not always see eye to eye. But I believe that Daffydd will support Llewellyn. In order to do so, he will have to continue on his present path and go through Two Hills Keep."

"Why wouldn't he go by sea, or take some other route?"

"I have the entire coast blockaded. He cannot go that way. Any other route would take too long."

"Unless he rode his horses to death."

"Aye, 'tis a calculated risk I am taking."

Haven looked closely at his king, surprised that Edward would leave anything to chance. The sparkle of mischief in Edward's eye had become a vivid gleam of satisfaction. "Of course," Haven spoke softly, "you have a plan to prevent any possibility of succor for Llewellyn from his brother."

"Indeed, you will proceed to Two Hills Keep. From there, you will seek out Daffydd's forces and drive them south into Edmund's army. Mayhap you will even crush Daffyd. Either way you *must* capture Two Hills Keep and hold it for me."

Haven swallowed disappointment. He had hoped to be with Edward in the battle against Llewellyn. "Aye, my liege. I will need more men if I am to battle Daffydd and his army."

"I will give you a writ to command any man you need who is not yet in service. By the time your own men arrive, and if you go by boat from here to Twynn, you can be at Two Hills Keep in less than a se'ennight. Daffydd should still be in the south, since few yet know of my plans for Llewellyn. That will give you time to fortify the keep."

Haven grimaced. He hated traveling by boat. On the journey to and from the Holy Land, he had been most vilely sick. The only consolation had been that others were just as sick. Roger, especially, had nearly starved to death for the inability to keep food in his stomach.

That memory brought the widow to mind, and Haven smiled. He could not possibly drag her and her son on so urgent a journey. Not only would he finally be rid of the widow, but also he had a battle to look forward to at the end of his travels. Mayhap he could tolerate a few days in the belly of a boat. "If the fleet is as busy as you say with blockades and supplying the army, will boats be available at the port in Chester?"

"I have already sent a messenger to the port with my orders. All will be in readiness." Edward nodded and sat in a chair next to the far wall, gesturing Haven to a small chair opposite his own. A pitcher and goblets stood on a table to the right of the chairs. "I want you to remain as Lord at Two Hills Keep, even after we defeat Llewellyn."

Haven kept silence despite his surprise at the king's order.

"I said earlier that I will crush the Welsh who support Llewellyn. 'Tis my intent to forbid them their homes. In fact, under no circumstance must you allow any Welshman within one hundred paces of Two Hills Keep."

Haven noted the unusual emphasis on this last order. "Who will till the fields, my liege?"

"I will send English families, good solid yeoman, whose loyalty and oaths I can trust. The first group should arrive at Two Hills Keep before the winter."

"How many, liege?"

"In toto, one hundred families, roughly three hundred able-bodied Englishmen, women and children."

"Isn't Two Hills one of the smaller Welsh castles?"

"Aye. So I will send a castle builder as well. St. George, if he is available; if not, one of his apprentices."

"Thank you for your trust in me, Sire."

"You are welcome. Now, my friend, tell me about the widow," said Edward.

Haven nodded. "She waits without."

Edward refilled his cup, then offered the pitcher to Haven. "Is she as beautiful as the women we had in France on our return from the Holy Lands?"

The memory of the widow's nakedness arose at the question. Haven shifted uncomfortably. "She is nothing like those women." That much was true.

"Then how did she bewitch Dreyford into treason?"

"I do not know. She seems more interested in her son's well-being than kingdoms and politics."

"Were I the widow of a traitor, I too would be concerned for his heir's welfare." Edward sipped and considered. "I should hang them both and be done with that nest of vipers."

I swear to protect your son and all his family. Haven's own words echoed in his head. If he were ever to fulfill his promise to Roger, now was the time. "Sire," Haven paused, choosing his words with care. "For the love that we both once bore to Roger Dreyford, do not hang his widow and child."

Edward's look sharpened. "I cannot rule a kingdom on sentiment."

"We have no proof that she is directly involved."

"We have no proof that she is not involved."

"You are a powerful man with many resources; need you hang her?"

"Aye, but right now all of those resources are sorely taxed."

"Surely one of the convents . . ."

Edward raised his hand. "Do not talk to me of convents. The abbesses I can trust already harbor other hostages for me; at great expense, I might add. I will not spend more of my exchequer to encourage them to take in an impoverished widow and her child."

"Could you not ask the pope?"

"The whole world knows of my disagreements with the pope about taxing the land-holding clergy. I cannot afford to give him so much as the possibility of leverage by asking his minions to guard a traitor's widow. Also, I am uncertain that I wish to place such a dangerous woman within his grasp."

"Liege, I have served you long and well. You know I did so for love of you as well as for the hope that you might someday reward me with lands to hold for you. You have given me Two Hills Keep, in feoff. I freely return to you those lands and renounce all claim to any of your favor, if you will spare Roger's family." Am I losing my mind? Haven wondered.

Edward lifted an eyebrow. "You promised Dreyford that you would keep his family safe. Did you not?"

The king's perceptiveness failed to surprise Haven. "Aye."

"Did you swear an oath to him?"

"Aye." Haven felt a great lump of worry grow in his throat and cast his glance to the floor.

"That was a foolish thing to do, my friend, for I have already decided the fate of the widow and her whelp."

Edward's hand touched his shoulder gently.

Haven raised his head to see rare sympathy in the king's long face. The expression lingered an instant. "I am sorry, Haven. I have no time for explanations." Then Edward called out to his secretary. "Bek, get your quills and ink. I've work for you to do."

"Aye, my liege." The fellow bowed.

To Haven the king said, "Go, my friend. Bring the

widow to me. You will find a priest sitting to the right
of the door. Bring him as well."

Haven squared his shoulders, stood and turned to the
door. *I have damned myself.* Guilt washed over him. He
had brought not only his dearest friend to death, but
that friend's wife and child as well. He deserved to be
damned for his pride and his broken oath.

Certain of the trust and affection the king held for
him, Haven had not hesitated to swear that he would
sway the king's favor and keep safe Roger's widow and
son. Now it was too late. As his failure loomed over
him, Haven saw himself denied all hope of heaven,
condemned to a life of penance followed by eternal
death in Hell.

Gennie bit her lip and wished the friar to the devil. He'd
approached the instant Haven left. She'd acknowledged him only because not to do so would prove even
more awkward than trying to remember where she'd
seen him. The holy man resolved her dilemma. He reminded her that he had often heard confessions from
Roger and herself when visiting the Dreyford demesne.
He then remarked that he was sorry for her loss. She
thanked the friar for his sympathy and tried to excuse
herself. But he insisted on reiterating the entire boring
story of his travels since he last saw Roger Dreyford.

In the midst of this recital, the door opened. At the
sight of Haven's pallor, Gennie broke off her conversation with the friar. Her hand went to her throat. "What
is it?"

"The king wishes to see you now." Haven's words
came strangled from stiff lips.

Gennie watched him turn to the priest seated on the
opposite side of the door.

"And you also, Father." With movements as stiff as his words, Haven turned and disappeared into the room.

The priest rose. "After you, milady."

Genvieve entered the king's council chamber. At the far end of the room stood Edward, a richly dressed clerk bent at a table by his side. The clerk's papers whispered like the rustling of a shroud being wound about the body of the dead. She would be hanged, but her body would receive no shroud. Such care was not given to traitors. Nor would she be buried. Instead, her body would be left as carrion for crows and other vermin to devour. A public reminder of the consequences of treason.

The king gestured her forward. The closer she got to his tall, lanky form, the more she trembled. So much, that when she finally stood next to de Sessions, she did not even try to curtsey. *What would happen to Thomas?*

A smile leered across Edward's face, and he drew the priest forward to stand beside him. "You may begin, Father."

Begin what? Gennie wondered. Images of the priest administering the last rites ran wild in her mind. What kind of man was the king to take such joy in the death of one woman?

"Is this the couple, then?"

What was the priest talking about?

"Aye."

"They must join hands."

"Do as he asks, Haven, madame."

"Huh?" Haven grunted the question.

Gennie looked at him and saw as much confusion in his eyes as she felt in her heart.

"Join hands, you dolts."

131

Exhausted, Gennie shifted at the same moment as Haven, bumping his shoulder. Startled, she looked at him. Brown eyes glared down at her. The king reached forward and grasped her hand. Gennie jerked in surprise, but the king's grasp remained firm until he placed her hand in Haven's. Heat from Haven's palm sizzled up her arm. She felt dizzy. The councillors at the end of the room stared. Gennie blushed. The father's words droned past her ears.

"We gather here in the sight of God . . ."

Chapter Twelve

"I do." Haven's statement echoed throughout the chamber.

Gennie shook herself from her exhausted daze. "You do what, Sir Haven?"

Anger blackened his face. Several discreet coughs from the end of the room distracted her. Something was not right. Closer to hand, the priest glared at her interruption. Edward looked fit to burst. What was going on?

The priest continued. "Do you Genvieve Eloise des Jardins Dreyford take this man as your husband, promising to obey him in all things, to adore him with your body, pledging him your fealty, cleaving to him as your liege lord and giving him all your worldly goods, saving only that which you owe to Christ?"

"What? Take de Sessions as my husband? Of course not."

The coughing increased.

"Are all those men ill?" Gennie asked. "Sir, send for

a posset, and I will tend to them." She started for the opposite end of the chamber, but Haven's hand held hers fast. "Please you, Sir Haven, let go. I may be dead an hour hence, but I will not stand by idle when others are sick and in need."

"They are not sick, madame. You must remain and answer the priest."

"I have already answered the priest, and I will not wed you. What would be gained by such a foolish action?"

"It would please me greatly." Edward's soft words accompanied a dagger-sharp look that even Gennie in all her weariness could not mistake.

She swallowed in an attempt to moisten her suddenly dry throat. "Well, I . . . uh . . . that is, I suppose no harm can come from it. We can always hold the execution afterwards, but I insist on having a shroud to wrap my body."

"By all means, madame. You have my oath as King of England, that when you die, you will have the finest of shrouds. Continue, Father."

Gennie blinked at the brilliance of Edward's smile. From the corner of her eye, she saw one of the men at the end of the room fall to his knees, moaning. She moved toward him once again, but Haven's grip remained strong. "The priest, madame."

"Do you take this man as your husband, madame?"

Gennie looked into Haven's unsmiling face. He squeezed her hand and nodded. "I do," she said, and felt as if the hangman's noose had just tightened around her neck.

"Do you have the rings, sir?"

Gennie saw Haven swallow.

"Bek, where are those rings I gave you?" Edward shouted to his secretary.

"Here, sire."

A heavy circlet of gold filled Gennie's palm. The priest's words faded as she stared at the ruby-eyed lion that crested the ring. She felt Haven shove a golden band onto her finger, and she fumbled to follow suit. Unable to meet his cold eyes, she focused on their joined hands.

"I pronounce you man and wife. Go with God."

Haven's grip loosened, and Gennie shook his hand off. "Now I will tend that poor man who collapsed. After that"—she glanced toward the king—"we can proceed with my hanging."

The king waved dismissal at the councillors crowding near the door. "That will not be necessary." Edward took Gennie's arm, guiding her to the table where Bek had laid out documents, quills and ink.

She ignored the items. "Not necessary? Of course it is necessary. Someone so ill requires immediate care."

"You may note, Lady de Sessions, that the man has already been taken care of." Edward pointed to the now empty far end of the room.

"I do not understand. How . . . ?"

"His friends took him away to get him help. Naught remains but to sign the marriage contract." Edward smiled and held the quill out to her.

Lady de Sessions. He had called her Lady de Sessions. Was she well and truly married to the man who had effectively killed Roger? "But . . ."

"Come." The king put the quill in her hand. "It is too late now to protest. Sign and then we shall have a marriage toast."

Gennie dipped the quill in the inkpot, then scratched her name on the vellum.

Haven snatched the quill from her hand and scrawled his signature below hers.

The clerk dusted the documents with sand and when they were dry handed them to Haven.

A servant brought wine at the same moment that a dusty messenger entered the chamber. The king moved aside to read the message, then turned to Haven. "I must leave immediately. A slight detour is required before I can march on Llewellyn. I regret that you must take Milady de Sessions with you into Wales, for there will be none here to have a care for her or Dreyford's family. See to your lady, and when your men rejoin you depart with all haste for Two Hills Keep, as we discussed."

Edward does not know the widow, Haven thought. Else the king would realize that with her in tow, all haste would be very slow indeed. Regardless, Haven chastised himself, Edward Plantagenet has given me a task. It is up to me to see it carried out.

Within moments, the king and all his attendants disappeared. Haven stood alone with Gennie in the empty chamber. He looked at the two cups the servant had placed in his hands before departing and held one out to Genvieve. "Milady, will you share our wedding toast?"

She wore a dazed expression. Her brow wrinkled in confusion as she took the cup. "Wine would be welcome, sir."

He watched her put the cup to her lips; lips that he knew were tender and sweet. Her throat, that delicate column of ivory and rose, rippled as she swallowed. He waited, hoping she would break the silence that weighed as heavily as the marriage into which the king had coerced him.

With all the councillors looking on, he had had no choice but to go through with the marriage. Edward had known that. The king had also known that Haven would refuse if asked to marry Dreyford's widow.

But Edward wanted the woman in the care of someone trustworthy. Who more trustworthy than a man who honored his vows to his king over a friend's life? Edward had gotten exactly what he wanted. Haven supposed he should be grateful. Because of this marriage, his soul was no longer in danger. Roger's wife and child would live. So why did Haven still feel as if he had betrayed his promise to protect her? Why did he want to smash something?

". . . before my execution, sir?"

Haven shook his head, set aside his untouched wine and allowed Genvieve's words to pull him from his thoughts. "What did you say?"

"I asked if you wished to consummate the marriage before my execution."

The thought of Genvieve's slender neck in the hangman's noose put torch to all of Haven's frustrations. He grabbed her by the shoulders, lifting her from the floor. Furious with her, with Edward, with himself, Haven kissed her. It was an ungentle echo of their sudden wedding and boded ill for this unwanted union.

He lifted his face a breath from hers and snarled, "Edward has condemned us both, milady. There will be no execution. This marriage will be consummated, but only when I am damned good and ready to do so." He dropped her back to the ground, then turned on his heel. His long legs took him to the entrance in a trice. The door slashed open under his grasp. He paused on the lintel. "I will send a servant to show you to our chamber." Then her husband was gone.

"So, Sir Husband." Gennie paced away from the gaping door and addressed the vacant room. "You will consummate our marriage when you are 'damned good and ready.' And should I not be ready, will you perform this consummation by yourself?

"Ooh." She shook her fist at a sunbeam that pierced the gloom from a high narrow window. "No one ever tried my patience as Sir Haven de Sessions, not even Roger at his worst. *Vraiment,* to be de Sessions's wife is a fate worse than death." The end of the room halted her progress and her tirade. She braced one hand against the wall, then leaned forward, resting her hot cheeks on the cool surface. Covering her face with her other hand, she sobbed.

"Dear God in Heaven, how can I tolerate this? He has made me cry. I swore that I would never again cry because of a man, especially a faithless man." And who more faithless than a man who betrays a friend? she reminded herself.

Gennie wiped tears from her cheeks and lips. Her mouth was still swollen from that punishing kiss. "Is not that like a man, to take out his anger on a woman's body? Does de Sessions think this marriage is of my making? Mayhap I enchanted the king into deciding on this travesty?"

A cough sounded from behind her. "Milady."

Gennie spun round, holding back a startled sound with a hand over her bruised lips.

The servant bowed. "I am to guide you to your chamber."

How long had he been there? She could hardly ask. Nor could she ask if he had overheard her outburst.

She shook out her skirts and followed the servant from the room. What did it matter if the servant heard or talked of what he heard? Surely de Sessions knew how she felt. Servants' gossip could not make that any worse.

The servant preceded her in silence. Too much has happened, she thought. She was not to die. Instead, she was chained to a man she could not trust, a man who confused and sometimes frightened her. Please God, he will never know how much. De Sessions was right: Edward had condemned them both. Try as she might, she could see no way out of this situation.

Somehow, she did not think that de Sessions would carouse himself into treason and death as Roger had. She might dislike Haven, but she knew he was no drunkard. Haven de Sessions was a very dangerous man. A man who held complete authority over her.

Wrapped in her thoughts, Gennie nearly knocked the servant over before she realized he had stopped and opened a door. He gestured her inside.

"Will you need anything else, milady?"

Gennie looked at the room, unseeing, then looked at the servant. "No, that is, yes. My husband will be hungry when he returns." Men were always hungry. "Please bring us food and drink."

"Very well, milady." The servant left, closing the door behind him.

Gennie stepped toward the fire. She sank down upon a footstool and warmed her hands at the blaze. She wished the fire could warm her thoughts as it did her hands. But all she felt was the cold chill of worry.

How could she survive another marriage, especially marriage to Haven? How would he treat Thomas? She had no wish to trust de Sessions with anything, least of all Thomas's safety. Yet, thus far, Haven had displayed no inclination to show Thomas cruelty. Indeed, de Sessions had been extremely patient with her son's needs as they traveled toward Chester. She had no true choice, after all. As de Session's wife, she must yield all to him whether she would or no.

That being so, mayhap this marriage had one bright spot. Surely she could submit to de Sessions for the sake of her son. The knight was a powerful man, after all, and a friend of a very powerful king. Gennie straightened her shoulders. *Oui,* as bad as this marriage might be for herself, for Thomas it was a good thing.

Determined to accept her fate, Gennie waited for Haven to return.

The sound of voices roused Gennie. She blinked sleepily and peered into the dimness surrounding the door. Her husband loomed, solid and dark, talking to a servant who placed supper upon a side table.

"No matter what the hour, I want my man Soames brought to me as soon as he arrives." Weariness pervaded de Sessions's curt words.

"Aye, sir. Will there be anything else?"

"Nay."

The servant left. The door closed. Gennie watched as Haven ran a hand across his eyes. Firelight flickered over his sharp cheekbones and stubborn chin, skimming past thin lips that wore a downward turn. He exhaled a small sigh.

About to rise and serve him, Gennie settled back when he dropped his hand to the table and began assembling a trencher. Perhaps he hadn't seen her. Despite the square set of his shoulders and his proud stance, she got the impression he carried some great weight—a weight that caused him pain and anger. Unwilling to add to that burden, she remained silent.

"Would you prefer your fruit with or without clotted cream?"

Gennie's head jerked. How had he known she was awake? "Without, please." Her voice was shaky. Not wanting him to see her anxiety, she shifted toward the fire. She was aware when he sat on the floor next to her, but she refused to look at him. She was afraid. Afraid to draw the anger that she suspected lay beneath his bleak frown. Roger had never hesitated to vent his anger on her. Would de Sessions do the same?

He set the trencher before her, along with a richly carved goblet. Her thoughts focused inward. She plucked bits of food and ate without tasting, too aware of the man who sat unmoving beside her.

She chewed slowly, unable to bear the silence yet uncertain what to say. She swallowed and waited, sipping at the wine all the while. The trencher was for both of them. Good manners dictated that she not eat more until he had taken food. A sideways glance showed that her companion stared morosely into the fire.

"You do not eat, sir?"

His blazing tawny gaze turned on her. "What?"

She leaned away from the leashed emotion she saw there, then gestured toward the trencher. "You serve us food, yet you do not eat."

He grunted and without looking at the trencher took some fruit and cheese into his hand. He devoured the food, as though starving, but did not reach for more. His darkling glance returned to the fire.

"What troubles you, sir?" Gennie asked the question quietly, praying that she would not provoke that earlier intensity from him.

141

He studied the flames. "King Edward told me that he ordered our marriage 'in order to prevent more treason.' "

Gennie gasped but held her outrage to herself. No protest on her part would change de Sessions's opinion of her, nor the king's.

"Those were his exact words?"

"Aye." Her husband continued to stare into the fire.

"I see. You must find marriage to me distasteful at the least."

He turned his hard gaze on her. "And does this marriage please you?"

Gennie placed the goblet on the floor between them. She twisted her hands together in her lap and looked past him, into the fire. *"Non."*

"Then you understand my problem."

Gennie shook her head slowly. "Did you wish to wed another?"

"Nay. Did you?"

"Non."

"That is good."

"Yes."

"Will you do your duty?"

What was he asking? Did he expect her to turn a blind eye to his whores as well as share his bed? Or need she only run his household? Tend his wounds? She had sworn before God and king to be Haven's obedient and faithful wife. How could she do else? *"Oui,* sir. Will you likewise perform your duty?"

"I will."

I will, he says. And just what does he mean? Gennie wondered. *Will he slake his lust on me and me alone? Protect and provide for me? Raise my son to be a good, strong man?* Experience had taught her not to expect

142

too much from a man's promise to perform his duty.

Gennie raised the goblet, took a drink and stood. "Then I will await you in bed."

Haven grasped her wrist, holding her in place. "First, I would have wine."

Gennie looked toward the table where she saw a pitcher, but no other goblet. "There is but one cup." She held it out to him.

"We are man and wife. We share trencher and cup. . . ."

His hand left her wrist and covered her own fingers around the goblet. The warm, vital strength of his grip sent shivers through her.

". . . just as we will share a bed."

She eased her hand from beneath his, but the warmth of his stare held her in place. She watched as he put his lips to the cup. Did he realize that 'twas the same spot where she had sipped moments ago? He swallowed, and the muscles in his throat moved. Her own throat went suddenly dry. She licked her lips. He lowered the cup, and Gennie's hand went to her neck. There was more than heat in his eyes now. She fled.

As Gennie began to disrobe, Haven turned back to the fire. It should be distasteful to bed his friend's widow. He thanked God that nature was taking its course. For even as he had asked his questions, he had felt the rise of desire in his loins. It was simple lust, recalled by the firelight playing over her face as candleglow had over her body that one time he entered her tent unannounced.

In this case, the church sanctioned his lust. He need feel no guilt over an act that it was his duty to perform. So why did he hesitate to join his wife in bed? Did he really fear that Roger's ghost somehow stood between them? He could hear Roger's words from the gallow's steps. "I cannot trust my wife." Haven shook the thought from his head. Roger was dead. Gennie was no longer his best friend's wife, she was *his* wife. And tonight they would consummate their marriage before God as was proper.

He should feel no guilt. Gennie had by her own admission agreed to share that bed with him. He was not forcing her. No more so than he forced himself. Haven shook his head. This bedding was a duty, and neither his feelings nor Genvieve's were important. If neither of them received pleasure, at least their souls would be safe. He grimaced and drained the cup, trying to sweeten the bitter taste that duty left in his mouth.

Chapter Thirteen

From the bed, Gennie watched Haven drain his goblet. He set the empty vessel on the mantelpiece. Her husband stood for a few moments, staring into the flames that cast the only light in the room. Then he stretched his arms above his head, reached over his shoulders, grasped the back of his tunic and swept it over his head.

At the sight, Gennie's face flushed, and her chest felt tight. Merci Dieu, *Haven cannot see me.* She had seen many men as tall as Haven; Roger had been one. She had seen many men whose backs were as broad as Haven's. Even a few who had shared both height and breadth. But none had combined that height and breadth with the same sleekness of muscle and beauty of form that Haven displayed.

An upbringing fostered on legends and housewifery had not given Gennie the words to describe the muscles shaped by strength of sinew and length of bone into one of God's most alluring creatures. Gennie felt as if Lancelot and Gawain combined had stepped into her chamber. The flutter that twisted her abdomen and the fanciful turn of her thoughts unsettled her. She drew the sheet up over naked breasts that suddenly acquired an almost painfully pleasant twinge.

Haven shifted, tossing the tunic toward a chest that sat beneath one of the chamber's two narrow windows. The air stirred, and Gennie caught the faint scent of leather and man. He leaned forward, bracing his arms against the mantel. Firelight danced across muscles that rippled and stretched. His hose tightened around thighs that swelled with tension. Gennie felt her insides melt.

What was he thinking? she wondered. Roger, the only other man who had shared her bed—and that rarely—had never paused or hesitated. He had climbed into bed, spread her legs and thrust himself upon her as quickly as possible. He had even insisted she sleep naked so that her nightrobe would not inconvenience him. All men were the same, were they not? So what was de Sessions waiting for?

"Are you ready for me?"

The soft question exploded in Gennie's ears. Was he being considerate? "*Oui*, I am ready." As ready as any woman could possibly be to have her body invaded, she thought.

Haven turned around and bent to remove his hose. Gennie lay back and tried to relax before the coming onslaught. She closed her eyes. She did not want to see him. She just wanted to get the bedding over with, so she could go to sleep.

The covers lifted away, and Gennie felt the cooler air of the room sift over her body. The fire's heat was weak and did not reach the bed. Gennie shivered a bit as goosebumps roughened her skin. The delay was intolerable. "What are you waiting for?"

"I wish to look at the woman who will bear my children."

It was not enough that he had to examine her like a broodmare, he had to remind her of the real purpose for this mating. There would be no affection or love in this marriage. How could there be between two people who bore so little trust for each other?

Gennie cracked her eyelids. Fair was fair, and if he would examine her, then she was entitled to a peek at the very least. He was magnificent. All thick thighs and narrow hips. Lean-fleshed and sculpted like the ancient heroes she had been raised to admire. A dusting of golden brown hairs glittered across his chest narrowing down, down to his . . . Gennie shut her eyes again.

She did not want to see. Did not want to know the too solid evidence of life that throbbed and pulsed within him. That would soon pulse and, *Sacre Dieu*, grow within her, if he was as potent a man as he looked to be.

The bed sagged. Gennie felt the covers slide back up over her. Heat from his body seared her. An answering flush sprang from the nerves that burned beneath her skin. But Haven did not touch her. Not even the faint mist of his breath stirred the fine hairs at her temple.

"Open your eyes, wife."

Gennie obeyed, staring ahead into the semidarkness. At least he had finally called her something besides "madame" or "widow."

"I will try not to hurt you." His easy rumble crossed her ears and sank through her body. Its vibrations joined the dance of butterflies that shifted from her breasts to her toes, causing her stomach to jump and

147

her thighs to tremble. Was this some trick? Roger had never given thought to her comfort; why should Haven?

"I am not untried, sir."

He had the ill grace to chuckle.

"Thomas is ample evidence of that. Nay, 'tis not lack of experience that would cause you harm." He placed his hand on her arm and stroked from shoulder to fingers and back.

"What then?" Gennie's mind scrambled for the possible cause of his words. Better to think than feel the terrifying tremors that shot through her at his touch.

The gentle caress continued, shifting by slow increments from arm to body, belly to breast, where his large hand finally came to rest. "Suffice it when I tell you that I've been about the king's business for these past three months."

He leaned closer to her. Gennie felt his lips on her forehead, her eyes, her cheek. He grazed her temple with his tongue and scraped his teeth over her earlobe. His palm closed around her breast, then opened, rubbing tiny circles across the sensitized tip.

Surely her heart would burst through her chest, it beat so hard and furious. She would bloody the sheets with such a violent death.

"You are not breathing, Gennie." His lips moved constantly. Flickered over her ear, down her jaw. "You have to breathe."

Mesmerized, she opened her mouth to obey. Those lips settled on hers. She sucked in air and his tongue, all in one life-giving gasp.

"Mmmm."

That groan of satisfaction. Was it hers? His? It hardly mattered. No sooner had her mouth whispered its delight at being plundered than a thousand other parts of her body shouted their discontent at his benign neglect. Haven seemed intent on pleasing all of them. And her body, traitor that it was, seemed greedily intent on helping him.

She tried, she really tried to remain still and compliant as Roger had expected of her. But Haven's wandering hands drew surprising urges from within her. His breath upon her face produced shivers throughout her entire body, as his lips, firm and soft, traversed the skin from her mouth to her ear and down her neck. When his mouth finally settled on her breasts, laving each nipple with delicate strokes, heat flooded her belly. Her fingers itched. She clenched them against the desire to grasp his head, to press him more solidly to her breast and soothe the ache he stirred there. She would not be the cause of his displeasure in this mating. His teeth closed on her breast in a gentle bite. She could not prevent herself from arching her back or uttering a small cry.

". . . so good." His voice came to her as if from a distance. "Gennie, touch me."

Touch him? Roger had never wanted her to touch him. "Wh . . . where?"

"Here." Haven grasped her hand and placed it on his hip.

Her palm uncurled of its own accord. Her fingers tested the texture of his skin and slipped around to his buttock.

"Yes," he breathed into her ear. "More. Please touch me more."

"Where?" She asked again, hardly daring to think as her fingers traced circles over his back.

"Anywhere, everywhere."

His mouth closed over hers again.

She didn't think, simply reveled in the strength and texture of him. How different the male form was. How unexpectedly wonderful, to touch a man. What delicious torment to stroke her hands over him, to arch her body closer to his. She felt the press of his knee against her limbs. Her legs shifted beneath his weight. She flung her head to the side, breaking the kiss.

He propped himself on one elbow and cupped her cheek with his free hand. "What is it, Gennie? Did I hurt you?"

"Nay." She looked at him, looming over her, his eyes agleam in the dark. "I . . . I don't know what it is. I feel so strange, so . . . needful."

The sheen of his teeth revealed his smile. "I feel needful too."

"What can we do about it?"

"Let me show you?"

She should fear him, this man who had betrayed his friend to seek the king's favor, but in this moment, she could not. Somehow he created such desire in her that she would risk all for the satisfaction he promised. She nodded.

His hand left her face and traveled the length of her body to the patch of hair where her thighs met. He rested there a moment, then pressed with his palm.

"Ahh," she breathed. Her legs parted and she lifted her hips.

His fingers slipped between the folds of skin that hid her womanhood. She felt the slickness that his handling drew forth. Dear Lord, what was he doing to her? She thrust her hips against his hand. It wasn't enough.

She felt his legs slide between hers. The hair of his thighs tickled the sensitive skin of hers. She spread her legs wider. He moved his hand upward to her breast.

His hips sank down on her. His manhood pressed at the entrance to her body.

She closed her eyes. 'Twas madness surely to let this man she didn't trust take her body so easily, the thought skittered through her mind. But he was her husband, and the madness was so very sweet.

"Gennie, look at me."

She lifted her gaze to his.

He eased his way into her and out again, then again. She felt her body stretch and clasp around him. She moved beneath him and drew from him a groan. He thrust faster, so she shifted her hips again. His groan became a roar. He lifted her legs over his shoulders, exposing her to his touch. She sobbed with each stroke of his body, each flick of his finger over her sensitized flesh. She reached for his hips. Her nails sank into his flesh. He thrust deeper and harder until her body lifted from the bed and she tumbled into a fantasy of splintered darkness and heat where Haven was the only solid presence. She clung to him, certain that she would be lost forever without him.

Haven drifted back to reality. He felt Gennie's heart pounding beneath his own. Heard her shallow breathing. The musk of sex swamped the lavender he had come to associate with her. He lifted himself away, and her breathing eased. He looked down at her. Her body, flushed and sweaty in the firelight, was more beautiful than any other woman he had ever met.

In her he found delight and wonder. So sweetly untutored, when he demanded she touch him and she asked where. He had shown her. She became ravenous in search of her satisfaction, and his. He smiled, settled beside her and brushed a finger against the lashes that dusted her cheeks. He wanted to see once more those green eyes dazed with passion and desire because of him.

What kind of man had Roger been to find such a treasure unappealing? Haven thought he had known his friend better than anyone, but he had not known that Roger would treat women with callous selfishness. And he had not believed that Roger was capable of treason all on his own.

Guilt flooded Haven. What kind of man was he to slake his body so thoroughly on a woman he couldn't trust? To lay with Roger's widow, when he was sworn to protect her, despite that lack of trust?

He gathered Gennie to him, pulling the covers up to ward off any chill. She may have been Roger's widow, but she was his wife now. The tenderness he felt for her at this moment frightened him. He was unused to fear and did not understand how this woman could inspire it in him. He shoved the feeling aside. He would keep her safe for the sake of the children she would bear him. And since he could not bring himself to trust her, he would guard his heart against her.

Gennie wakened to the feel of Haven's arm around her waist, anchoring her back to his chest. *Merci Dieu*, bedding with Roger had never been like that. If all men were alike, she wondered, then who was the aberration, Roger or Haven? For the sake of every other woman in the world, Gennie prayed that more men were like Haven than Roger.

Guilt flushed over her. How could she wish that more men be like Haven? He had betrayed Roger to the king without a thought for the consequences. He took no heed of a child left fatherless or a sister left homeless before doing what he claimed was his duty. Yet here she lay in the arms of a man she did not love and could not trust, wishing only that he would wake and take her to that sweet oblivion again. *Vraiment,* lust was a powerful temptation.

Mayhap she did not completely trust her new husband. She certainly could not like him. If the rest of their nights would be as this one, she would have no trouble performing her wifely duty. But she might have difficulty keeping safe her heart.

Gennie lay on her side, her back pressed against Haven's chest, and watched the light change from dark to dim. She worried over Thomas and Rebecca. Were they safe? When would they arrive? They traveled in the cold and rain, without decent shelter, while she slept in comfort and warmth.

Three nights since, she and Haven had married, and each night the same. She had no idea where or how Haven spent his days, but he never failed to return with enough energy to do his duty as a husband. And such a duty.

Her present liking for marriage duty troubled her greatly. She had never experienced such lust with Roger. She had hoped for it, especially in the early days of her marriage, before she discovered that Roger preferred whores to his wife. But look where Roger's lusts had led him. Mayhap she was as inconstant as he? The thought terrified her. Was she? Would her desire for Haven's body and what he could do to hers lead her into a mire of betrayal like that where Roger had met his death? Surely her soul was in danger if she allowed this to continue.

Beside her, Haven stirred but did not wake. Gennie smoothed a hand across her lower abdomen. Would she quicken with his child as soon as she had with

Roger's? Worse, would Haven, once assured of a child and possible heir, leave her for whores and other women?

Gennie flung the covers aside. She sat up and dragged on the robe that she had left at the bedside. Roger's penchant for whores had taught her well. She survived before; she could do so again. She paused in tying the sash around her waist, surprised at the physical pain even the thought of Haven with another woman caused. Straightening her shoulders, she finished fastening the garment and made a decision. This time she would not suffer a faithless husband. Somehow she must find a way to make her marriage work without succumbing to temptation. And the first step was to confess her own guilt.

Haven paced the battlements, watching the sun sink into the clouds that hovered low on the horizon. He had been in Chester three days. Even with Thomas and the others in tow, Soames should have arrived by now. How could they get to Two Hills Keep before Daffydd ap Gruffydd if the men didn't show up soon? Worse yet, Edward had been unable to give Haven more warriors.

"Here is my royal order giving you the right to compel to service any able-bodied man with or without horse. Between now and the time your own men arrive, you should be able to gather a reasonable force with which to garrison Two Hills Keep." After a few more words, Edward had ridden away, confident that Haven would succeed. And why not? Haven had never failed his king. But how he would succeed at this with only twenty-five mounted men and no archers, Haven didn't know.

He reviewed what he did know about Two Hills Keep. The small holding overlooked a vital roadway into the mountains, and Edward expected Haven to hold the keep and the roadway against Wild Daffydd at all costs. Once again, Haven faced failing in his duty.

Haven frowned. He not only had missing men and a nearly impossible task to worry him, he had the widow too. No, Genvieve was a widow no longer. She was his wife. His wife; now there was an irony if he had ever encountered one. He had wedded her out of loyalty to his king. He had bedded her out of duty. He had expected to find that duty onerous, despite her obvious attractions. Instead, he had found himself looking forward to the evenings they shared.

She was well schooled, intelligent and a thoughtful, challenging companion. Even better, she didn't talk too much, seeming to know when he needed silence. And then there was the bed play.

What was it about the . . . his wife that drew him mothlike to her honeyed flame each night? Gennie wasn't skilled in the amorous arts. He knew because he had learned lovemaking from experts in the Holy Lands, Rome, France and the English court. He shook his head at the thought of the female whispers about his *perfection* in bed.

At the sound of a door opening, Haven turned and saw Gennie enter the courtyard. In the new blue cloak he had given her, she was comely enough. She was still too thin. Her skin remained pallid. But her bruises had healed. He thought her beautiful. Was that it? He had never been drawn by mere physical beauty before. He liked partners who were not only pleasing to look at but vocally enthusiastic, if not downright lustful. Gennie spoke very little in their bed play.

Not far from his wife, a friar stood haranguing a group of stable lads who gambled in a corner of the bailey.

The same friar Gennie had been speaking with outside Edward's audience chamber. How had his wife come to know the robed beggar? He watched her approach the itinerant priest. She and the holy man conversed for a moment, then turned toward the chapel. What was she doing? Haven followed the battlement on a course that paralleled his wife's. Lady Genvieve de Sessions was a puzzle.

She greeted him enthusiastically, even lustfully, in bed. Yet she barely uttered a sound when he touched her. Just an occasional gasp, a moaning cry or an innocent question. Still, if her voice had been restrained, her body had more than made up for it. He had hopes of coaxing a tender word or two from her lips this night.

Haven watched her halt at the chapel door. The friar entered. Gennie looked about her, as if she wished to remain unobserved, then slipped inside the building. Still trying to figure out what drew him to a woman he couldn't trust, Haven sped down the nearest stair.

If, as she had stated, she merely performed her marital duty, she did so with an unstudied, albeit silent, generosity that lured him in a stronger fashion than the most skilled Saracen women. That was probably it. Gennie was simply a passionate woman who didn't realize the power she held in her body. Haven wasn't about to tell her. Thus far she had found no whip with which she could goad him to treason as she had Roger. As long as she remained ignorant of the lust she inspired, Haven was safe.

By the time he crossed the courtyard and entered the church, Gennie had disappeared. Haven stopped. She couldn't have gone far. The chapel had only one other door. He paced, soft-footed, down the center aisle. Just as he reached the nave, he heard the faint sound of voices. He followed in their direction, until he stood before a confessional tucked into an odd corner beyond the chapel proper.

The door to one of the confessional chambers remained cracked open on a wedge of blue material, like that of Gennie's cloak. Were it not for that, Haven would have left by the other door and never found his wife's destination. He turned to go, but quiet words held him in place.

"Forgive me, Father, for I have sinned."

The response was indistinct, but Haven had no doubt that it was the friar who heard Gennie's confession.

Haven debated only a moment. If he stayed, he would have his own confession to make. But if he left, he might never know what his wife had done for which she sought God's forgiveness. He stayed, creeping closer to the confessional.

"I have lusted in my heart for a man."

Again the confessor murmured.

"*Oui*, he is married."

Another response mumbled through the secure door on the prelate's side of the confessional.

"*Oui*, I have lain with him."

Haven's rage blotted out all other sound. So she acted the innocent for him and spent her days in bed play with some other man. He wanted to put his fist through someone's face. He turned and left, before he snatched open the confessional door and murdered his adulterous wife. He needed time to think, and a place to beat his anger into submission.

Gennie exited the confessional. The friar had understood her problem, but the penance for a cardinal sin like lust was stiff. She must not only abstain from all carnal relations until after her woman's flow, but she must wear a hair shirt next to her skin for all the days of her abstinence. The friar assured her that only in mortification of the flesh could her soul be purged of the stain that unrestrained lust had poured on it.

She sought out the castle tanner. He had several hair shirts. One he pointed out was of soft lambswool and would do little harm to her skin. She would not shirk her duty to her soul, so she asked for the stiffest shirt he had.

He shook his head and handed her a dark lump of material. The hairs felt more like boar bristles than fur. Gennie held it up to her body. The fit would be tight.

So much the better. No one could possibly accuse her of cheating on her penance with such a garment. Her conscience at rest for the first time since her wedding, Gennie paid the tanner and departed for her room. Now all she had to do was inform Haven of the friar's dictates.

Haven had spent hours on the training field, exhausting his rage on the bodies of the castle garrison. He ached from the few blows that had gotten past his guard. As he had hoped, the pain cooled the first blaze of anger.

His feet dragged on the stairs to his chamber, and he thought about the woman with whom he shared that space. On hearing her confession, the friar had probably assigned penance for the sake of her soul. But Haven doubted that hours on her knees at prayer would teach her body to respond to only one man—him.

He was her husband, and by God's holy shroud, he alone would stir Gennie to ecstasy. He imagined her naked, on her knees, begging and pleading for sexual release. He would refuse until she acknowledged that only he could satisfy her. Then he would keep her in bed until she forgot other men existed.

Haven's body hardened and his aches faded. He climbed the stairs faster, eager to teach his wife a much-deserved lesson about lust.

Chapter Fourteen

Haven shut the door behind him, closing out the world. Lady de Sessions knelt at the prayer bench below the window of their chamber. *Lady de Sessions indeed. Lady Deceit was more like.* Haven listened to the clack of rosary beads and observed her still form.

He crossed his arms over his chest and leaned back, watching the play of firelight in that flow of red-black hair. Like her hair, she was never the same from moment to moment. Just hours ago in the bailey she had seemed colorless and drab. Yet in bed some inner light flashed, and her body at least came alive, despite her armor of almost complete silence. Haven found himself wondering what he would find, if he could pierce that armor. Would he discover a woman willing to risk her heart as well as her body? A woman who might trust him, as he longed to trust her? For he did wish to trust her, he realized. The knowledge that he could not hurt him more than he liked.

Gennie rose from the prayer bench. She stood and extinguished the candles with great care, as if those simple movements caused great pain.

Haven frowned.

His wife turned and saw him. One hand flew to her lips, but a gasp emerged before she could silence herself.

"Good even', milady wife."

She dropped her hand. "*Bon soir*, sir. Have you been waiting long?"

"Long enough." He walked up to her and took her hand, placing a kiss on the fingers that had so recently touched her mouth. "Do you pray for me?" He sent her a sideways glance.

"*N . . . Non.*"

"Too bad. I've been thinking of you for hours." He lapped at the pads of her fingers and felt her hand tremble. He hid his smile in her palm and breathed a question. "For what did you pray?"

She tried to tug her hand from his tender assault.

Haven held firm and whispered his lips over the delicate skin of her wrist.

"For God's mercy." Her voice strangled on the words. "Please, husband. Do not touch me so."

It was a start. He let her fingers slide from his and turned to study her face. She looked like a wounded animal—too much in pain to run but too fear-filled to remain. Haven knew very well that passion and pain were close akin, but such a reaction from a mere kiss of the hand was very odd.

Regardless, she wouldn't escape him or his plans for her. He placed a hand on her shoulder to draw her close.

She flinched.

"What?" He grabbed her upper arm.

A choked moan escaped her.

"What is wrong? Are you hurt?" The memory of her feet, bloody and blistered, her bruised body and face, rose in his mind.

"Nay," she shrilled, tearing herself from his grasp with a sob. She threw herself across the room, placing the bed between them. "Do not touch me."

"Madame, I am your husband. Should I wish it, I will touch you." He pursued her. Caged her with a hand placed on either side of her head. Stroked her body with the slow side-to-side movement of his own.

She wept.

Nothing felt right. Not her tears, not her protests, not her flight, not her body. Her body; what was it that didn't feel right about her? Keeping his gaze on her face, he put his hand on her breast.

She bit her lip, but Haven saw the effort that restraint caused her. He felt too the peculiar textures beneath his hand. Her breast was there, but between his hand and her flesh lay more than cloth.

"What are you wearing?"

Her eyes closed. Tears seeped from the corners. Her head moved from side to side.

"Then I will find out for myself."

Haven unlaced her tunic and drew it over her head. The undergown quickly followed. He should have been staring at rose-tipped breasts and a dusting of auburn curls at the juncture of her thighs. Instead, ugly brown leather covered her from shoulder to elbow and knee.

"A hair shirt? You are wearing a hair shirt!" Haven couldn't get over the obvious. He was a good Christian, but this . . . this was sinful. "Why?"

"P-penance." She trembled, and even though he no

longer touched her, another tear leaked from her eye.

"Penance!" Haven grabbed the shirt and ripped it down the seam from neck to hem.

Gennie moaned.

Haven stared at her body. She could only have worn the shirt a few hours, yet her skin screamed an angry red everywhere the shirt had touched.

"This isn't penance. This is folly."

Gennie's moans quieted to whimpers.

"Get in bed."

"I can't."

"What do you mean, you can't?"

Gennie turned around.

He should have known. That blistering red covered as much of her back as it did her front.

"Stay there." Haven strode to the chest, opened it and removed the salve for treating small wounds and burns. He had used it on Gennie's feet. He hoped he had enough left to ease the worst of her pain. He grabbed his softest cloak and returned to Gennie.

She remained as he had left her, braced on her forearms against the wall. Her head rested on her clenched fists.

Anger warred with sorrow. He tossed the cloak on the bed. "I am going to put salve on your skin. It will hurt at first. When I am done, you should be able to lie down."

Gennie nodded. Her body tensed.

Haven placed a scoop of slave on her left shoulder and began to smooth the ointment across and down her back. He turned her round and repeated the process over the entire front of her body.

As he knelt before her, stroking the cream into the

reddened skin of her thighs, a furious pounding came at the door.

The portal opened. Haven dropped the salve, tossed the cloak at Gennie and reached for his sword all in one motion. When he turned to face the intruders, it was clear that Soames had gotten a very good look at Haven's wife before she had been able to cover herself.

"What is it?" Haven snarled.

"You asked that I attend you the moment I arrived."

Haven took in Soames's mud-stained clothing and nodded. He placed his sword back in its scabbard. "Aye, I did. Step outside. I will join you in a moment."

Soames left.

Haven turned back to Gennie. "Madame, we are not finished."

"Non."

"I expect to find you in that bed when I come back."

"But . . ."

"No. You will sleep. I will bring food and a priest and wake you when I return. Until then you will, for once, do as I tell you."

"Oui."

Haven turned on his heel and left. "Women," he muttered as he closed the door.

Across the hallway, Soames nodded.

"So you find the widow attractive after all?"

"Unless you want to lose all your teeth, you'll close your mouth on that smile," Haven ground out. "The widow is my wife."

Soames smile fled. "How?"

"In the usual fashion, at a wedding. Ordered by Edward, so it was unavoidable."

"Tell me."

"Aye, that I will. But first we have the king's business to prepare for."

Gennie didn't see Haven again until the next day. She did receive a visit from a priest. Father Jonas arrived with servants and food in tow. The round little man refused to let her rise from the bed.

"Sir Haven explained some of your problem to me. Please remain as you are. We will break bread together and see what may be done to set your conscience at ease."

Gennie wanted to protest, but the priest turned away to supervise the servants. He had them move a table and a stool near the bed and set the meal in place. Then they disappeared with a wink and a smile from Father Jonas.

The priest served Gennie a small piece from the trencher and watched as she ate and swallowed. Before she could speak, he placed a goblet in her hand. "Drink." His mild tone revealed an unshakable faith that his orders would be obeyed.

Gennie drank.

Father Jonas began to eat. Betwixt bites, he asked, "Do you wish to share your confession with me, child?"

"I—I don't know. I've already confessed."

"Yea, and done penance too from what I was told."

"*Oui.*"

"Perhaps you have more on your mind than what you told your other confessor?"

The priest's perception comforted Gennie. "I hardly know where to begin."

"Start wherever you like, child. I will listen."

Gennie told the priest her entire story. From the moment she had left France to marry Roger, to the horrible

165

embarrassment of lust for her new husband that had led to wearing the hair shirt. She even confessed that she had not yet told Haven that she must not lay with him for several weeks.

The telling took a long time.

When she was done, Father Jonas refilled her goblet and his own. He sipped at the wine, then sat back and folded his hands together across his large middle. "Child, child. Your zeal is admirable, but the friar counseled you to folly."

"Do you tell me that lust is not a sin?"

"Nay," he chuckled. "I tell you that excess is a sin, even in penance. And such pain as you endured is excessive, especially when your *sin*, as you call it, is not so heinous. You have suffered enough. The church absolves you of all further penance in this matter."

"I do not understand, Father. I do not love my husband. How can my lust for him be anything other than sinful?"

"Many married couples do not love one another. Had your mother been with you when you married, she might have taught you this."

"I do not know. My father loved my mother deeply. He told me stories about other men and women who loved as they did."

The priest patted her hand. "Yes, my child, but those are only wondrous stories. Fancies for entertainment. Were such fancies common they would not be wondrous, would they?"

"No." Gennie twisted her hands around her cup.

"Lady Genvieve, the lust that men and women feel for one another has a holy purpose when sanctioned by marriage vows. That purpose is twofold. First to bring forth children to God's glory. Second to strengthen the bond of marriage begun with the vows into a love that will last a lifetime."

"But I felt neither lust nor love for Roger Dreyford."

"Aye, and he had none for you."

"I doubt Sir Haven has either love or lust for me."

The priest regarded her in silence for a few moments. "Your marriage to Haven de Sessions is young yet. Give it and your husband time. Even if he does not bear tender feelings for you, accept the passion you have for your husband's body. The blessings that come to you may surprise you."

Gennie wrinkled her brow. "You speak in riddles, Father."

The priest rose. "So Christ's words often seemed to his apostles. Your faith is strong, milady. God rewards the faithful. Now, let us pray."

When the priest had gone, Gennie lay back in the bed. She believed what Father Jonas had said. But did her husband believe it too? They didn't trust one another. She blamed him for Roger's death as much as Haven blamed her. He saw loyalty to the king as the ultimate good. She believed in loyalty to more than a mere man, no matter how powerful. How could she and Haven ever surmount such differences and create a strong marriage? Without trust in each other, how could passion alone be enough to nurture love?

If passion was not enough, could she survive another marriage like her first? At this time she had little choice in the matter. Suffice that for now she and Thomas were still alive and would soon be together. She must place her faith in God, as Father Jonas advised. But believing did not mean she understood. Her mind whirling with confusion, Gennie fell asleep.

*   *   *

A day later, Gennie held her son's hand and crossed the narrow plank to the boat that would carry them to Wales.

"Will the boat sink, Mama?"

"What makes you ask, Thomas?"

"It's raining. Won't the boat fill up with water?"

"That's possible, but not very likely. Even Noah's boat didn't fill up with water when God made rain for forty days and forty nights."

Thomas nodded.

Gennie followed him to the far side of the boat, where he clambered onto a coil of rope. They stood watching the harbor over the boat's rim.

"Mama," Thomas broke the silence. "Becky says you married Sir Haven."

"I did."

"Why?"

"Because the king ordered it."

"Will the king order me to be Sir Haven's son?"

Gennie's heart twisted. She placed an arm around Thomas's small shoulders. Events had wiped clean his familiar life. Of course he wanted to know what his place was in his now uncertain world. What better place for a boy than that of son to a man of strength and reputed honor?

Haven appeared at the boy's other side. "A knight does not take his own sons as warriors until they've been fostered to someone else. Since you are already one of my warriors, you cannot be my son."

Thomas's lower lip trembled.

Gennie tightened her hold on his shoulder. She prayed that young as he was, he would accept the place Haven offered.

"Mama was my father's wife. Now she is your wife. Does that not make me your son?"

"Nay, Thomas. Being a wife or husband is a matter of man's law. Being a son or daughter is a matter of God's natural laws. Do you understand?"

The boy raised his head. "I understand that I am your warrior, but whose son am I?"

"You are your father's son."

"But Papa is dead."

"That does not change who you are."

Thomas nodded and squared his shoulders. "I hope we see a sea monster."

Haven ruffled Thomas's hair. "Go find Soames. He has work for all my warriors."

Thomas grinned up at him. Haven's hand fell from the boy's head to cover Gennie's over her son's shoulders. "Aye, Sir Haven."

With a speed possessed only by small boys, Thomas was gone. Gennie turned to make her way to the rear of the ship.

"Stay a moment." Haven's hand still held hers. "I would talk with you."

"As you will, husband."

A voice called an order to loose all ropes. The ship lurched. Gennie wobbled a bit as the boat left the quay.

An unhappy expression on his face, Haven grasped Genvieve and she held steady.

"Did Father Jonas speak with you?"

"Oui."

"I would know why you wore the hair shirt."

Gennie stared at the sea and gripped the ship's rail with her free hand. "I told you. It was a penance."

Haven twined his fingers in hers and with his other hand turned her face toward him. "Do not try my pa-

169

tience too far, wife." His cheeks paled and his mouth tautened.

Gennie swallowed. For the sake of her soul she must tell Haven all. Yet she could not bear to reveal such weakness to this man. He was so perfectly strong in both body and will. Gennie squared her shoulders. She couldn't hope to match him in worldly strength, but her faith was as firm as any devout. She would draw on that. God would guide her.

"I . . . I sinned."

Haven's lips twisted. "That is the usual reason for penance. How did you sin?"

"I felt lust"—Gennie's face burned—"for a man I do not love."

Her husband frowned and tightened his grip on her hand. "Who was this man?"

Gennie hesitated. What could she say? How could she make him understand, when she didn't understand herself?

"I am waiting."

Chapter Fifteen

"You." She snatched her hand from his and covered her flaming cheeks. "Do you understand? I felt lust for you. Are you satisfied now?" She dared him with her eyes to push for more.

Haven puffed out his cheeks. His forehead wrinkled as if in pain. "Nay!" he groaned and leaned over the ship's rail.

What? Gennie suppressed a gasp of surprise and looked closely at Haven, who clung weakly to the side of the ship. "You suffer *mal de mere?*"

Her big, brave, oh-so-strong, oh-so-perfect knight uttered a truly pitiful groan followed by protracted sounds of wretching.

Automatically, Gennie rubbed her hand over his back. When Thomas was sick the soothing strokes always helped.

"It is no sin to lust for your spouse." The faint words

floated toward Gennie just before another bout of nausea shook Haven's back.

He was wrong, but she would not argue with him now. Now all she wanted was to find some fresh water and get him to a cot. She stopped a burly seaman, who promised to bring the water "right quick like."

Haven's groans ceased, but periodic pains wracked his body.

Gennie continued to stroke him. She murmured soothing sounds, assuring him that he would soon feel much better.

The seaman returned. He helped Haven to sit on a rope coil and steadied him while Gennie wiped his face.

"Can you stand?" She had to get Haven to the shelter at the back of the boat, and standing was the first step.

"Of course I can stand," he croaked. Suiting action to words, he rose and would have toppled face forward had the seaman not caught him. "God, I hate the sea," Haven muttered.

"Sea prob'ly dunna like ye overmuch either." The sailor grinned. "Seein' as we ain't left t'harbor yet."

Gennie put the basin down. "Can you help me get him to a bed?"

"Aye." The seaman suited actions to words.

Aware of the effect that seeing their leader laid low might have on Haven's men, Gennie shook her head. "Let us try together first."

"Verra well."

Gennie took up a position on one side of Haven. With the seaman on the other, they managed a credible imitation of a casual walk to the wooden structure that housed the beds where passengers might sleep.

Gennie loosed her hold. The seaman lowered Haven to one of the small cots.

"Thank you very much."

The seaman nodded. "He be the first, but 'twill be plenty more 'fore we've been at sea a day."

"Are you sure?"

"Aye. Most passengers don't take well to the sea, nor the sea to them."

"Then I will need Marie. Will you get her for me?"

"Which one is she?"

"The short, round woman with red hair."

"I know the one, a fair buxom wench."

Gennie grinned. Haven moaned, drawing her attention from the seaman's apparent fascination with her son's nurse. "Ask her to bring water, basins and cloth."

"I will have her to ye 'fore two turns o' the wheel."

"My thanks again." Gennie slipped the words over her shoulder and stroked her hand down Haven's face. He looked slightly less pale. The grim lines about his mouth faded.

Haven's lips moved.

Gennie strained to hear his words. Failing, she leaned closer.

His eyes opened and his brown gaze searched her face. "My thanks to you, wife."

This time she caught the faint words. "Think naught of it, husband. A little rest will see you back on your feet again." Unaccustomed to his vulnerability and his thanks, Gennie rose, intent upon finding Marie.

Haven's hand caught hers with a weak squeeze. "Nay. I cannot feel so vile and not die."

Gennie looked down at him and could not help the small upward turn of her lips. He looked so much like

173

Thomas when life threw some unexpected obstacle between him and his current great desire.

"I do not doubt that you feel most wretched. But truly, you will recover, especially if I can find Marie to help us."

"Stay with me. Please." His eyes closed.

She could have broken his grasp with a small shake of her hand, but her determination faltered in the face of his plea.

"*Oui*, I will stay with you. But you must promise to sleep."

Haven's hand dropped to the bed. " 'Twill be no burden, to sleep with you near. I would . . ."

His words trailed off as Gennie resettled herself beside him. His breathing evened, and Gennie knew he slept.

Moments later, Marie bustled into the hut, her arms filled with everything needed to tend the sick.

"So that sailor told the truth. I had not thought anything as simple as the sea could lay your husband low, milady."

" 'Tis reassuring to know that he is not as true and perfect as rumor would have us believe."

"Surely you can not wish this *mal de mer* upon him?"

"*Non*, I do not wish anyone ill, Marie. But you must admit that he can be somewhat daunting."

Marie studied her mistress, then set about preparing the sickroom. "Mayhap, milady. I confess I know little about men who daunt. Most of the ones I know be just like babies, yelling whenever their will be cros't."

"Sir Haven does not seem to yell near as much as Roger did."

"Well, there's yellin' and yellin'. Some men do so in a quieter fashion than others."

Gennie nodded. In the few weeks of her acquaintance with Haven de Sessions she had become very familiar with his quiet authority, coming into conflict with his determination on more occasions than she cared to admit.

"Marie, that sailor who fetched you to me, said others would be struck with *mal de mer.*"

"Aye, milady. You recall how it was on our voyage from France."

Gennie shuddered at the memory of the foul stench and pitiful moans that she and Marie had encountered as they tended the other passengers. "Is there nothing we can do to prevent such sickness?"

"None that I know of, milady. Indeed, most folk recover before any treatment could be of use. We only need worry for those who don't recover within a day. They must have water and naught else. And we must watch for fever. That'll be our worst enemy."

"How long would it take for fever to set in?"

" 'Tis hard to say. Some are sick for days but show no sign of fever. Others I've seen become feverish the minute they take to their beds. Had we a goodly supply of willow bark, I would not concern myself too much. But we've little left, and the sailor didn't seem to think there was any on the ship."

Gennie frowned. "Think you Thomas will fall victim to this?"

"I cannot say. But he is your son, and you showed no signs on the boat from France."

"True, but he is also Roger's son, and I heard that my first husband sickened most severely on his voyage to and from the Holy Land."

"Mayhap you should check on the lad, then."

Gennie looked at Haven, torn between duty to her husband and worry for her son. "But . . ."

" 'Twill set your mind at rest. I can tend Sir Haven until you return."

Gennie nodded and rose. "I will return the moment I have seen Thomas."

Haven woke to the sound of moans and wretching. His stomach hurt, but he didn't think he would vomit. The thought surprised him. The past few days, he had spent most of his waking moments bent over a basin. Someone, usually Marie but sometimes Gennie, would wipe his face and give him water. Then he would fall back exhausted and sleep.

The swaying of the cot told him they were still on board the ship. His stomach churned at the realization. Haven quelled the sensation. He had been laid low too long. Plans must be made for the coming battle with Daffydd. The ship's master must be made to give up some of his archers. Determined to conquer his weakness and get on with his work, Haven sat up.

A slim hand pushed him right back down again.

"I must rise."

"Nay, husband. Not when you are so weak that a touch as small as mine puts you flat on your back."

"But . . ."

Her finger against his lips silenced him.

"Not another word until you've eaten the sops I brought you."

Haven's stomach twisted in protest at the mention of food. He turned his face, and her finger trailed away down the side of his neck. "I hate sops."

"Oui," she agreed with more cheer than anyone on

a boat should possess. "Now hold my shoulders, and I will help you sit so that you may eat."

"I won't eat that mess." Nevertheless, he fixed his hands on her and let her pull him upright. Her scent smothered the other nauseating smells in the chamber. Deliberately he slid against her, so he could linger a moment near her lavender softness.

"You need to eat to regain your strength."

"I will not grow strong on pap."

"Until you keep the sops down, 'tis all you'll get."

Haven knew that he could not fight her and win in his present condition. So he must use guile. "You really wish me to eat that?"

"*Oui,* it would please me greatly."

"And what will you do to please me in exchange?"

He watched his wife blush. Having Father Jonas speak with her had been a good idea.

"You cannot mean . . ." She cast a look about the room.

"Nay, wife." He took the bowl she had picked up from the table. "But I must speak with Soames before we regain the shore."

"That will be impossible."

"Why?" Had he the strength he would have bellowed his displeasure.

"Because Soames is just as ill as you were two days ago."

Two days? He had been ill two whole days. That meant the boat would dock in another day. The need to have his plans in place became more urgent. But how could he accomplish preparations without Soames?

Haven felt a spoon against his lips. He opened his

mouth and swallowed the soft, fragrant stuff without protest.

None of his men had the leadership skills that Soames's experience gave the older warrior. Haven didn't know enough about the new men . . .

Since the food Gennie spooned into his mouth was too soft to sink his teeth into, he chewed on the thought.

The new men; that was it. Owain had all the skills needed. Could Haven trust the man? Did he have any choice? He lifted his hand and took the spoon from Gennie. "Owain—is he ill?"

"Non." She eyed him suspiciously.

"Good. Get him and bring him here."

"But your food?"

"I can feed myself."

She raised an eyebrow.

"See." He shoved a heaping spoonful of the sops into his mouth and nearly choked trying to swallow the large mass.

Gennie smiled.

"It would please me greatly, wife." He purposely echoed her earlier words.

"Well, I suppose it would not hurt you to talk to Owain."

"Thank you."

"But only for a few moments."

Gennie was gone before Haven could correct her. The plans he must make would take some time. Quickly he finished the sops and set the bowl aside. His stomach still felt somewhat shaky, so he leaned back against the wall that bordered the cot. Owain must not see his leader prostrate with sickness.

The man entered the chamber moments later.

Haven looked beyond the man-at-arms. "Where is Milady Genvieve?"

"Since she knew I would be with you should the seasickness overtake you again, she wanted to take the air."

"A fine nurse you'll make, I am sure," Haven grumbled. "Still, 'tis best that this conversation be as private as possible. Are the others asleep?"

Owain surveyed the sickroom. "Aye, they seem so."

"Good enough. Tell me how you've kept the men busy."

"All who are not sick sharpen their weapons, tend the horses or help the crew?"

"How many are sick?"

"Oh, no more than two or three at a time. You and Soames have had the worst of it."

"Will they be fit for battle?"

"Aye. We have a three- or four-day ride to Two Hills Keep once we dock. Plenty of time to settle stomachs. I am more worried about you and Soames than about the men. None of them has been ill for more than a day." Haven frowned at Owain's clear implication. "I have never failed my king. I will not fail now."

"And Soames?" Owain raised a brow.

" 'Tis a good thing he's asleep and not able to hear you question his abilities."

"Only a fool goes to battle when he is ill."

"Soames is no fool. If I order him to remain behind, he will do so."

Owain nodded. "What plan do you have for the battle?"

"Since I do not know if Daffydd ap Gryffudd has gained the castle at Two Hills or not, I've prepared two plans. If Daffydd occupies Two Hills Keep before we arrive, we will need sappers."

"We can find diggers at Twynn."

"I am counting on it. I will lay siege until I can breach the castle. Then I shall crush Daffydd and his force within."

"We will have to take care not to alert Daffydd as to our arrival."

"True. We will send two men to scout the situation in advance. Then approach by night."

"And if we arrive first?"

"We will occupy the castle. We'll set patrols at two leagues out, keeping watch for Daffydd. My understanding of the ground is that the castle sits on a small rise, with another similar rise about one league to the east. I want men posted on that rise. No fires. I want Daffydd to think our entire strength is in the castle."

" 'Tis a sound plan. Do you know the strength of his force?"

"Only estimates. But, with the aid of ten good archers, thirty mounted men should be able to hold the castle and the road."

"Your pardon, sir, but we have no archers."

"True, but this boat has a complement of forty all told. And I have Edward's writ to compel any man I need who is not currently in service."

"The ship's master may argue that those archers are in service to him."

"Have you seen any enemy ships?"

"Nay."

"And has the ship been threatened by a force from land?"

"Nay."

"The ship is to return to Chester the moment we've

been put ashore. Since there is neither current threat nor danger of future threat before replacements can be gotten, I do not see that the archers on board this vessel are in service. The master can spare me half his archers without fear."

"And if he refuses?"

"It is your job to see to it that he does not refuse."

Haven followed the last of his men down the gangplank and stepped ashore. For the first time in days he felt his stomach settle. That offended organ immediately growled at him, announcing its hunger. Food. Yes, food was the first order of business. Then they would proceed to Two Hills Keep.

"Watley."

"Aye, Sir Haven."

"Saw you where my lady wife went?"

The young man ducked his head. Haven could swear he saw a blush decorate his squire's cheek.

"I believe she went with the men who carried Soames to the inn at the end of this street."

"Good. When you have seen to the horses, join me there."

"Aye, sir."

Haven walked down the street, savoring the feel of solid ground and the thought of well-cooked mutton. As he neared the inn half a dozen people hurried out, shaking their heads and muttering in Welsh. Shouts came from inside.

"I won't." Rebecca's mulish whine was unmistakable. Haven was too distant to distinguish the quiet reply.

"You can't make me."

He crossed the lintel and heard a crash.

"Rebecca, calm yourself. These things do not belong

181

to us, and we cannot afford to pay for them." Gennie's voice was low but strained.

"Get your brute of a husband to pay for them. He has the king's favor. He must be rich."

Haven decided to charge through the door to the common room and deliver a much-deserved lesson, when Gennie's voice brought him up short.

"That comment is unworthy. Haven is no brute, and you should not expect anyone to pay for your ill temper but yourself."

"Ill temper?" Rebecca shrieked. "I will show you ill temper . . ."

"*Non*, you shall not."

An outraged howl followed. "Look what you've done. How could you?"

Haven dared a look into the room. Like a drowned cat, Rebecca stood, soaked to the skin and spitting, at the far end of the room. Gennie faced her a few feet away, shoulders stiff, an empty bucket in one hand.

The girl continued to wail. "You know I have no other clothing. This wool will never dry, and I will die of ague. I hate my life."

Haven watched his wife's shoulders slump. She put down the bucket and reached for Rebecca. The girl crumpled into Gennie's arms. What was going on here?

"Please don't forbid me to see him. He's the only person who's shown the least bit of kindness and understanding since we were tossed from our home."

Haven leaned back against the wall outside the room and ground his teeth at the girl's blatant ingratitude. From the moment his escort started, nothing had been asked of Rebecca but that she have a care for her nephew. She no longer lived as a titled lady with lands, money and servants, but she lived. As the sister of a traitor, she barely deserved the life she so despised.

"There, there," Gennie soothed. "I know this has been a difficult time for us all. But you must see that a connection between you and Watley is most inappropriate."

"Why? Is he not a gentleman? Are we not of equal rank? Does he not faithfully serve that awful knight you married despite the man's unfeeling rudeness?"

Watley! Gennie was right. A connection with his squire was more than inappropriate. How long had the girl been flirting with the lad? He thought back. Thomas! At least since the boy had disappeared. She had mentioned that she had been talking to Watley when the boy went missing. Haven should have warned the squire of the dangers Rebecca represented. He had thought about it and forgotten in the rush to find her nephew.

"Rebecca, you make me most angry when you spout such vileness about Sir Haven. You will not say one more word against my husband. Do you understand?"

There Gennie went, defending him again. Haven ventured another look into the room. The two women now sat on a bench near the fire. Rebecca faced the flames, her back to the room. Gennie sat next to her, facing the opposite direction. His wife's hand lay on her sister-in-law's cheek.

The girl gave a damp nod.

"*C'est bon*. Now, as for Watley . . . Yes, he is a gentleman who serves his lord with admirable dedication and sacrifice. However, you are not his equal in rank."

"What do you mean? He is not a knight, and thanks to de Sessions, I am no longer a titled lady."

"Rebecca, I warn you, do not blame de Sessions for your brother's foolishness."

"I am sorry, Gennie."

"Watley is not a knight now, but he will be. If he has lands, he will certainly not wish to wed the sister of a traitor. If he has no lands, he will wed where he can gain them, regardless of whatever feelings he claims for you."

"But . . ."

Over the girl's shoulder, Gennie's glance caught Haven's. *"Non.* No more of this nonsense. Learn to accept your place. As my sister-in-law, you share de Sessions's protection. When this war with the Welsh is over, I am sure Haven will see to it that you make a proper marriage."

His wife sought a promise he might not be able to keep. Nonetheless, he would try. No matter how ungrateful Rebecca was. He owed Roger this much, to see his sister well cared for and his son trained as a knight. Haven nodded his head and entered the room.

"Wife."

Rebecca started. Gennie put her hands on the girl's shoulders, holding her in place. Then his wife rose and curtseyed to him. She stood before Rebecca, shielding her sodden embarrassment.

Haven held out his hand. If nothing else, he could rescue Gennie from Rebecca's self-pity. "Come, I have procured us a room in this hostelry, and we have much to do if we are to depart in the morning." He smiled suggestively, so she would know he had heard her defend him.

"Qui, husband." She took his hand and looked up at him.

He pulled her against him, wanting her to feel the hard throb of his manhood that leapt to life at her mere glance.

Gennie gave him an arch look. She brushed her body across his. "What is it that we must do before morning?" Her face wore a guileless expression, but she leaned into him. For the briefest of instants his chest burned where her breasts rubbed over him. Then his whole body ached with loss when she turned and preceded him from the room, invitation clear in the slow sway of her hips.

Haven's groin tightened painfully. With a low growl, he plunged after her down the darkened hallway.

Behind him Rebecca frowned into the fire. *Watley loves me. I know it. Oh, he hasn't said so, but I know it all the same. Everyone seems to think that because the king has taken away my family's lands and titles that I no longer deserve respect and courtesy. Gennie uses me as a spare nurse whenever that awful Marie is busy. Even Therese, my own maid, thinks nothing of going off and fornicating with the enemy when she should be tending her mistress. Only Watley shows the consideration that is my due by birth.*

Gennie was wrong. She had been forced to marry de Sessions and couldn't possibly understand what it was like to be worshipped. Rebecca nodded to herself. She would wed Watley whether Gennie and her horrid husband approved or not.

Chapter Sixteen

Haven watched his wife fuss over Soames. She was too softhearted. Why had he never seen this side of her? Or had he? He recalled the past weeks. She had treated Rebecca with gentle firmness. Her concern for her son was boundless. Even in the worst of circumstances, she showed constant smiles to his men. And she had cared for him with tender patience during his shipboard illness. Had he simply refused to see beyond his belief in her treason? How could a woman capable of treason be capable of such tenderness and understanding? Even more, she defended him. This woman, who reviled him to his face for betraying his best friend, excused those same actions to her sister-in-law. Why?

"Gennie, we must go." He slapped his gloves against his thigh.

"*Oui.* I shall be right there."

"Please, milady. I will be fine in a day or so and catch up with you before you ever miss me," Soames said.

"Thomas misses you already."

"Watley will keep the lad out of mischief." Soames looked past her to where Haven glowered at them from the doorway. "You had best leave before someone else starts trouble."

Gennie glanced over her shoulder at her husband. "I see what you mean." She stood, finally, but turned back to Soames. "I left the last of our medicaments with the innkeeper. Be sure to use them all."

"Aye, milady."

"Genvieve!" Haven imbued his voice with as much threat as he could muster. Although what he would do if she continued to delay, he wasn't certain. Fortunately he wasn't forced to find out.

With a swift peck on the older man's cheek, Gennie spun about and left the room. "Well, Sir Husband." She spoke from the top of the stairs. "What are you waiting for?"

Haven opened his mouth, but before he could speak, she disappeared below. What indeed? he wondered.

That first day out of Twynn, Haven set an easy pace. Two Hills Keep lay roughly ten leagues to the northeast down a well-traveled road that paralleled the river emptying into Twynn's small bay. Everyone, himself included, seemed drained by the four days at sea. Everyone, that was, except his wife and her son.

Despite having to attend more sick beds than she had probably ever seen in her life, the sea voyage had invigorated Gennie. She had an energy and a glow that had been missing before. She smiled often, laughing at the jokes of the men and her own fumbled attempts to learn the Welsh tongue from Owain and some of the archers.

Haven smiled, looking forward to the evening's halt

and having his wife to himself. The discovery that Gennie was innocent of adultery eased his mind. Even more, the assurance of Gennie's lust for him pleased him mightily. Lust carefully tended could grow into . . . He frowned. Had he imagined even for a moment that Gennie might come to love him? Such thoughts were folly. Roger's death stood between Haven and any hope of Gennie's love. Be satisfied with the passion you share with her in bed, he chastised himself, and turned his thoughts toward the coming evening.

Much distance would pass before that pleasant interlude, and Haven reminded himself that he still must talk with Watley. He searched the party for his squire and found him pacing his horse next to Rebecca's. The young man held Thomas in the saddle before him. The boy chattered amicably despite the frown on his aunt's face.

Haven joined them. "Watley, give Thomas to his aunt and come with me."

"Aye, Sir Haven."

Rebecca jerked on her reins, bringing her horse to a halt.

Haven rode off to the head of the column before she could complain.

Until Watley arrived, and they had put a small distance between them and the rest of the party, Haven remained silent.

"Watley, you became my squire as part of your training to become a knight, did you not?"

"Aye."

"And you know that a knight must always be prepared to face danger?"

"Aye."

"Do you know what danger is?"

"Aye. Danger is a threat to the safety of life or property."

"And in what forms does danger show itself?"

"Danger shows itself as either natural, as in fire, or beasts or as a human enemy and the tools he uses such as Daffydd ap Gryffudd, his men, their swords, spears and arrows."

Haven nodded. "Indeed, these are the most obvious dangers that a knight must face. But there are others."

Watley wrinkled his brow. "Do you mean dangers like the seasickness and hunger, or like those temptations that endanger the soul?"

"Those are dangers too, Watley, but not the particular threat I have in mind."

"Then what else?"

"Women."

Watley chuckled. "You cannot mean that, Sir Haven."

"Believe me. I have faced many anxious moments because of one woman or another."

The squire guffawed. "I do not believe it. Women call you perfect. How can that be a danger?"

Haven ground his teeth. The business of instructing his squire in the ways of women proved much more difficult than he had expected. His mouth thinned, and he looked about, checking to make sure no one rode to join them. The party remained a good distance in the rear.

"The danger lies in the woman's status and intent. Married women and women of low birth pose little threat to a knight. The first already have husbands. The second expect nothing but a pleasant toss. However, most unmarried women of gentle birth see a knight as nothing but a potential husband."

"I understand. One should not marry where one cannot trust. I shall be as careful as you have been."

Haven felt the stab of his squire's statement. Subtlety was not getting him anywhere. "Trust is important, and difficult to attain. It comes with maturity."

"If a man is prepared with the knowledge you have given me, I do not see the danger."

Haven sighed. "Let us take, for example's sake, my wife's sister-in-law, Rebecca."

"Yes. What say you? Would she make a good wife for a knight?" Eagerness lit Watley's eyes and curved his lips.

"She is too young."

The squire's mouth straightened. "She is past the age when many females wed."

"Youth has less to do with age than you might think," Haven remarked. "Also, her position as a traitor's sister is precarious."

The light in the young man's eyes dimmed. "I know, but . . ."

"She can bring you no lands, and you have none of your own."

Watley frowned. " 'Tis true . . ."

"Let me be blunt. I forbid you to court or flirt with the girl."

Watley's expression became mulish. "You have no right."

"I have every right. I am your overlord and, until Edward says otherwise, the girl's guardian. A match between the two of you would be a grievous mistake. I will not see either of you fall victim to her sly manipulations."

Haven watched Watley clench a fist against his thigh.

He took a deep breath and compressed his lips. "As you will, Sir Haven."

"You will thank me, you know."

"But not at this time. May I return to my duties with Thomas?"

"Aye. Go, but think carefully on my words."

Watley gave a salute in acknowledgment, turned his horse and left Haven in solitary thought.

Why, Haven wondered, do I think I made a mess of that?

That night Haven went looking for Gennie. Rebecca, Thomas and the female servants would occupy the tent. For privacy he had made a bed to share with his wife a short distance from the main camp. He found her just beyond the tent. She stood with her arms crossed over her chest and frowned out into the trees.

"What troubles you, wife?"

"Rebecca is once more in tears."

"Her tears are cheap. Do not spend your worry upon them."

Gennie cast him a sharp look. "These tears may prove costly."

"How so?"

"Watley caused them. She is heartbroken and like to do something rash."

So his squire had paid attention. Haven suppressed a smile of satisfaction. "You told her to avoid my squire, did you not?" Haven reminded Gennie.

"*Oui,* but in this case she was not flirting. She simply asked Watley to assist her. He refused most abruptly."

"I did not train my squire to be rude."

"No doubt, but it seems he was rude."

"Could you and Rebecca have misunderstood what he said?"

"That is possible, and I was not close enough to hear every word. However, their voices rose quite a bit toward the end of their argument. I distinctly heard Watley call Rebecca sly and manipulative. She's an inexperienced young woman. Why would he say something so hurtful?" Gennie faced her husband.

Haven couldn't prevent the flush that heated his neck. He hadn't expected Watley to repeat those words to Rebecca.

Gennie's dropped her jaw. "Husband, what do you know of this?"

"I know nothing of what passed between Rebecca and Watley, save what you have told me."

"But you suspect something." She began tapping her foot.

Haven wouldn't be bullied, especially by this woman. He leaned forward and thrust out his chin. "I warned Watley about the dangers of courting inexperienced, gently bred young women."

"No doubt you phrased your warning as an order."

"What if I did? It is my responsibility to train my squire for knighthood. If he will not listen to reason, I must supply that training through any means possible, including orders."

Gennie shook her head and cast her hands skyward. "Husband, there are moments when I believe you are a most true and perfect fool."

"But . . ."

She turned on her heel and disappeared into the tent.

Haven made to follow her. He would settle this disagreement, and Gennie would share his bed. The sound of rosary beads and the words of the Pater Noster brought him up short. He spun away from the tent and stomped across the clearing to the bed he had made and would now occupy alone.

Be damned if he would share his bed with Gennie and her prayers. He tossed within the furs that covered the pine boughs and cursed at the world. Because of his thickheaded squire and Gennie's addlepated sister-in-law, Haven could not sleep. Lavender and cream should have mingled with the scent of pine. Gennie's soft sighs should have harmonized with the breeze. She should have joined him in marital ecstasy. He hoped her prayers would keep her warm.

Gennie was still praying. Haven rode at the front of the party where he had been for the past two and a half days. He still had not figured out a way to make her stop. He might have to apologize.

The sound of a horse approaching from behind halted his thoughts. Maybe Gennie had come to apologize for calling him a fool. Even though she had been right, it would be nice to have her soothe his vanity.

Owain's voice dashed that wan hope. "Your men complain much."

"I know this."

"She used to try praying at Roger."

"And what did Roger do?"

"He sought more pleasant company."

"So that's how she drove him to treason. She prayed him into rebellion."

Owain laughed.

"I see naught funny about it."

"Think what you like, but Roger would have left her anyway. Fidelity was not in his nature."

Haven held his tongue, unsure how he felt about

Roger these days. The picture painted by Gennie and some of the others cast his old friend into a new and different light. A light that showed just how lacking Roger had been as a husband. "So, once he had left, did she stop this constant praying?"

"Eventually. Think you of leaving us for a while?"

"Nay. That would be foolish this close to Two Hills Keep."

"Aye. Think you we will get there before Daffydd?"

"I know not."

They rode in silence for a few moments.

"The men's grumbles distract them from their purpose."

"Have you any suggestions?"

"You could kiss her into silence."

"The thought has occurred to me, but to do so would profane her prayer and cast sin upon us both. I've no desire to trade her praying for penance."

"Then she must be distracted."

"Aye, but how?"

"She has a most tender heart."

"Aye, too tender."

"One of the Welsh archers tells me that a village lies less than a league beyond the keep."

"So?"

"So villagers often have stray cats or dogs that they would be glad to be rid of, especially for a price."

"You think I should give my wife a pet."

"I think a peace offering never hurt. And an offering that strikes her most vulnerable spot is best."

" 'Tis a good plan. Mayhap you can find me a pup in this village."

"Then you will take the puppy from me and give it to your lady wife."

Haven looked Owain straight in the face. "Nay, I will give it to her son."

Owain cocked an eyebrow in thought, then laughed out loud. "Sir, you are a most devious man."

Haven nodded. "Truly, where my wife is concerned, I am."

"I will see you anon." Owain turned back toward his post at the rear of the party.

Haven slowed his own mount to a walk. The clear tones of Gennie's prayers floated on the air. Haven smiled.

They had just forded a small stream when Haven raised his hand, bringing the party to a halt. The birds had stopped their song, the squirrel's chatter ceased. The beat of galloping hooves shattered the silence.

The advance guard's horse broke into view, its rider bent low in the saddle over the lathered animal.

"Lindel, take nine men. Escort the women back across the ford. Protect them at all costs."

"Aye, Sir Haven."

As the warrior departed, the guard reined in.

"Report."

"Welsh warriors. About fifteen mounted. Some bowmen, but I was spotted before I could take their number."

"More than ten?"

"Less."

"Did you see Daffydd's standard?"

"Nay, but their mounts reveal them to be Welsh. None is taller than a large dog."

"Do not underestimate the advantages of a small horse. What of the terrain ahead?"

"Just around that bend"—the man pointed down the road—"is a small rise. The height would give our arch-

195

ers advantage. The trees are thin there. We could array our horse to defend the flanks of the archers."

Haven nodded. "Form the archers and march out double quick. I will organize the mounted men and come on behind you."

"As you wish, Sir Haven."

From the opposite side of the stream, Gennie watched the battle preparations. Haven's men had gained experience during their long journey from Yorkshire. Confusion was minimal. In moments, two bands formed and moved out.

Behind her Gennie heard a commotion.

"Let go this instant," Rebecca snapped the command. "I must see Watley."

"But mistress, we are ordered to stay here."

Gennie turned, ready to make peace and calm Rebecca, when the girl's horse shot by, splashed through the stream and headed straight toward the point where the first warriors rounded the bend in the road.

"Lindel, go after her before she causes more harm."

"But, milady, Sir Haven said . . ."

"Think you that those men want fear for Rebecca to stay their arms in battle? Go now!"

Lindel nodded and leapt into pursuit at a full gallop.

But Rebecca had gotten a good start. "Watley!" Her shriek echoed through the trees.

Haven and two of the men at the rear of the troop turned in their saddles.

At that moment, an arrow sliced the air.

Chapter Seventeen

The Welsh poured out from the surrounding trees. Haven pulled his sword from his scabbard and kneed his mount to face the nearest opponent. "A de Sessions," he shouted and swung. The Welshman fell. Haven's cheek twitched. He wheeled his horse.

Three grinning enemies separated him from his men. The melees in the Holy Land flashed through Haven's mind. Unbidden, the ululating battle cry of the Saracens welled up from his chest. The sound so startled the three men that he spitted one and unhorsed a second in the time it took the third to land a blow against Haven's chest.

Haven ignored the pain and sliced at the exposed shirt under his opponent's outstretched arm. The enemy sword dropped, and the fellow turned tail, opening the way for Haven to join his men. His horse was already in motion when Haven saw a burly Welshman wrestle Rebecca from her mount. The girl clawed at the man, making things as difficult as possible. She managed to delay him long enough for Haven to change directions.

He prayed she would keep fighting just a few moments longer. From the corner of his eye he saw Watley, with surprising agility, dispatch two enemies and start toward Rebecca on a course intersecting Haven's. Good; the squire's aid would be welcome.

Haven's horse faltered over some obstacle. He gathered the reins and tried to help the animal regain his stride. As the steed crashed to the ground, Haven flew over the saddle, straight into the squire's path. The breath smacked out of Haven on impact. Watley would never be able to stop. Still Haven tried to call a warning.

Time slowed and sound vanished. All Haven could see were the hooves of Watley's mount aimed squarely at his head. The horse lifted in midstride. From below he watched the animal pass over him. Haven would have sighed his relief had he breath enough. The thought hit him at the same time as the rear hoof of Watley's mount.

Haven's vision cleared slowly. His head throbbed. He had to stand up. He had been warned. The Saracens spitted any enemy unable to stand. If he wanted to live, he had to stand.

"Haven. Haven, can you hear me?"

From a long way off a woman's voice called. What was a woman doing on a Saracen battlefield? Where was Roger? He shook his head to clear it and moaned as pain pounded through his skull and twisted his gut. Despite the agony, he rolled to his side and emptied his stomach onto the dirt and grass. Dirt and grass, not sand. This wasn't the Holy Land. Wales. Gennie. Rebecca. Watley's horse. *Roger is dead, because of me.* Pain pushed the thought aside.

Haven groaned and sat up, cradling his aching pate in his hands.

"Husband, lie down." Gennie's hand touched his shoulder.

"Nay." He shrugged off his wife's hand and her concern and stood. The world spun, and Haven was grateful for Gennie's quick support. A glance showed his men to be the victors. Most of the Welsh had run off or lay dead. Two sat bound, their backs braced against a stone. Owain knelt to talk with them.

Haven wanted to know what the Welshmen said. Still leaning on Gennie, he stepped forward. A sharp pain in his side joined the pounding in his head. He bit back a gasp and touched his hand to his ribs. His fingers came away red. "I am bleeding."

"*Oui*, and you should be lying down, not dancing around a field of battle."

"I am grateful for your consideration, wife. Now, if you will guide me to yon stone, I will cease dancing, as you put it."

The short walk to the stone exhausted him. Haven did his best to conceal his agony from Gennie. He failed.

"Owain, keep you this lunkhead from toppling over and doing himself further injury while I seek out medicine and bandages."

"Aye, milady."

Uncertain which was more troublesome—his pain or his wife—Haven growled a curse at her retreating form.

"God will punish you for your ingratitude, husband."

Haven, who knew he had already received sufficient

punishment for his sins, ignored his wife's taunt. "What say our prisoners?"

Owain frowned. "Pah. The braggarts say we will never find Daffydd. That he is already flown north to aid Llewellyn."

"Do they speak true?"

"Who can tell? My people were ever given to exaggeration. They talk of a battle three days past and sapping some castle that might or might not be Two Hills Keep. One describes a crossroad and two hills. The other claims but one hill and a ford."

"What were they doing on this road?"

"Again they gainsay each other. They are either innocent travelers headed to market in Twynn or they are part of Daffydd's rear guard."

Haven eyed a growing pile of weapons deposited by his men as they cleared away the mess of battle. Then he eyed the Welshmen's chain-mail hauberks. "I doubt innocents would be so well prepared for a fight."

"Aye. Shall I beat the truth out of them?"

"Nay. Two Hills Keep is less than a day's ride from here. Most likely the truth is completely different than what either of them says. We'll find out soon enough."

"What shall we do with them?"

"Keep them with us until we get to the keep. Once we determine its strength, we can send them to the king along with our report."

"As you wish, Sir Haven." Owain lifted the Welshmen to their feet and shoved them toward the ford, calling for a guard as he went.

De Sessions closed his eyes and slumped where he sat. If Daffydd had slipped past before they could arrive, securing Two Hills Keep became even more important. It now sat at the most likely route of retreat for Llewellyn's forces, should he somehow escape the net that Edward cast over northern Wales.

Weariness sapped Haven's stamina. He had not fully recovered from days of seasickness, and the battle had left him drained. Yet he knew he could not afford to rest.

"Husband, you must lift your arm if I am to examine your wound."

He opened his eyes at Gennie's quiet order. "Aye, wife." Gritting his teeth against the pain, he stretched his arm over his head.

Gennie bent to look closely at his rib cage. "Your mail is embedded in the cut. Watley, help me get Sir Haven's armor off."

"Aye, milady. What would you have me do?"

"I will loosen the metal from the wound. As soon as I have it worked free, lift the armor and the shirt from my husband's body. Haven, raise your other arm."

Tired as he was, Haven complied.

"Now, husband, this will hurt."

"Aye, so get it over with." He set his jaw against any cry that pain might steal from him.

An age later, Watley whipped the shirt over Haven's sweat-drenched head. Haven dropped his arms and drew in huge gulping breaths.

"Watley, get Sir Haven water to drink."

"Aye, Lady Genvieve."

Haven felt Gennie dab at his side. He looked down. Blood covered the entire left side of his chest and still seeped from the ragged cut that decorated his ribs. "That doesn't look good."

She finished cleaning the area and began to wind a bandage around his rib cage. "You are right. It should be stitched, but I have no needle or thread with which

201

to do so. You should have medicine, a poultice for the wound itself and potions to ward off fever and infection. I have none of those either. The best I can do is to bind the wound tightly and tell you to rest." She looked up at him. "I don't suppose you will listen to me."

"If I could, Gennie, I would. But I must get to Two Hills Keep. Perhaps I can take a day of ease once the place is secured, but not before then."

"Then I must check this bandage at every halt. Even now you lose blood. Riding will not help you heal, and if the bleeding does not stop, you will faint. Then you will rest whether you want to or not."

He put his hand under her chin. He wanted to do more, but the effort was too great. "Thank you for your care of me."

"Much good your thanks will be when you sicken with fever or collapse from loss of blood."

"Ah, but then you will have me at your mercy. And you may punish me as you wish."

"Do not tempt me."

Haven smiled. "We will not talk of temptation. Now go and tend the others. I know I am not the only one with hurts."

"But you are the worst, and I fear to leave you alone."

"Here is Watley with my water. He will aid me should I need aught."

"Very well."

Haven watched her walk away. He took the cup from Watley, then said, "Go fetch my horse. 'Twill take long for me to mount, and I would be ready before the others."

"Are you sure you should, Sir Haven?"

"Verily, I am certain I shouldn't. But there are needs

greater than my own, and I must see to those first. Now do as you are bid."

The young man hesitated. "Sir Haven?"

"What is it, Watley?"

"Your horse. It fell in the battle."

"Ah." Haven paused for breath. He had no time for the sorrow he felt. "A sad loss, that. He was a good horse. I will not get another as well trained any time soon. Well, find me what steed you can; just don't give me one of those Welsh animals. My knees would drag the ground."

Gennie watched Haven weave in the saddle. The sword wound had stopped bleeding, but it wasn't healing cleanly, and he still had headaches. Despite her many requests that he rest, he refused, insisting that duty to his king came before all else.

He didn't realize the effect his stubbornness was having. She had spent a good ten minutes assuring Thomas that his newfound hero wasn't going to die. No sooner had the party gotten underway than Bergen, Lindel, and Sutherland in quick succession made discreet inquiries about her husband's well-being.

Watley shared his guilt with her. She gave him what assurance she could that he had done his best to avoid harming Haven. She offered praise for his persistence in battle and his rescue of Rebecca. He thanked her but fell silent when the object of his rescue joined them.

Rebecca rode a small horse taken from her would-be captor. The mount she had ridden since York had been given to Haven as replacement for the steed he had lost in Rebecca's defense. It was the only consequence Gennie could think of that she had the ability to enforce. Fortunately others in the party let Rebecca know by their actions what they thought of her foolish behavior. None would speak with her. Even Therese, who took every opportunity to complain, refused to honor her mistress with a word.

"Did God answer your prayers?" Rebecca asked.

Gennie considered carefully whether or not to answer this conversational gambit. Like her brother, Rebecca rarely concerned herself with the needs or wishes of others.

"God answers all prayers."

"He did not answer mine."

"Truly?"

"If God had answered my prayers, I would still have fine clothes and a home. I would not be riding this ridiculous beast."

Had the girl no understanding? Gennie couldn't believe her ears. She observed the stern look in Watley's eyes and the painful longing in the set of his mouth.

"Perhaps that ridiculous animal, as you call it, is the answer to your prayers." His words hanging in the air, the young man rode off.

Gennie looked to Rebecca. Astonishment showed plain in the girl's open mouth and wide eyes.

"What did he mean by that?"

"Perhaps he means that God sometimes says no, even to our most heartfelt prayers."

"Oh." Rebecca fell silent.

Gennie let the silence continue. She had her own worries, foremost among them her husband. She looked ahead to where he rode at the front of the column. His horse paced quick and straight under his urging, but Haven seemed less steady than before. Every now and then his body shuddered, as if he felt a chill.

"Do you think Watley still cares for me?"

Gennie almost didn't hear the quiet question. "Do you wish him to?"

Rebecca paused a long while before responding, "More than anything."

"Then you might think carefully on the things he says and does."

"You mean about how God answers our prayers."

"That and other things."

"Like obeying Sir Haven's orders."

"Perhaps. I will let you be the judge of your own thoughts."

"Thank you, Gennie."

"You are most welcome, but for what?"

"No one else will talk with me."

"Ah."

"I think I will go and offer Thomas a ride on my ridiculous beast."

Gennie acknowledged Rebecca's smile with one of her own and watched the girl ride off. Clouds massed on the horizon, and Gennie caught the rumble of thunder on the rising wind. More rain. That would do her husband no good. How could she help Haven if even the elements were against her?

Owain's horse fell into step beside hers. "Your husband is a stubborn man."

She frowned, still trying to discover a way to surmount the weather and her husband's obstinacy. "He has proven so throughout the short time I have known him."

"You are well matched."

Startled by his blunt comment, Gennie lifted her head to get a good look at his expression. "Do you suggest that I am stubborn?"

He smiled. "Oh, nay, milady. A woman who prays for

days on end is merely determined, not stubborn."

Gennie relaxed a bit. "I have had to be."

"Aye. Roger was not an easy husband."

"De Sessions is far from easy."

"But a very different man than Dreyford."

"Oui."

"Sir Haven is the better man."

Privately Gennie agreed, but she was not about to say so. "Roger had his good points." She hoped Owain would not press her to name any, for at that moment she couldn't think of a single one.

The warrior raised an eyebrow. "True. Dreyford was game for any pleasure, and he always had a ready story."

Thunder grumbled in concert with the memory of the many times she had sat ignored by a husband who sought greater attention with his antics and tales. Gennie told herself that Roger's neglect had been a blessing in disguise. Had she been more dependent upon him, she might never have survived his ultimate neglect— treason. *"Oui.* Roger could be very entertaining."

"Did you ever notice that most of his tales were about his great and valorous friend, your present husband?"

Gennie looked at the darkening sky and thought back. She recalled the small amount of envy she had experienced early in her first marriage. She had soon become used to being last in Roger's regard and armored herself with prayer against his preference for whores and distant friends over his own wife. *"Non,* I had not noticed. Why do you mention this?"

"You and Sir Haven seem to be often at odds for such a well-suited couple."

"And you think the praise of my former husband is a recommendation. Why should I attend the words of a traitor well known for his foolishness and disreputable associates?"

"I had hoped that you would not hold such a recommendation against Sir Haven."

The wind soared, thrashing through the branches.

"I am not so foolish."

"Are you not?"

Gennie gasped at his audacity, but the warrior continued.

"Why then do you resent him so?"

Gennie had no reply. Despite her prayers that God would remove her anger, she did harbor resentment. It had been easier to blame her changed circumstances on the unknown Haven de Sessions than where they belonged—on Roger's foolishness. But with each day, her resentment toward Haven became harder and harder to maintain. Mayhap God was answering her prayers. Now she prayed that Haven would live long enough for her to discover the truth of her own heart.

Drops of rain spattered against the leaves. Ahead, the road rose and left the trees behind. Haven's horse dropped to a walk. She saw his hands go slack on the reins. Owain must have noticed too, for he kicked his horse into a trot with Gennie.

They should have acted sooner. Haven's mount halted at the top of the rise. Focused on her husband, she saw him lean forward and start to dismount. His movements lacked his usual grace. Certain that he had reached the last of his strength, Gennie pressed the animal beneath her into a canter. In the moment that her husband crumpled to the ground, she pulled her horse to a stop next to him and leapt down.

"*Non!* You will not die." She bent over his still form, listening for the beat of his heart. She heard it; faint, but there nonetheless. She lifted his shirt and tore aside the bandage. The wound was closed, but an angry red showed around its edges. It was hot to the touch.

Next she checked Haven's head. The swelling left by the impact with the hoof of Watley's horse had gone down. A bruise remained, but the heat coming in waves from Haven's forehead concerned her more. Her hand came away drenched in sweat and rain as the clouds burst over them.

"How far is it to Two Hills Keep, Owain? We must get him to shelter."

"I believe that may not be possible, milady."

"Not possible?" she shouted over the downpour. "What do you mean?"

"Look."

208

Chapter Eighteen

Gennie folded her cloak and placed it on the ground beneath Haven's head. Then she shifted to look where Owain pointed.

"*Mon Dieu.*"

"Yes. Daffydd ap Gryffudd got here before us."

The road divided the valley below from southwest to northeast. The river that had paralleled the road for most of their journey since Twynn veered off, splitting the valley from west to southeast. The road crossed the stream just in front of the two hills that gave the keep its name. On the taller rising sat the keep, or rather what was left of it.

Gennie stared at the roof-to-foundation gap in the central tower's wall. Piles of rubble littered various spots in the curtain wall. Through the holes she could see the burned husks of what she presumed were out buildings—stable, granary, kitchen and more. From her rainy vantage, the only undamaged part of the entire castle was the bridge and the small gatehouse towers that flanked the broken portcullis. "Owain, tell me it's not as bad as it looks."

"It isn't good. But we cannot know how bad until we send men to see."

"Then do so immediately, please. My husband needs shelter."

Owain was already turning back to the men. "Aye, milady. Lindel, Blacksund."

"Yea, Owain." The two men came forward from the ranks that formed a semicircle about their fallen leader.

"Go scout the keep. Search first for remaining enemies, then look for a safe place where we may shelter Sir Haven. Signal with a white cloth when you are satisfied the place is secure. Do you understand?"

Both men nodded.

"Hurry, then. While you complete that task, we will assemble a litter for Sir Haven. I want to be able to move him as soon as possible."

The scouts left. The remaining men stood by silently. Gennie understood their silence. What could anyone say? She wished she might offer some comfort to the men whose leader lay so still in the rain. But she had none to offer herself, and so none to share.

Owain's voice broke into her thoughts. Soon all the men, even Thomas, scrambled to perform some small task, as if their very speed and diligence might save Haven. Six men dismounted and formed a roof of shields above his body, diverting the rain onto themselves. Humbled by their actions, Gennie choked back the urge to weep. As long as she had something to keep her occupied, she had been able to avoid fear and worry.

With one hand she clasped Haven's hot, damp fingers to her breast. Her other hand stroked the slick sheen of sweat and wet, matted hair from his face, while she watched the shallow rise and fall of his chest. Cling to that, she told herself. Cling to the fact that he breathes yet and pray that he recovers fully.

Owain's hand touched her shoulder. How long she had knelt there, praying in the mud, she didn't know.

"Milady, we are ready."

Gennie saw a white cloth waving from atop the gatehouse. She surveyed the ground nearby and found a makeshift litter at Haven's other side. *"Oui."*

"You must let go of Sir Haven's hand so that we may lift him."

It was silly, she knew, to fear letting go of Haven. Logic told her that her touch alone did little to keep him alive. She lifted bleak eyes to Owain and saw equal worry on his face.

"Just for a moment, Lady Genvieve. We will be careful and take him to the keep slowly. You will be able to walk by his side, and you may hold his hand again as soon as we raise the litter."

"Oui." Gennie rose. Thomas came and hugged her. The small embrace warmed her as nothing had since Haven's horse had topped the rise.

"Will Sir Haven die?" The boy's question echoed her own.

"I don't know, Thomas, but we must pray very hard to God that he will not." She looked into her son's worried face and felt her own fear lessen a tiny bit. Surely God would not disappoint such unconditional love as Thomas bore for Haven de Sessions. "Come walk with me. We will keep each other company."

Thomas nodded and took her hand.

The men lifted Haven onto the litter. He neither

211

shifted nor groaned, but lay still as death save for the
small movement of his chest.

The men squeezed themselves and the litter into the
small, chilly room atop the gate tower. Designed more
as a lookout post than a chamber, the room held only
enough floor space for two armed men to turn around.
But it was dry and could be made warm.

Haven was shifted from the litter to a mound of ticking that one of the men had salvaged from a dry corner
of the main keep. Gennie asked Lindel to bring the few
tapestries she had kept as Thomas's inheritance and
use them to cover the arrow slit and two doorways.

She sent Bergen away with a plea to find a braiser or
some other fire-safe container that she could use to heat
the makeshift chamber.

One by one, the men left with her requests, each of
them eager to help his master and grateful that they had
something to occupy them. At last only Owain remained.

Gennie twisted water out of a rag and arranged the
dampened cloth across Haven's brow. Did all men
taken with fever lie so still? Those few times that illness
struck Thomas, he had thrashed and moaned. But he
was a boy. Gennie didn't know what to expect of a
man's sickness.

Beside her, Owain shifted from foot to foot.

"What bothers you, Owain?" She kept her eyes focused on Haven.

"I . . . I am uncertain of my authority."

"You swore fealty to my husband and are therefore
his man, *non?*"

"Aye, I did that."

"You are the most experienced warrior here?"

"Aye."

"Do you think I would question your loyalty?"

"Not to yourself, milady, nor to your son. Because I am newly come to Sir Haven's service, some of his men question my loyalty to him."

"You proved your loyalty in battle and by your care of my husband afterward. Whoever says otherwise speaks false. I will be happy to correct them, should you wish me to do so."

"Nay, lady. You are needed here."

Gennie spared a brief glance at Owain's concerned expression.

"I believe I may speak for my husband when I say that until Soames arrives, you must act in my husband's stead. Those who dispute you may come to me for reassurance."

"Thank you, Lady Genvieve."

"You are most welcome. Before you leave, perhaps you would share with me your plans for our defense."

"I would be most happy to do so. What do you wish to know?"

"Rebecca, Thomas and the servants will reside in the opposite tower, I assume?"

"Aye."

"How will you occupy the men?"

"Those men who are not on guard or hunting will work to rebuild the curtain wall."

"I know my husband expects Soames to bring a castle builder with him. Won't the wall have to be rebuilt then, and if so, why do it now?"

"Even poor defenses are better than none, milady."

"*Oui.* Where will you quarter the men and horses?"

"The men will sleep in the driest portions of the keep proper. We shall picket the horses in the bailey."

"And what of supplies? Hunting will fill our bellies, but a rabbit cannot provide medicines, nor can a quail make us mortar."

"I have two men scouring the countryside for the local peasants. If they know we intend to defend the keep, rather than loot and destroy, they may be willing to help us."

"I pray it is so. You have much work to do, Owain. I will not keep you from it."

The warrior left, recognizing dismissal when he heard it.

Gennie frowned in thought. Owain shared his plans with her out of courtesy. He needed neither her approval nor her permission to act in Haven's stead. She had asked because of the concern she had read on the man's face. She hoped her questions would give the sergeant-at-arms time to absorb the extent of Haven's condition and come to terms with the temporary necessity of filing his place with the men. At least she prayed it would be temporary.

Haven felt the hot winds of the desert blow across his face. The moving sand whispered, ominous before the battle to come.

"So you find my wife irresistible?" A chuckle followed the words.

"Roger?" Haven called out. Where was his friend? "I can't see you."

"I am here, at your back. Saving your life, just as you saved mine."

Haven could smell blood and sweat. He tried to turn his head and couldn't. There were so many dead, falling on him, crushing him back. If he could just push enough of them away, perhaps he could find Roger. "Where are you?"

"Here. Inside your heart and soul." The voice chuckled some more. "Where all good friends reside."

"No!"

"Yes. I am right here, along with all the lies you tell yourself. I always thought that you weren't as *true* as you wanted to believe. Now that I am dead, I know it. Of course," the voice breathed, "I am not surprised, since you were less than true to our friendship."

"What do you mean? I kept my vows."

"Yes, you kept your vows," the voice hissed and spat. "At the cost of the best friend you ever had. And look what those vows got you. A wife, a son and a holding. Not bad for a Judas like you."

" 'Tis not so. I wanted none of that!"

"Oh, you know better. Remember how we talked of our children's marriage? Of you gaining lands near my holding in Yorkshire? You betrayed me out of jealousy, admit it. Your vows, your duty were just excuses."

"You lie."

The voice mocked him. "*You* lie. *You*, Haven. *You* are the one who is false."

Shadows danced just beyond Haven's vision. He threw his arms outward but found nothing. How could he hear Roger so clearly and not be able to see him, touch him, find him?

That taunting voice echoed in his mind, endlessly repeating, "*Lies, lies, lies, lies . . .* "

Haven gripped his head and sat up. If the chanting didn't stop soon, he would go mad.

"Tell the truth now, Haven. How does it feel," the leering tones inquired, "to know that you love a woman more than your precious honor?"

"Nay!" Denial exploded hot and fast, like a killing blow. "I don't love her. I don't love Gennie."

"Yes," the voice said, dying. "You do . . . you do love Gennie . . ."

A hand pushed Haven down. He offered no resistance. He heard weeping but couldn't feel the tears on his cheeks.

Gennie wiped her eyes and prayed that she would never again have to hear her husband admit that he didn't love her. She had known he did not, and still she was unable to guard her heart against him. His lack of feeling for her should not hurt so much. She must take greater care with her heart. But she feared it was already too late. The best she could hope for was to keep her feelings from Haven so he could not use them against her.

She had watched over Haven for two days. Taking her meals with him. Leaving only when absolutely necessary. When exhaustion demanded, she slept on the floor beside his makeshift bed. She had known he didn't care deeply for her, but hearing it from his own lips hurt much more than she expected.

Was this how Roger had felt when Haven arrested him, choosing duty to king over love for his friend? Would the pain of Roger's execution gape ever wide between herself and her husband?

In the early hours before the third dawn since their arrival at Two Hills Keep, she had wakened to Haven's shouts and thrashing. What demons he fought she could not tell, for he spouted nonsense and argued with phantoms. But despite his illness, he had more than once tossed her across the small room. She had been forced to summon Watley and two other men to help her hold him down.

Owain had come some time later. With him, he brought an old beldam. "Milady, this is Gwyneth. She has herbs and other potions that may help Sir Haven."

Gennie fell on her knees before the peasant woman and clasped her hands in a fierce grip. *"Merci, merci. Pour grace de Dieu, aidez mon coeur."*

A string of rapid Welsh issued from the woman.

Gennie looked to Owain. "She speaks so quickly. Please, what does she say?"

"She says that in exchange for her help, she wants a place by Sir Haven's fire for the rest of her life."

Lady Genvieve didn't hesitate. "Anything. Anything I have."

Another spate of Welsh, and Gennie looked again to Owain.

"She asks that you remain here with her. She wants you to learn what has happened to their people as well as how to use the potions that will heal Sir Haven."

Gennie smiled. "She could not make me leave. I will be happy to learn all I can from her. In turn, I will teach her English."

Owain left one of the Welsh bowmen to act as interpreter for Gennie. Then the sergeant-at-arms went off to get the items Gwyneth said she needed to heal Sir Haven.

The next day and a half sapped every ounce of Gennie's reserve. The treatment of Haven's fever required reopening the wound; draining and cleaning it, stitching it shut and applying a poultice. The beldam insisted on alternating hot and cold compresses.

Haven tossed, shouted and fought with distressing randomness. They had to wait until he exhausted himself before feeding him, or he would spill more food than he ate.

During the few moments when he slept, Gwyneth told Gennie of the horrors that had visited Two Hills Keep since Daffydd had decided to rebel against the English. If Gennie hadn't expended all her tears on Haven, she would have wept over Gwyneth's tales of orphaned children, families burned alive and women raped.

All the folk in the area had lost their homes. Crops had been destroyed, and there was no money to purchase replacements for the winter. Worse, it seemed that both the English and the Welsh rebels visited these horrors on the people of the region.

Two mornings after the beldam arrived, Gennie had slipped into a weary doze. Loud voices from the bailey roused her from the only rest she had gotten in more than a day. She glanced to the corner near the braiser where Gwyneth had taken up residence. The woman nodded, and Gennie rose. She stretched the kinks out of her back and legs, then descended to the courtyard to discover what the yelling was about.

Chapter Nineteen

In the bailey she found that Soames had arrived with two strangers. They stood in the open with Owain. All four men shouted at once.

From the top of the stairs, Gennie used her firmest tone and said, "Stop that yelling this instant."

The effect was minimal. Obviously stronger measures were called for. She marched straight up to the group, elbowed her way between the two strangers into the middle of the bellowing males and knelt in the mud. She folded her hands and began.

"Our Father . . ."

A groan fell into the stunned silence, but no one interrupted her. ". . . Amen."

A chorus of *Amens* rumbled over her head.

She smiled and made to rise. Four hands shot out to assist her.

"Milady, that was unnecessary." Owain actually looked hurt.

"Was it? I disagree. My husband rests peacefully for the first time in almost a week, and you can find nothing better to do than shout down the walls below his chamber."

Soames and Owain had the grace to look embarrassed. The two strangers chattered in Welsh.

"Now, what is this all about?"

"Soames says the Welsh cannot . . ."

"Owain doesn't realize the harm . . ."

Welsh words came from the other two men.

Gennie put her hands over her ears. *"Arretez!* One at a time. Please, Soames, you first."

"But . . ." Owain objected.

"Non, you'll have your turn. Now be silent until Soames finishes."

"We have a serious problem, milady. Owain has allowed the Welsh to work and trade at the keep. I understand some of them even live here."

"The Welsh hereabouts have been much abused. In exchange for our protection, they help us to rebuild and secure supplies. I do not see a problem."

"King Edward gave Sir Haven specific orders not to let the Welsh anywhere near this place."

"Did he so? I wonder why?"

"That I do not know, Lady Genvieve. But Sir Haven will be angry if he recovers to find the Welsh have overrun the keep."

"My husband may prove more reasonable than you expect." Gennie hardly believed her own claim. She offered it nonetheless, knowing that the men needed to hear it.

"Maybe, maybe not."

"We shall have to see. Is there anything else?"

"The walls and keep must be reconstructed. We've

not the laborers nor the supplies with which to do it. Then, there's this fellow and his assistant." Soames gestured with his thumb at the two Welsh strangers.

"What is the difficulty with these men? We have little, but we can offer what hospitality we may."

" 'Tis not a matter of hospitality. That black-haired fellow is the castle builder."

Gennie studied the engineer, who unabashedly studied her right back. "I am confused, Soames. Everyone knows that Edward's master builder is James St. George d'Esperanche. This man is Welsh. And did you not just say that the king did not want the Welsh anywhere near Two Hills Keep?"

"Aye, I said all that. But seems the master builder was needed elsewhere, so he sent this fellow Arthur Pwyll in his place."

Upon hearing his name, Pwyll spoke in careful English. "I studied with Master St. George for ten years. Your king has many castles he wants to build. Too many for one engineer. My master has permitted me to supervise construction on some of the smaller keeps. I have letters to confirm what I say." He reached into a sack at his side and offered a rolled and sealed parchment.

"Well then, Soames, that sounds well enough. If Pwyll has letters authorizing his work here, all we need do is read them and comply."

She looked from Soames to Owain and back, then took the parchment from Pwyll. "I will read the letters. Soames if you are finished, I will hear from Owain."

"Aye, I am done."

"Milady," Owain began, "we must have the Welsh to aid us."

221

"I do not see how that will be possible if the king expressly forbids it," she countered.

"And what of your promise to Gwyneth?"

"Oh, my. I cannot unsay that promise."

"No, milady, you cannot."

"You should never have made such a promise in the first place," Soames interjected.

"Did no one tell you that I made the promise because Gwyneth claimed she could save Sir Haven's life? She did as she claimed. I would make the same promise and more if I had it to do again."

Soames's face flushed. "No one spoke of this to me."

"Now you understand. It is not only Gwyneth but also others of the local Welsh who have made it possible for us all to survive. I will hear no more about removing them from the keep unless my husband decides it must be so." Which he never will do, if I can prevent it, she thought.

"What else, Owain?"

"Soames does not agree with me as to which task to undertake first."

"What say you, Pwyll?" Gennie asked.

"I disagree with both of them."

"Soames, can we not divide our men and the Welsh workers into three groups, and thus make progress on all tasks?"

"Aye, milady, that might work."

"An excellent idea, Lady Genvieve." Pwyll's bow accompanied the statement.

"Thank you, Pwyll."

"You are most welcome, milady. If you will permit, my assistant and I will begin our examination of the keep and grounds."

"By all means do so." The Welshmen left, and Gennie

turned her attention to Soames and Owain. "If all is settled, I must return to my husband."

"Stay a moment, Lady Genvieve. There remains one small matter."

" 'Tis foolishness to bother her ladyship with such a small disagreement," Soames said.

Gennie sighed. "What disagreement is this?"

"Your son, milady . . ." Owain hesitated.

She had seen her son but briefly in the past week. Guilt and concern choked her. In an impulse to still the worried beat of her pulse, Gennie's hand went to her throat. "What of Thomas? Is he well?"

"He is fine, milady," Soames assured her.

"It's just that the dog . . ."

She cut Owain off. "Dog, what dog? Please tell me he's not been bitten by a mad dog?"

"The boy is fine." Owain muttered from behind clenched teeth. "But he has found a dog and has grown attached to the beast."

Relief nearly stopped her heart. She could not have born to lose Thomas. "Is that all?"

"It is a most inappropriate creature, milady," said Soames. "The boy even named the cur Caesar."

"It is a puppy, and 'twill do the lad good to have a playmate," Owain argued.

"Sir Haven will be most displeased," countered Soames.

Gennie laughed. "I would hardly worry about Sir Haven's displeasure over a hound that I allow my son to have, when we will no doubt suffer more than frowns over the issue of the Welsh workers."

Soames and Owain both nodded, as if she had uttered some sage wisdom.

"Good; now I must go. If you see Rene, would you

ask him to send some sops for my husband with my food?"

"We'll see to it, milady."

Gennie turned and mounted the stairs to the gate-house room. She could not help but smile as the two warriors' voices rose in discord behind her.

Gennie licked his ear. It felt good, very wet, but good. Still he had rather she licked his . . .

"Bad dog. Get out."

Bad dog? Get out? Haven felt tension form between his eyebrows. He opened his eyes, but the dim light made his head ache more. He hurt all over, yet even with his eyes closed, he struggled to rise. He had no idea where he was, nor to whom that voice belonged. Nonetheless, he would not stay where he was unwelcome.

"Nay, Sir Haven." The strangely accented voice cackled, and a hand met his chest, restraining him.

Despite his difficulty rising, Haven fell backward, surprised to discover just how weak he was.

More words crackled from the odd voice, but the sounds made no sense. He heard shuffling footsteps.

He had a vague vision of a battle with the Welsh. The three warriors, Rebecca, falling in the mud, Watley's horse . . .

Haven braved the increased headache and opened his eyes. Stone walls, a few tapestries, a braiser and a heap of furs met his glance. *Where am I?*

More footsteps sounded, lighter and faster this time.

"Haven? Haven." Gennie burst into the room, a smile beaming on her lips. *"Merci le Bon Dieu.* Gwyneth said you had awakened, but I needed to see for myself."

She sat by him and fussed with his covers. She

224

seemed determined to touch him everywhere. Weak as
he was, he could not prevent his body's natural reaction.

"I only stepped out for a moment, to tell Thomas he
must keep that dog out of this room. Getting you well
has been a trial, and I don't want that mongrel bringing
pestilence in here."

Mongrel? Thomas? Why would Gennie call her son a
dog? And where in Hades were they? He grabbed his
wife's wandering hands and grimaced. Even that small
movement hurt.

"What is it? Are you in pain? Where does it hurt?" Her
words rushed, panic-driven, over his face.

"Everywhere," he gritted out. "Now be still. It will
lessen the pain."

"But husband . . ."

"Nay. Please, where are we?"

Gennie blinked at him. "Why, at Two Hills Keep.
Where else would we be?"

"I know not. The last thing I remember is falling in
the mud and Watley's horse leaping over me.

"Oh, my poor dear Haven." Gennie removed one
hand from his. Her soft fingers moved over his face,
pushing back the hair that fell across his brow. "You
remember nothing of the two days that followed that
battle?"

"Nay."

Gennie caressed his cheek.

Haven shuddered.

"You refused to allow me to treat your injuries, but
insisted on pushing forward. You would complete the
task your king had set you or die trying."

He lost focus as she spoke. He narrowed his field of
vision, clinging to the sight of those plush lips, moving

225

a hand's breadth from his. She had called him her dear Haven. Had he somehow managed to capture a small portion of her affection? More like she simply felt sorry for anyone in pain.

"We at last arrived at Two Hills Keep, and you collapsed. I was certain that you had no strength left, but it might have been from the shock of seeing the keep destroyed and the knowledge that Daffydd had been here and gone before us."

Instantly his gaze shifted back to her eyes. "What do you mean? If the keep is destroyed, where are we, exactly?"

"We are in the gatehouse. It was the only shelter left standing."

"How do we know it was Daffydd who did this?"

"I am not certain. I suppose Owain might know, or Soames."

"Soames? Soames has arrived?"

"*Oui*, and the castle-builder with him."

"Good. I must speak with them and Owain immediately."

"Nay, husband. First you will eat. Then you will rest. And after that, if you are strong enough, you may have a short visit with your men."

"But . . ."

"*Non*. You are in no condition to gainsay me. Food first."

He glared at her.

Gennie smiled.

A moment later, a crone entered the chamber carrying a tray.

"Good, our meal is here." Gennie took the tray and set it on the floor near Haven's bed. The beldam honored Haven with a nod and a long look, then jabbered at Gennie in a mixture of Welsh and English.

Gennie shook her head. *"Non.* I can manage alone." She turned to Haven. "Husband, this is Gwyneth. You owe her your life, for when you lay sick and I could do nothing to help you, she offered her herbs and her skill, and asked only a place by your fire in return. I promised it to her, of course. 'Twas a small price for my husband's life."

Edward's order to keep the Welsh from Two Hills Keep sprang to Haven's mind. Gennie's statement bothered him so much that he didn't even protest over the sops that she fed him. When he was done, he lay back and closed his eyes. He was tired. Soames and Owain would have to wait. He blinked against pain and frustration. How could he tell Gennie she must put Gwyneth out in the cold?

Chapter Twenty

Gennie lowered the tapestry and left her husband asleep.

Gwyneth would return in a moment and watch over him. With swift strides she descended the gatehouse stair and crossed to where Thomas watched Owain and Arthur supervise work on the last of the holes in the curtain wall. Her son circled a wide stick around the inner edge of a large vat.

"Look, Mama, I am helping to build the wall."

"You look very busy, Thom. What is it you do?"

"I am stirring the mortar. It makes the stones stick together."

"That sounds like a very important job."

"It is." He nodded seriously. "Arthur says if the mortar isn't stirred well, it won't work right, and the stones will all fall down."

"Then I am very proud that he chose you to do the job."

"Aye, milady. The lad has been a great help." Owain spoke, approaching with Arthur on his heels.

"I thank you for your care of him, Owain. I've been so busy . . ."

"There is no need, Lady Genvieve. We all know where your attention has been and would not have it otherwise. Would we, Thomas?" The sergeant-at-arms bent, bringing Thomas into the conversation.

"I had rather Sir Haven weren't sick at all."

Gennie knelt beside her son. "Well, I've good news, then. He is much better. Today he sat up and ate all his food."

"I eat all my food."

"Yes, you do, sweeting. And you are a good boy."

"Arthur, my arms are tired. May I stop stirring now? I want to play with Caesar."

Arthur looked to Owain, who answered. "Aye, young Thomas, but leave the stick in the vat and ask Bergen to take your place before you go."

"Thank you." He let go of the stick and flew across the bailey to where Bergen sat outside the wrecked stables.

Gennie surveyed the yard. Much had been accomplished, but much more remained to be done. The curtain wall neared completion, but they still had no real shelter other than the gatehouse.

Arthur reached for her elbow. "Excuse us please, Owain. I would consult with Lady Genvieve on the repairs to the keep itself."

Owain nodded and returned to his work. Gennie and Arthur moved toward the keep's tower. Wooden structures had been added to prevent the broken walls from toppling further, but the huge space still gaped.

"You have done so much in such a short time, Pwyll."

"Aye, but I cannot proceed until I know what Sir Haven wants. I also seek your opinions on some matters of comfort."

"I will be most happy to assist in any way that I can."

"The basic plan here is good. The kitchens and stables are far enough from the tower for safety, but close enough for convenience and easy defense. With your permission I will rebuild the out buildings on their original foundations."

"With the exception of the stables and the kitchens, I approve."

"What changes do you suggest?"

"I wish the main kitchen where it is, but I would like you to add a small keeping room on the lowest level of the tower. I would have a place to warm foods before they are brought to table."

The castle builder's eyes lit. "That sounds ideal, milady.

'Twill give me a chance to try building a chimney instead of a central fire pit."

"Is that not dangerous?"

"Nay, milady. The fire pit is actually more dangerous."

"Then why have them?"

"Until recently we did not know how to build the chimneys needed to vent a fire placed against a wall."

"It sounds cold and drafty to me. The fire will heat one side of the hall and the other will lack heat."

Arthur rubbed his chin. "We could put in a second chimney on the opposite side."

"That, Pwyll, is a perfect idea. How long will it take to construct the chimneys and make the other repairs?"

"With the current number of laborers, I doubt we'll finish before this time next year."

"That long?"

"It could be longer, if the winter is early and harsh."

"Is there any way to close off enough of the keep that the men and workers could have a dry place to sleep?

"That could be done in a matter of weeks. It is the chimneys and the new walls that will take time."

"And if you had more workers, you could do it faster?"

"With two hundred workers and ten skilled artisans, I could finish before winter this year."

"Then I will find you more workers. Can you write me a list of the skilled men you will need?"

"Certainly. But where will you find enough men?"

"I do not know yet. But find them I will. Is there aught else you wish of me or need?"

"I want to know if you would like a solar or other private chambers."

"A real solar?"

"Aye, I know of no other type." Arthur chuckled.

"Silly; I haven't seen a solar since I left France. My . . . my first husband's family was very old-fashioned, believing that privacy was vanity."

"Do you agree?"

"*Non,* in France we had three private chambers. One for my parents, one for me and one for guests."

"I could rebuild this keep with three private rooms, but four would be best and easier to do."

Gennie smiled and hugged him. "Pwyll, you are a treasure."

The young man's face colored. "Yo . . . you mentioned the stables."

"I must insist you consult with my husband before beginning work on the stables. He should be able to speak with you in a few days. And it might be best if you came prepared with some drawings. He has not seen the castle, nor the extent of the damages."

"I understand completely, Lady Genvieve. Thank you for giving your advice on these matters." The Welshman kissed her hand.

"You are most welcome, Pwyll. Now I have a few errands to run before I return to my husband's bedside."

He watched her go and shook his head. He had been unable to resist placing that small formal kiss upon her hand. You are a fool, Arthur Pwyll, he told himself. The woman is not only married but clearly in love with her husband. Respect her, but do not touch her, he reminded himself.

She was determined to torture him. Haven watched Gennie snuggle into the furs that made her bed on the opposite side of his sickroom. While Gennie touched him constantly, it was only to help him move or arrange his blankets. Neither her gestures nor her expressions hinted at passion. And Gwyneth still occupied the corner by the braiser. He wanted Gennie in his bed and the old woman gone.

The distance he felt growing between himself and his wife surprised him. He had not recognized what they shared as closeness. How had he come to admire her determination and the strength with which she faced the worst that life could hand her? When had he come to rely on her, to expect her sunny smiles and gentle touch? What had happened to the laughing temptress Gennie had revealed herself to be during their stay at Twynn? Had she recalled the barrier Roger's death raised between them?

He had told no one of that terrifying voice from his

delirium. The remembered whispers still haunted him. "Yes, you do . . . you do love Gennie." That thought frightened him more than the idea of lying sick in a keep still vulnerable to attack. Even worse, he could not say why. The nightmares had left with his fever, but the memory of Roger's face on the scaffold had not. His words, "I cannot trust my wife," as he begged Haven's vow, those remained painfully fresh. Haven needed to talk with Gennie. But how could he, when she came near only to tend his wounds?

He sighed and shifted. The headaches had faded, and his pain had become a dull but constant twinge. Now his greatest hurt was one of the heart. He doubted whether he could heal it.

"Husband, are you well?" Gennie's disembodied voice floated out of the dark.

"No," he grumbled and shifted again. "I am not well at all."

His wife emerged from the gloom and laid a hand on his brow. "You are not fevered. What troubles you?"

"My bed is empty. That troubles me mightily."

Gennie looked at him and the bed. Confusion wrinkled her brow. "But you are in the bed, sir."

His patience at an end, Haven grasped her wrist and tested his strength with a short tug on her arm.

She fell into his lap with a satisfactory gasp of surprise.

"Now, wife, my bed is no longer empty."

"Oh." She hesitated.

He could imagine her blushing.

"But what of Gwyneth?"

"Gwyneth is asleep. And since we shall sleep too, I do not see that Gwyneth is a problem."

"But . . ."

233

"But what, wife?" His eyes searched her face in the dim light cast from the brazier.

"Nothing." She shifted, placing herself under the covers and stretching along his side. "Nothing at all. Good night, husband."

It was progress, he told himself. Content, but far from satisfied, Haven folded his arms under his head and closed his eyes. "Good night wife."

Gennie slapped a sodden shirt against a rock and pretended it was her husband's head. The man was torturing her. During the day he was cranky and cross. Gwyneth decreed that Haven should not rise until all trace of pain disappeared. Haven argued with her, each then enlisting Gennie's support. Gennie fled, taking refuge in chores that, as lady of the keep, she didn't have to do. Today it was the wash.

But the nights were worse. At night Haven would shift and sigh, utter an occasional moan and shift again, until Gennie was forced from her bed to discover what ailed him. He would insist that he could not sleep without her near. She would lie down beside him, and they would both fall sleep. If that had been all, she might have tolerated it.

Two days ago, she had woken to the stroke of his fingers across her breast. She had elbowed him. He had grunted and turned over. The next night it had been her fingers that had wandered. Haven's groans had awakened her, and she had snatched her hand away from their intimate clasp. This morning the heat from his hips pressing against her bottom had burned sleep away. He had been snoring. How her gown had twisted above her waist, she didn't know. But she remained awake until he shifted in his sleep.

Thank heaven for Gwyneth's presence, or Gennie might have given in to temptation and had her way with her husband. What kind of woman was she? The man had not yet left his sickbed. If she succumbed to her baser urges, he might not leave it for another se'ennight.

Was this what Father Jonas meant when he said that one purpose of lust was to strengthen the bond of marriage begun with the vows into a love that would last a lifetime? How could that be, if Haven did not love her? Even if she did love him, he had denied any love for her. Shouted it in his delirium. Yet he still wanted her in his bed.

And what of her own unspoken fear that Haven would one day betray her as he had Roger? Were her husband forced to chose between wife and knightly duty, which would he pick?

Mayhap she should sleep in the other gate tower chamber with her sister-in-law and son. Doing so would certainly protect her heart, even while her body might ache for Haven's touch. Although not fully recovered, Haven was much better now. He hardly needed both herself and Gwyneth keeping watch over him at night. Yes, that would be best.

She rose, leaving the remainder of the laundry to the Welsh women. They had come with their husbands, fathers and brothers when, at Gennie's request, Gwyneth had spread the word that work could be found at Two Hills Keep. She nodded and called a farewell to the women, who nodded and smiled back.

She dawdled on her way back to the gatehouse. She had decided the right course, but somehow she couldn't bring herself to put it in place. She played with Thomas and Caesar. Consulted with Rene on the state

of supplies for the winter. Listened to Soames, Owain
and Pwyll report on their progress. Pwyll was quite
pleased. Due to the extra laborers, the repairs making
the keep habitable would be complete next week. Then
he could concentrate on the improvements. Soames
and Owain too seemed optimistic about their projects,
and reported frequently to Haven.

Dark descended and Gennie could delay no longer.
She took the tray with Haven's dinner upon it and
climbed to their room. She entered the room and set
the food beside Haven's bed. He was sleeping, and she
didn't want to wake him, so she went to the corner
where she kept her few things. Determined, she rolled
up her sleeves, knelt and folded her belongings. She
lingered a moment, stroking the soft wool of the blue
cloak Haven had given her as a wedding present. She
shook her head, then stood with the pile of clothing
and turned to take them across to the other chamber.

"What are you doing, Gennie?"

Haven's voice brought her to a halt.

"I had thought you asleep."

"I was."

"If my work disturbed you, I am sorry."

"Nay, 'twas not your work. You were most quiet."

"What then?"

"The scent of lavender."

She smiled. "That is ridiculous. Flowers don't wake
anyone from sleep. In fact, lavender is known for its
soothing properties."

"I do not find it so."

"I am sorry. I will cease to wear the scent."

"Nay. I insist you wear it always."

"But you dislike it."

"I said it did not soothe me. I did not say I dislike it."

236

"Very well." Gennie shook her head at his nonsense and moved toward the doorway.

"Do not go."

"I must put these things in the other chamber."

"Why?"

"Because you no longer need two nurses at night."

"But if you go, I shall have none."

"What do you mean, husband?"

"Gwyneth agreed to move to the other gatehouse chamber, so that you and I might have some privacy."

"Oh."

"Oh, indeed. Now put those things down and come here."

Gennie swallowed. She put her folded clothing back in the corner and approached the bedside. Haven patted the surface next to where he lay. Gennie sat. She bent and lifted a plump berry from the tray. "Are you hungry, husband?"

"Aye, wife. Feed me."

Chapter Twenty-one

Haven opened his mouth and watched Gennie lean forward. Her eyes widened, and she licked her lips. She hesitated, as if she expected him to bite her or worse. Wise woman, his wife.

"Do you like berries?" she asked, her voice soft but far from soothing

Haven looked at the fruit in her hand. Juice ran down her wrist and arm. He watched the liquid drop from her elbow to a spot at the top of her thigh. He lifted his gaze to her breast. "I love berries. Especially if they are firm and plump."

Her hand crept forward, until the tidbit rested against his lips.

He raised his eyes to hers, while his tongue darted out and plucked the fruit from her fingers into his mouth. He held her with his gaze and closed his lips around her forefinger. He engulfed the digit, savoring the mix of berry juice and Gennie. With small nibbles, he pursued the small stain into the sensitive web of flesh that linked fingers and thumb. He watched her shudder and close her eyes. Then he covered her thumb, suckling there, letting his tongue play with the tender pad and his teeth scrape over the soft flesh.

Haven released her hand. She all but fell into his arms. He reached down beside the bed and found another berry. Rolling over, so Gennie was on her back, he pressed the sweet to her lips with his own. The explosion of taste and texture so overwhelmed him that his hips shifted to the rhythm of his tongue.

Gennie responded in kind. Her tongue sought his, her hips lifted against him. She moaned.

Yes! Haven lifted his mouth and chest away.

"No," Gennie whispered. "You are not yet well."

He forced himself to be still. He gazed down at Gennie's kiss-glazed eyes. "I am well enough." He flexed his hips, rubbing the evidence of his health against her.

"Yes, please," she murmured.

He kissed her eyelids. "First, I will have these clothes off us both.

Gennie smiled. "Let me help."

"Certainment, mon coeur." He lay back and allowed her to remove the nightshirt, which he had taken to wearing to preserve his modesty in front of Gwyneth,

She pulled the cloth over his head. "Are you sure you are up to this?"

Haven smiled at her, then looked down the length of his body.

Gennie followed his gaze. "Oh, my. I guess you are." She reached out to touch the pulsing flesh. Her hand circled its steely softness. She stroked upward, then down, then up again.

Haven groaned.

Gennie let go.

"Nay, do not stop."

"But you are in pain."

He caught her chin with his hand and looked into her eyes. "Surely Roger taught you . . . ?"

Gennie could feel herself blush.

"No, I guess not. I am sorry, I keep forgetting how stupid my friend was with regard to his wife." He leaned forward, brushing her mouth with his. "I will continue to be in pain unless you do as you just did."

She resumed her stroking.

Haven sighed at the sweet tension that she built in his body.

"I still do not understand."

The woman would drive him mad. He grasped her hand, pushed it away from his body and over her head. In a blink he had her on her back and was lifting her skirts.

"Wait." She mumbled from inside the swath of over-tunic and chemise that covered her head.

"Nay, I will not wait to make you understand."

Her clothes now lay in a tangle around her raised arms.

Haven sat back on his knees between her legs and grinned.

"What are you doing?"

"Enjoying the view."

Gennie cast a glance down her exposed body. "I see nothing of interest."

"Really?" He looked at Gennie's nipples, coming erect in the cool air. Haven licked his thumb. He passed its dampened pad across the very tip of one partially distended crest.

Gennie's reaction was instant and obvious. A red

flush colored her from chest to brow. Her back arched slightly, and she uttered a sharp, "Oh."

Haven repeated the action several times, until he had thoroughly soaked that one taut bud. Then he blew gently on it and sat back once more.

Gennie wore a mixed look of pain, pleasure and surprised understanding on her face.

"Do not stop."

"So, you understand now?"

Gennie studied him.

He bent slightly and breathed on her quivering breast.

"You are a cruel man."

"I can be."

"Yes," she gasped. "I understand."

"Good, because I have no intention of stopping again for a very long time."

Gennie smiled. "Excellent. Now take these clothes off my arms."

Haven stretched out beside her. He reached up and brushed the hair from her face and neck, then leaned over, placing his lips on the pulse just below her earlobe. "I think not," he whispered.

"But I cannot touch you."

His teeth closed around her earlobe. When he heard her breath hitch, he let go and soothed the flesh with gentle flicks of his tongue.

"I am pleased that you wish to touch me, but for now it is best that you do not."

Her lower lip emerged in a pout. "I disagree."

"Ah, but I have the upper hand." To prove it, Haven set about pleasuring her with all his skill.

Gennie knew she was going to die. Haven had touched and stroked, licked and suckled, teasing her with his passion until she nearly screamed at him to have done. He refused. Instead, he had loosed her arms and started again. He praised her body and urged her to touch his. He had questioned her, refusing her favored caress of the moment, until she spoke her most lustful desire. Then he fulfilled that desire tenfold.

He was relentless, driving her from murmurs and pleas to screams with the most intimate of kisses. Never had she felt so admired, so valuable. Never had frustration been so enjoyable. She moved beneath him, restless, needy, anxious for the ease that would come when he had finished killing her with pleasure.

"Gennie, look at me." The dark rasp of his voice stroked down her body.

She opened her eyes. His body was a shadow made tangible by the throb of his sex against hers. His gaze shone above her, a faint gleam in the web of heat that surrounded them.

"I need you, Gennie. Give yourself to me."

It wasn't a question, but she felt his plea in every corner of her being. Her heart clutched. He spoke of need, not love. If she gave to him now, she would gain nothing. Dare she trust him and risk her heart? Dare she love him, when he did not love her? Could she prevent it? The emotion that welled in her would have to suffice for them both.

She lifted her hands and grasped his hips. Her eyes focused on his, she pulled him into her, and all thought shattered. She tumbled headlong into the maelstrom. His thrusts tossed her from crest to crest with increasing speed.

Like a wild rose, need vined through Haven, caught him against its thorny pleasure and burst into bloom with a shout. He folded a dewy and dreaming Gennie into his arms and drifted. For that moment, with her secure next to his heart, he knew he could trust her.

Slowly, Haven descended from the gatehouse to the bailey. The sun was well up and the keep bustled with activity, yet no one had disturbed his privacy with Gennie. He smiled. After last night, she could have no doubt about her place in his life.

He looked about him. He had been abed too long and needed exercise. Sharp skills were a key part of survival, and he insisted his men practice wherever they were. Where had Soames set up the practice yard?

As he wandered in search of either his second-in-command or the sounds of mock battle, the construction progress he saw pleased him. Soames and Owain both had reported on the condition of the keep during the course of his recovery. The curtain wall was completely mended. Several outbuildings had been restored, and more were in progress. Even the central tower of the keep would be habitable in the next day or so. He must remember to find the castle builder and praise him for his efforts.

In fact, Haven was surprised that so much had been accomplished. The more he saw, the more he wondered how it had been done. Both Soames and Owain, on the few times he had seen them, commented on the shortage of labor needed to achieve repairs in a timely manner. His inspection had shown hundreds of men and women at work on various tasks. So where had all these workers come from? Edward had said he would send one hundred English families to ensure the countryside remained loyal to the crown. Could so many of those families have arrived so soon?

On closer examination, Haven frowned. The voices

he heard were not English but Welsh. Over the past weeks Gwyneth's gabbling had become so familiar that he could recognize the Welsh tongue when he heard it. Edward's orders regarding the distance the Welsh must stay from the keep were quite explicit. This situation could prove disastrous and must be rectified immediately. Haven might persuade Edward that one old Welsh woman was harmless, but not several hundred able-bodied men and their families. Even if work on the keep came to a dead halt, the Welsh would have to leave.

To that end, Haven intensified his search for Soames. He found the older man with a group of the other warriors. They were busy clearing stones and rubble away from what appeared to be a cistern. It was menial labor and beneath the dignity of a warrior, but with so much to be done, it made good use of the strongest backs.

Haven waited while Soames and five other men lifted a huge slab of stone. Simply watching the strain evident in each man's effort exhausted Haven. So he sat. The slab was tipped up on end and then allowed to crash back to earth in the opposite direction from which it was lifted. The impact shattered the stone, making it easier to remove. Soames ordered the men to cart the pieces to the wall, where Haven could hear a Welshman supervising a team of masons.

Soames approached. "Good day, Sir Haven. 'Tis wonderful to see you up and moving about."

"I have been too long from my duty."

"Mayhap, but you were gravely ill. We feared for your life until Owain found the beldam, Gwyneth. I didn't want to let the woman near you, but Lady Genvieve argued strongly that without Gwyneth's aid you would die of a certainty."

Gennie's concern pleased Haven, although he regretted causing anyone anxiety, Gennie most of all. He must thank her when next he saw her. In the meantime, orders banishing the Welsh workers must be given. "Do you recall what I told you of Edward's wishes regarding the Welsh?"

"Aye, Sir Haven. And it caused me no little discomfort when your wife promised Gwyneth a place by your fire, then asked the crone to spread word throughout the countryside that shelter and food could be had for work done at the keep."

"I should have known my wife was behind this. You had the authority to override her, Soames. Why did you not?"

"Lady Genvieve is a determined woman. You have firsthand experience of how strong her will is. Would you have opposed her in my position, when her prayers would be inflicted not on myself, but on a man who lay defenseless in his sickbed."

"I doubt my wife would have inflicted on me prayers meant for you. But I understand your concern. Still, we are left with hundreds of Welsh in the castle, when our king has ordered that none come within one hundred paces of the outer curtain wall."

"What's to be done, sir? If the Welsh leave, we'll not finish repairs to the keep before winter."

"I understand, but they must leave all the same. I will give the order. Please assemble them to hear it."

"Aye. But it goes against the grain to do so. These people have borne much abuse from Daffydd. They work hard and ask little in return. Less than many English peasants would in a similar case."

" 'Tis another reason the Welsh must leave. Edward is sending loyal English workers here. We must feed, house and clothe them through the winter, until they can grow crops and build homes of their own. I doubt that our supplies will stretch to feed the Welsh as well."

" 'Tis a shame nonetheless. I will call the Welsh together in front of the gatehouse. Will that be satisfactory?"

"Certainly. While you do that, Soames, where might I find the engineer the king sent?"

"Why, right over there, sir." Soames pointed at the young man Haven had heard earlier.

"You jest, surely. The man is Welsh."

"Nay, 'tis no jest. He has papers from the king, proving him a student of James St. George, d'Esperanche, and explaining why he was sent in the master builder's place.

"And who saw these papers, Soames?"

"Your lady, sir. She read the papers and confirmed what they said."

Would she save his life only to plot treason beneath his nose? A worry niggled at the back of Haven's mind and was immediately denied. Nay, the woman who shared his bed last night, the woman who had nursed him and defended him, that woman couldn't possibly do so. Gennie's word would suffice. He would not ask to see the Welshman's papers.

Aware that Soames waited, Haven nodded. "Then he must stay."

"Shall I bring him to you?"

"Nay. I will speak with him after I deal with the peasants."

"As you wish, sir." Soames snapped a salute, then left the keep. On his way, he spoke to the Welsh engineer. The man in turn spoke to his workers, who put their tools down and followed Soames out of the building.

246

The engineer stared at Haven as the masons filed past. Haven wondered exactly what that intense gaze meant.

Gennie followed Pwyll from the gatehouse at a run. She could not believe what Pwyll had told her. After all the work the Welsh had done, Haven would not cast those people to the elements. The man she had come to love could not be so cruel.

But it seemed he could. From the bottom of the main tower's stair, she saw Owain standing before the keep with Haven. The Welsh gathered before them in the bailey. Haven was saying that King Edward had forbidden the Welsh within one hundred paces of any castle held by the English. Haven was sorry, but they would have to leave.

Grumbles came from the crowd before Owain finished translating.

"Nay!" She would stop this foolishness now. "Husband, I have given these people my promise. Would you shame us both?"

"You should not have given your word. You did not have the right."

"I had the right every goodwife has to support her husband."

"Aye, and for your intentions I thank you. Nonetheless, the king's orders must stand over your promise."

"Even when the king's wishes will cause more war? War is costly. Surely Edward will see the benefit in saving both money and lives."

"No one knows better than Edward the cost of war and the benefits of peace. Should he change his mind, I will welcome these good people to Two Hills Keep at your side."

247

"Edward will change his mind all the faster if he is shown the error in his thinking."

" 'Tis too great a risk; besides, even now the king sends one hundred loyal English families to populate this holding. With winter less than a season away, and no crops or supplies in our stores, how will we care for them, let alone all these Welsh?"

Gennie faced defeat. She could not let Haven remove the Welsh. "I do not know, husband. I can only pray that God will provide, as I pray you will recognize a greater good than absolute loyalty to your king." Having loosed all her arguments, Gennie turned and walked away.

Chapter Twenty-two

Haven watched her leave. She held her shoulders straight and her steps even. He could imagine her just so, leaving her home in the rain after Dreyford's disgrace. She would find a place to pray and then act on her prayers, as if God's answer were a foregone conclusion.

He looked at the people who stood before him. Many shook their heads. Some mumbled curses, clear from the accompanying gestures if not the Welsh words. One by one they drifted away, following his wife's path.

Haven sat where he had stood and cradled his head in his hands. His wife's course had nearly cost her life, for it hadn't prevented her first husband's treason, nor had it softened Edward's heart. As Haven thought back, he could not recall that any of Gennie's frequent prayers had been for herself. She had prayed for him, for her son's safety, for many, many people, but never for herself.

Her reward for such sacrifice had been stoning and marriage to himself. A man who had betrayed a friend.

No wonder she felt no respect or love for him. It was a daunting thought, and shame gnawed at his soul.

His own loyalty to Edward over Roger had sent Gennie penniless into the rain. Could he do so again? This time it wouldn't be a lone woman with a small band but hundreds of men, women and children who would be homeless. He owed his life, so he had been told, to one of those people. He owed his shelter to many others. The evidence of their labor stood at his back.

The Welsh had worked not out of loyalty or any other compelling reason. They had worked for a promise, given by one determined woman. A woman who, even after the death of a treasonous husband, held fealty to him. Despite whatever loyalty to Roger that Haven felt and the friendship they once shared, he could no longer deny the truth: He loved Gennie more than life itself.

For the love he bore her, if for no other reason, he would not let her promise be foresworn. He knew not how, but he would find a way to convince Edward to change his policy. Mayhap Gennie was right, and the proof of trusting the Welsh lay in the doing. Gennie trusted them and had her trust rewarded. Haven decided he could do no less.

With that small hope, Haven raised his head to find himself alone. The sun was sinking behind the curtain wall, and the bailey lay deserted. Where had everyone gone? Regret buzzed in his mind. It saddened him greatly that the Welsh had accepted his dictates so quickly. But his men's absence surprised him more. Their departure murmured of reproach. Of all those concerned, they could best understand why he had acted as he had. Perhaps he should not be surprised by their lack of faith in him, since he was about to enact a more grievous lack of loyalty to his king.

Regardless, he would humble himself however he must in order to get the Welsh to return to work. Guilt muttered loudly, urging him upward. He moved into the bailey, discovering that the sound of chorused voices was not the prompting of his conscience, but real.

Haven pursued the noise around the arc of the building. There, where the roofless walls of the new chapel abutted the tower, knelt the Welsh in prayer. Owain, Soames, all of Gennie's band, even Thomas, had dropped onto the muddy ground before the chapel's closed doors.

As if a mighty fist slammed into his chest and stole his breath, the sight halted Haven at the last rank. He had determined to put away pride. But when he had imagined himself on bended knee, it had been before a disdainful people who would stand in judgment on him. Joining them in prayer had been the farthest thing from his mind.

Gennie could swear she heard angels chanting. A glance behind revealed the building to be empty. She had no idea how long she had been kneeling before the chapel's makeshift altar, but a look upward through the exposed rafters showed only the evening sky dim with an oncoming shower. So where had that sound come from?

She bowed her head once more, determined to complete her supplications, but she had lost her concentration. She shook her head, crossed herself. As she stood, the noise came again, as if storm winds rose up, ready to visit nature's wrath upon the homeless. She could not let that happen. Haven would have to listen to her; barring that, she would simply defy him and call the workers back into the keep on her own.

Susan Charnley

She hurried from the nave. If she would keep the Welsh from being lashed by the elements, she must act quickly. The scent of the damp summer evening assaulted her as she opened the chapel door. No storm then, yet the thunderous sound continued. Not thunder, but prayer. A hundred voices and more raised in desperate hope. The force of so many Aves and Pater nosters halted her on the chapel steps and surprised her to speech. "Oh, my." Gratitude overwhelmed her and her voice fled.

A few of the folk near the steps heard her surprised utterance. Looking up, they ceased their praying at the sight of her. One by one the voices stopped, as each person became aware of his neighbor's silence. Until, finally, a single voice remained raised in supplication to the Lord.

The crowd slowly parted, and Gennie looked into the face of her husband. His eyes were closed in fierce concentration. His voice, strong and steady, pleaded with God for forgiveness and a solution to the many problems that would stem from asking the Welsh to remain. Gennie's heart went out to Haven at the same moment that she found her voice. "Husband."

Haven's eyes sprang open, alight with fierce emotion. "Have you changed your mind?"

He stood, swept the kneeling crowd with his glance, then stared at Gennie. "I will protect these people with my very life. This I swear before God."

The crowd greeted his oath with a rousing cheer. Both he and Gennie were lifted on the shoulders of the men and women and carried into the tower. Not until Gennie stood in front of one of the two newly constructed fireplaces, her hand held securely in Haven's, did she believe in his miraculous change of heart.

Someone struck up a tune. Men and women danced, shouting joyfully before her. Haven pulled her close. "Can you forgive my stubbornness, wife?"

"Can you forgive mine?"

"I think not."

Worried, she studied his face.

He smiled. "How can I forgive when there is no need? You said and did what you believed was right."

"We have many problems to overcome."

"Aye, but we have many hands to help us." He looked out at the celebrating crowd.

"Oui, we do."

"We will start working on those problems later. Now we should join our people in celebrating." He pulled her toward the dance.

Gennie hesitated long enough to say a silent prayer for the protection of this man who risked so much for so many, then followed him with all her heart.

She danced on joyful feet, meeting and parting from her husband only to rejoin him as the pattern of the dance required. They stopped to rest, and Gennie ordered ale brought up from the cellar. Haven arranged for a calf to be roasted. He watched indulgently as Gennie danced with half the men in the castle. When she showered smiles on Arthur Pwyll, Haven quickly took the engineer's place. He wanted those smiles for himself, and himself alone.

Much later, exhausted and laughing, he escorted Gennie to the chamber they shared. They paused on their way to look in on Thomas, who lay curled up with his puppy. The boy was happy and hale. In him Haven saw the promise of his own children. Children he would have with Gennie.

What better time to start those children than tonight,

when his love for Gennie shone fresh and new in his heart. He had already danced half the night away and perhaps taxed his wounds enough. Regardless, he would make love to his wife, for surely her touch would heal him more than the sleep he could find before dawn. But first he had to rid himself of the shadows cast by Roger Dreyford.

"Come, wife." He held out his hand to her.

She looked at him, remembering another time when he had held his hand just so. She arched a brow at him. "Do we have much to do, husband?" She placed her hand in his, and he led her along the battlement.

"Aye," he said as they walked. "Should it please you, I will keep you busy all night."

She felt hope glimmer in her heart. "To be busy with you, husband, always pleases me." She spoke quietly, afraid to reveal too much, afraid not to reveal enough.

They reached their chamber, and Haven drew her into his arms. "Gennie, I have refused to let myself love you."

She felt the pain of his refusal and tried to draw away.

He grasped her arms to keep her in place. "Nay, hear me out. I felt that my love for you betrayed my promise to Roger, to protect his family. And you were so loyal to his memory, I feared you would hate me if I confessed my feelings. I worried that you would see my love for you as a further betrayal of my friendship for Roger. I can no longer deny what I feel. I can only pray that my love for you will be a stronger protection than any sword or influence I could wield."

She stared at him, her mouth open in surprise.

"Gennie?" Concern colored his voice. "Are you all right?" He gave her a little shake.

Her mouth snapped shut, then open again. "You love me?"

"Aye, that is what I said."

She launched herself at his chest.

His arms closed around her. Haven stumbled backward and landed on the bed.

"I love you too." She thumped him on the chest with her fists. "How dare you have such feelings for me and not share them."

He clasped his hands around hers. Her fingers uncurled and linked with his. "I told you as soon as I could." He smiled.

She smiled back at him. "I never loved Roger."

"Truly?"

"*Vraiment.* I was his wife, and I gave him the fealty that my marriage vows required. But I never loved him, and I don't believe he ever loved me."

"Why?"

"He never made me feel as you do." She ducked her head, feeling shy and uncertain.

"And what way is that?"

"Sick with dread that you might never love me. Giddy with passion that you do."

"Passion, hmm?"

"Yes, passion, you knightly oaf." She worked one hand loose of his grip and thumped his chest again. Then she rubbed the spot.

Haven produced a satisfied growl in response.

Gennie continued, "Roger's touch never brought me pleasure, and his preference for whores gave me much shame. And I never wanted to caress Roger like this." She pulled up Haven's tunic, baring his chest. She stroked her hands over him and leaned across his torso to lave his nipples with her tongue.

Haven pulled her up onto his body, kissing her eyes, cheeks and nose. "Roger was a fool. Only a fool could want whores when he had you in his bed." His lips settled on hers, plucking with tender nibbles, begging her to open for him. Their tongues twined. She tasted his unique flavor, licking at him, showing him what she wanted. She pushed away from him, straddling his hips as he lay there. "Father Jonas said that lust could lead to an everlasting love. I pray that this is what happened to us."

"Gennie." His voice hoarse, Haven began to remove her gown. "I promise that I will never dishonor you."

Gennie's heart soared at his declaration.

Much later, as Haven lay snoring softly beside her, Gennie found her mind not yet ready for sleep. She could hardly believe Haven's actions this day. He had accepted her counsel, choosing to honor her promise to the Welsh, though it defied the king's direct orders. The responsibility for his decision lay heavily on her shoulders. She knew Haven had made the right choice, but how would Edward see it? Would he brand his true and perfect knight a traitor? Would he think Gennie had led two men to treason? She moved closer to Haven. Was their fledgling love strong enough to withstand a king's assault? She vowed it would be. For surely they had at last laid Roger's legacy of treason to rest and could build on the love they had declared for each other.

Even several weeks after leaving his sickbed, Haven was exhausted. Each day he joined one or the other of the work parties, clearing rubble, hunting food, cutting timber: the tasks were endless. Gennie was no less busy. She organized the women, the laundry, the meals, the search for berries and roots to supplement the meat brought home from the hunt. She instructed young girls in the care of the children. She furnished the tower, now that it had solid walls. Haven marveled at her achievements and boundless energy.

In a few days the keep's upper floor would be ready. Haven looked forward to sharing the new solar with Gennie. It had a stout door, which could be barred from the inside against untimely interruptions.

Each evening, after supper, they would sit by the fire with a few others and review the day, making plans for the next day's work and watching Thomas play with the other children of the castle. The group around the fire included Soames, Owain, Pwyll, Gwyneth, and one or two others who would join from time to time as various needs and concerns arose among them.

Across the great hall, young people would gather to laugh and entertain themselves. It did not escape Haven that Watley and Rebecca often sat together. Nor did it escape Haven that his wife paid particular attention whenever Pwyll chose to speak.

This night she leaned close and argued fiercely with the Welshman over the best ways to expand the castle to provide for the coming English families. While Haven debated with his men ways of acquiring supplies for the winter, he listened with half an ear to Gennie and Pwyll. Their conversation had devolved to the complications of storing supplies for close to two hundred and fifty people or more.

Gwyneth, who still preferred Welsh to English, would occasionally look up from her knitting to interject a comment that Owain would translate about the medicines and herbs she needed and how they should be preserved. Unless some source of food could be found, Haven worried that all their planning would be moot.

The hunting parties were able for the time being to supply the current need, but almost all the food was consumed and very little preserved against the future.

Worse, Soames reported that someone had broken into the small stores they had assembled on the keep's dungeon level. Nothing had been stolen, but a sack of precious grain had been split open and a few spare crocks tossed about and broken. Why anyone would do anything so senseless was beyond Haven's ken. Still, he meant to keep watch himself for the next few nights.

"What think you, Sir Haven? Should we add to the outbuildings or should we increase the space in the dungeon? Many of the men who help construct walls and roofs are miners by trade. Excavation would prove fairly easy and a more effective use of their skills."

Pwyll's words pulled Haven from his thoughts.

"I favor expanding the space belowground in the tower."

"But, husband," Gennie objected, "we have so many needs for storage. Surely it would be best if supplies were stored by purpose near the buildings where they will be used. 'Twould reduce the amount of traffic and disturbance within the tower."

"You make good points, wife. But I must say you nay. The tower keep itself is our last defense against intruders. I would not provide enemies with supplies that they could use against us. Nor would I give cause for my own people to starve because an enemy prevents them getting to grain and meat. You know that 'tis for this very reason that we are making a well inside the keep."

Gennie nodded at this reminder. "*Oui*, husband. I have felt so secure here that I had forgotten."

Haven smiled, pleased that she had confidence in his ability to keep her safe. He firmed his decision to do everything in his power to increase that safety, even if he must give up a few nights in their bed. Once he had solved the problem of the intruder in the dungeon, he could celebrate for a string of nights behind the door of the new solar.

Gennie didn't like it when he escorted her to the gatehouse and told her that he would be busy for the next few nights. She wanted to know exactly what he would be doing and where. How could she be assured of his safety if he wasn't in bed with her? Her concern touched him, but he refused to yield. This duty was his as Edward's vassal and the guardian of Two Hills Keep. Gennie would simply have to trust him. She had sniffed and told him to take his warmest cloak and some food, if he wouldn't accept her concern. He had nodded his agreement and left.

Now he sat in the dark dungeon, his blade drawn, his back pressed up against the wall opposite the stairs that led down from the keep's first floor. That floor rested on a stone foundation that raised it a good ten feet from ground level. That way the wooden stair that led into the castle from the bailey could be cut away from the building, leaving intruders with no way to enter the main tower. Still, the chinking in some of the stonework was imperfect, allowing a small amount of light to penetrate the gloom during the day. At night the place was pitch black. Even so, Haven's vision adjusted, and soon he could make out the difference between solid shapes and empty spaces.

As people retired, the sounds of the tower stilled. He waited, expecting that he would repeat the experience for several nights before his quarry returned. Haven sat in that cramped position, hidden by bags of grain, for a great length of time. He recounted in silence the exploits of Charlemagne and King Arthur, in order to keep himself awake.

A sound at the top of the interior stair rewarded his endurance. *The fool had returned early.* Haven put his hand to his sword and silently cautioned himself to patience. The stairs creaked under the person's weight. A halo of light surrounded the figure that moved downward, pausing at the bottom of the stair. Even better, the intruder had brought a lantern. The man was overconfident.

Still Haven waited. As much as he wanted to catch and punish the intruder, he wanted more to know what the man sought. The fellow was moving now, headed for a spot on the wall at Haven's left. The intruder set down his lantern and began to shift the sacks that topped a few ale barrels. When he had moved the barrels aside as well, Haven heard a scraping noise. Then the figure picked up his lantern and vanished from sight.

Silently, Haven rushed to the spot where he had just seen the man. There, behind the barrels, was a square opening in the cellar floor. A trapdoor was propped against the wall, and Haven could see the faint light of the intruder's lantern. Haven debated whether or not to follow the man, when the light began to brighten. He was returning.

Sword at the ready, Haven crouched behind a barrel and waited for his prey to emerge fully from the hole. The man rose from the ground. He placed his lantern atop one of the barrels and reached for the trap door. In that moment, Haven stood, putting his sword to the man's throat. "Hold and turn to me." The knave complied.

"You!"

Chapter Twenty-three

"What are you doing down here, Pwyll?"

"I could ask the same of you."

"But you won't because you know I am looking for you."

"True. I thought it a stroke of good fortune when no one remarked on the broken crockery and spilled grain from my last two visits."

"Well, your luck just ran out."

"Maybe. But perhaps you would like to see what I've found."

"Answer my question first."

"As you like. I was looking for a silver mine."

At this absurd response, Haven dropped his blade a few inches. It now pointed directly at Pwyll's heart. "You jest at your peril."

"Nay, sir, I can show proof."

"Where?"

"Here." Pwyll pulled a pouch from his belt and held it out to Haven.

"Empty it onto the barrel next to your lantern."

Pwyll did so. Several rocks slid from the pouch to the barrel surface.

Haven sheathed his sword and picked up one of the rocks. "And you claim this is silver?"

"Aye, Sir Haven. You can have this sent to the king. He no doubt has metallurgists who can verify my claim."

"Mayhap I will do so. Show me where this silver mine is."

Haven slid into bed beside Gennie and reached for her warm body. Even in sleep, Gennie sidled away from his cold grasp.

He didn't blame her, but he wanted to share his news with her, and he needed her warmth.

To look at the mine, Haven had followed Pwyll on a long and filthy walk beneath the bowels of the keep. From the way water dripped down the walls of the tunnel in places, Pwyll speculated that the tunnel ran under the river. Haven didn't care. Once he had seen the cavern where Pwyll had found the rocks, all Haven wanted was to return aboveground and wash the stink of moldering earth from his body.

On his way back to Gennie, he had stopped at the cistern in the bailey, stripped and sluiced his entire body with clear water. That left him clean but cold. He had dried his feet, picked up his clothing and run for the gatehouse chamber where his wife dreamed.

Haven pursued her across the ticking. When she could retreat no farther, she finally woke.

"You are freezing," she said, frowning, and blinked sleep from her green eyes.

Haven kissed her. "So warm me," he requested when he came up for air.

"With pleasure," Gennie purred.

Later, when Haven's breathing calmed and they lay twined together, he told her of Pwyll's discovery.

"Does anyone else know?"

"Nay, and they shall not, until we can determine how best to turn this discovery to our advantage."

"You cannot keep this secret for long."

"Long enough to get word to the king wherever he is and have him send a metallurgist and smelter to advise us."

"Must you tell Edward?"

"This is his castle, Gennie. The silver belongs to the crown. I hold it by Edward's grace."

"I see. But could you not use some of the crown's silver to make improvements to the crown's grace?"

Haven smiled. "I will certainly put that in my message to Edward."

A few weeks later, Haven went in search of Gennie and for the third time in as many days found her in close conversation with Pwyll. They sprang apart at the sight of him. What attraction did the young Welshman have for his wife? Haven shook the thought away as foolish. Gennie was so enthusiastic in their bed at night, she could have no passion left for another man. She had even said she loved him, a declaration he still found hard to believe, but one he reveled in every day.

"Sir Haven, well met. I've news," said Pwyll.

Gennie excused herself, saying she needed to consult with Rene on the evening meal.

Impatient with his wife's desertion, Haven spoke sharply. "What is it, Pwyll?"

"I found an entrance to the mine on the far side of the hill opposite the keep."

"Did anyone see you?" Haven asked, instantly interested.

"Nay. Nor is this other entrance easy to find."

"Good. I will have Soames add the location to our patrols."

"Won't he wonder why?"

"Mayhap, but more like he'll be embarrassed that he forgot to add it to the patrol in the first place. Behind that hill is an excellent place for an enemy to gather for a surprise attack."

Pwyll nodded. "I am not used to this business of keeping secrets. How long do you think it will be until the king sends a response to your message?"

"Who can say? It will take two weeks to get word to Chester and back. Since the king is elsewhere fighting Llewellyn, we must wait until the messenger finds him."

"Then there is nothing left to do but wait."

"Aye."

"If that will be all, sir, I will see to progress on the well. You are right that the cistern is vulnerable to attack. A well located in the dungeon will be much more secure."

"Aye. If you need more men, let me know."

Pwyll bowed and left.

Haven headed for the practice field that now occupied a large section of the bailey. On his way, he noticed Watley talking with Rebecca near a corner of the stables. Obviously, neither had learned discretion during his illness. The relationship could not be allowed to continue. Haven changed course, coming up on the couple from behind the stable. "Ahem."

Just like Pwyll and Gennie, they started apart, as if discovered in something sinful.

"Good day to you, Mistress Rebecca." Haven spoke as if he had noticed nothing unusual. "Watley, I understand that your training has been sadly lacking since I fell ill."

"Aye, Sir Haven."

"Then join me on the practice field."

"Aye, Sir Haven."

Haven waited.

"G . . . good-bye Rebecca."

"Good-bye Watley." She lifted her hem and walked off.

"I hope you are not being drawn in by her again?" Haven asked.

The squire remained silent.

Just as well, Haven thought. There wasn't much the lad could say. But he caught the glint in Watley's eye, and the tension in his jaw as they walked to the practice field. No doubt the squire wanted to teach him a lesson. Let him try.

There could be no better training than to fight a man you wanted to beat some sense into. Today Watley would learn to check his emotions before he joined in battle.

With a groan of relief, Haven settled into bed beside Gennie. Watley had gotten in several good blows before Haven could taunt him into carelessness and defeat the younger man. With that fight finished, it seemed that every available man wanted to test Haven's strength. He knew they needed confirmation that he was completely recovered, so he accepted every challenge.

And he bested them all, save Owain, which surprised no one, since Haven had taken the big man on last. Haven had hidden his aches and pains well from the men, but in the privacy of his own chamber, he could acknowledge how ill prepared he had been for this day's exercise. When Gennie snuggled next to him, Haven did no more than anchor her to his side with an arm about her waist before nodding off to sleep.

Had it not been for the dropping of his arm, Haven might not have noticed Gennie slip from the bed and leave the solar. As it was, between his own aches and Gennie's soft footsteps padding about the room, Haven came quickly awake. But Gennie was gone just as quickly, or Haven would have called out to her. He spent moments in thought, then followed her as rapidly as he could don his clothing

Either his pains had slowed him more than he expected, or Gennie was in a great hurry, for her blue cloak trailed around the corner at the bottom of the stair just as Haven reached its head. He dared not rush down the steps. New as they were, they had a tendency to squeak and groan. Thus, by the time he cleared the stairs, Gennie had disappeared.

Had the outer door of the keep not stood open, Haven would have guessed that she headed toward the new keeping room near the soon-to-be-finished well. But finding the door open was so odd that he had to pursue that path first. No doubt he had missed her and would find her back in bed on his return.

Haven eased out the door. He rested a moment, surveying the bailey below. A guard marched his post on the inner curtain wall from stables to gatehouse. Haven hurried across to him.

"Who goes there?" The words came at Haven in heavily accented English.

"Sir Haven," he told the Welshman. "Have you seen anyone pass this way?"

The man wrinkled his face and pondered, finally uttering, "Aye."

This wasn't going to be easy. "Was it a woman?"

Again that painful look of concentration. "Nay."

Haven should have known. Gennie was probably back in bed already.

" 'Twas a man and a woman."

"What?"

The guard jumped.

Haven reminded himself not to shout.

"I said, ' 'twas . . .' "

"I know what you said. Which way did they go?"

"T'the stables, sir," the guard added.

"My thanks. Return to your post."

The guard hurried away.

Haven paced soft-footed toward the stables. There too, the door stood ajar. Someone was being careless. Haven slipped through the opening and stepped into the shadows cast by the loft. At the far end of the building, two horses stood saddled and ready to ride.

In front of the horses, a man embraced a woman. Haven recognized Gennie's blue cloak. She had gone into alt when he had presented it to her as a wedding gifts, along with a trunk full of clothing.

The man wore nothing that revealed his identity. Haven watched as the two kissed, murmured and kissed again. It was obvious that Gennie was about to leave him. Through a haze of red, he debated letting her go.

Susan Charnley

But she knew all the keep's defenses, and she knew of the silver mine. He could not allow her to betray him or anyone else. The couple had to be stopped. The man would learn a valuable lesson about letting his cock guide his head, and the deceitful lady would get her just desserts.

Letting out a frustrated roar, Haven gave his opponent enough warning to let go of the woman. Then Haven grabbed the fellow, intent upon beating him senseless. The man's nose made a satisfying crunch under Haven's fist, but that only whetted his appetite. He throttled the man with one hand, picked him up and slammed him against the stone wall of the stable.

The woman screamed. Horses reared and snorted. The commotion drew footsteps. Amid the yelling and chaos, Haven continued to pound his fists into his victim's face and ribs. He didn't even stop when the first bucket of cold water hit him. To pull him from the man's bruised and bloody body required another dousing and two strong men. The haze cleared. Haven looked down at the man who dared to touch Gennie.

Chapter Twenty-four

"Watley, my love," Rebecca wailed. "That brute has beaten you like a churl."

What was Rebecca doing here? Haven stopped struggling against the men who held him. "Would someone tell me what is going on here?"

"Indeed, husband, I too would like to know why you attacked Watley."

Haven craned his neck to see his wife.

Covered in her nightrobe and shawl, Gennie stood in the doorway to the stables, surrounded by curious folk.

Haven shook his head. If Gennie wore her robe, then who wore Gennie's cloak? He turned back to the man and woman nearest him. Watley groaned on the stable floor. Rebecca knelt next to him. From beneath the hood of Gennie's cloak, the girl looked up at Haven with hatred clear in her eyes. "Beast," she spat out and bent once more over Watley.

Haven studied Gennie, who smiled and moved to his side. What did she have to smile about?

"Husband, have you been beastly to your squire again?" She took his arm.

"Again?"

"*Oui*, I understand that you defeated him most grievously at practice today."

"That was not beastly. That was training."

"Yes, husband. I am glad you cleared that up for us." She looked pointedly at Rebecca, then touched Haven's face. "You have a cut, sir."

He put his hand to where hers soothed his forehead. Given his fierce onslaught, Watley had done well to land any blow. Haven spent a glance on his squire. "Can you stand?" he asked the young man.

Watley tested his jaw, moving it from side to side. "Aye."

Haven bent and offered a hand.

The young man grasped it, hauling himself upright.

"I do not apologize for hitting you. You deserved punishment for defying my express orders to stay away from Rebecca Dreyford."

Watley nodded.

"I do apologize for mistaking Rebecca for my wife, and therefore for the extent of the punishment meted out."

" 'Twas an easy mistake to make," mumbled the squire, who continued to check that all his teeth remained in place.

"Well enough. Return to the barracks. Soames will get someone to tend to your hurts."

Watley left, pushing through the people who surrounded the stable door.

Haven frowned at the crowd, and they fled like sparrows before a hawk.

Gennie chuckled, "You are so very fierce, husband."

Haven turned his frown on her.

" 'Twill take more than an unhappy look from you to vanquish me, sir."

He cocked an eyebrow. "I will deal with you later." He straightened his expression and looked at Rebecca.

The girl stood in the corner of a stall, a vision of cowering defiance.

"You have much to answer for, Mistress Dreyford." Haven stepped toward her.

"Nay," the girl cried and burst into tears. "Do not touch me. You are a cruel man."

Taken aback by this outburst, he halted and felt Gennie's hand on his arm. He looked back at her. "Wife?"

"She is hysterical, husband. Permit me to take care of her."

Wanting no more to do with Rebecca than she with him, Haven nodded. "I will await you in the solar. But we will have words, wife."

With Haven gone, Gennie suppressed the impulse to hug and soothe. In the past, she had used gentleness with Rebecca to no avail. 'Twas time to be firm. Gennie advanced on her weeping sister-in-law. "I would have my cloak, Rebecca."

The girl turned tear-filled eyes on Gennie. "But 'tis cold out."

Gennie gripped her temper. "*Oui.* You are dressed, and I am in my nightrobe. Think you I feel the cold less than you?"

Chastened, Rebecca removed the garment, handing it to Gennie with a watery, "I am sorry."

Gennie donned the cloak. " 'Tis not enough this time, Rebecca."

The girl bent her head.

"I counseled you often not to give in to your affections for Watley, did I not?"

"Aye."

"Yet you ignore my counsel. Plot against my husband. Steal from me. And lead a young man astray to his detriment. 'Tis beyond understanding."

"But I love Watley, and he loves me."

"I do not doubt that you believe you are in love. Even if it is true, do you think love excuses your thoughtless actions?"

Rebecca twisted her hands together and mumbled a response.

"I could not hear you."

Gennie's sister-in-law straightened her shoulders and looked up. "No, my actions are inexcusable."

"That is better. Since you recognize your fault, I am willing to intercede with Haven for you."

"Oh, Gennie, thank you."

Gennie found herself in a fierce hug. "Don't thank me too quickly. You must do something for me in exchange."

"I will do anything."

"Think carefully before you agree. Your actions cannot go unpunished, Rebecca."

"Anything, I promise."

"Very well. You must accept with good grace whatever consequences my husband allots."

"But you said you would intercede."

"*Oui*, I shall try to convince Haven to permit your betrothal to Watley, but only if you hold to your part of our bargain."

" 'Tis unfair." The girl stamped her foot.

" 'Tis more than you deserve for treating others so unfairly."

More tears brimmed in Rebecca's eyes. She studied Gennie, then nodded.

"Good. Give me your promise once more, then get you to bed."

"I promise that I will accept with good grace whatever consequence Sir Haven decides is just for my actions this night."

Gennie hugged the girl. " 'Twill not be so awful."

"You cannot know that."

"I know my husband as you do not."

Rebecca nodded and left.

Gennie sighed. Nausea in the middle of the night was difficult. 'Twould be better if the sickness came later in the morning. Now she must face her husband, who despite his love for her clearly did not trust her. Did he doubt her professions of love? After all they had shared, how could he think she would steal away in the night with another man? Earlier, she had smiled at his jealous actions, but her good humor hid the pain his lack of faith had caused her. She resolved not to confront him about it. She needed him to place his trust in her completely and of his own accord. She would accept what he had to give and pray for the rest. She shivered. This night she would plead on Rebecca and Watley's behalf. The idea of persuading Haven not to act on his fury at Rebecca made Gennie weary to the bone. She was tired and would seek her bed soon, but first she must find someone to tend the horses left saddled at the back of the stables.

*   *   *

Haven watched his wife enter the solar and remove her cloak and nightrobe. She rolled her shoulders and rubbed at her abdomen as if they both ached. She had been through much this night. He rose and went to her.

"Sit down," he ordered and pointed at the sheepskin rug near the braiser that lit the room. Gennie sat. Haven seated himself behind her and lifted her hair from her neck. He stroked the fine bones of that delicate column, thinking what a strange mixture of strength and fragility was this woman who had come to mean so much to him in such a short time. Placing a hand on each of Gennie's shoulders, Haven rubbed at the knots he felt just beneath her smooth skin.

"Ah," Gennie groaned. "That feels good."

" 'Tis meant to."

"And is it meant to prepare me for a lecture about interfering in your authority?"

"Nay." Haven chuckled. "You would never do such a thing, meek and obedient wife that you are."

Gennie threw back her head, joining his good humor. Her eyes shone up at him in the dim light; her body glowed. No other woman could be so beautiful.

Haven bent and nipped her neck, then soothed the bite with his tongue. He drew away. They had problems to solve before he could allow himself to succumb to the passion she stirred in him.

"I cannot let Rebecca go unpunished."

Gennie nodded. "I know, Haven."

"She should suffer equally with Watley."

Beneath Haven's hands, Gennie tensed.

"Will you beat her?"

" 'Tis my right."

"*Oui.*" Her voice faded.

"What think you?"

274

"I think 'twould be a shame for you to prove to others what Rebecca already believes."

"And what is that?"

"That you are a cruel man."

"You think it is cruel to be just?"

She twisted and looked at him. "Mayhap, but you are not cruel. I think you will find a just solution that is not also a cruelty."

Haven cupped her cheek. "Would that I could do so, Gennie. Rebecca's thoughtlessness angers me so that I think she deserves a beating."

His wife smiled at him. "I understand how you feel. Rebecca is a very taxing young woman. She was much indulged by her family and completely unprepared to find herself homeless and deprived of rank."

"This does not excuse her selfishness."

"True, but she is not evil, husband. She can be taught."

"Perhaps, but not here. We both have too many responsibilities to constantly watch and discipline Rebecca."

"If not here, with her only family, where then? A convent?"

"Now there's a thought. She would hate the work. And 'twould teach her humility." He smiled.

"Oh, Haven, no. She is not suited to convent life."

"I agree, Gennie. But a few years in a convent won't hurt her."

Doubt gleamed in Gennie's eyes.

" 'Tis less cruel than a beating and should produce a more enduring result," he prodded.

Gennie rubbed her chin in thought. "You may be right. Especially if we soften the blow."

Haven sat taller and frowned. "How can a punishment be effective if softened?"

"What I mean is that Rebecca should have something to hope for when she leaves the convent."

"You mean like a reward for good behavior?"

"Exactly." Gennie trailed her fingers up his chest and around his neck to tangle with the hair at his nape.

Haven eyed her suspiciously. "What have you in mind?"

"Well, you could allow a betrothal between Rebecca and Watley."

"No!" Haven stood, rejecting Gennie's caress along with her suggestion. " 'Tis pure folly to allow a betrothal when neither party has lands or fortune. In addition, Rebecca's connection with Roger can do Watley's consequence no good."

Gennie rose, hands fisted at her sides. "Have I done your consequence harm?"

"Nay, but I am not an untried squire who has yet to earn his king's regard."

Gennie's hands relaxed, and she let out a gasp of laughter. "Is that all?"

Haven stared at her. " 'Tis more than enough reason to forbid the betrothal, think you not?"

"Forbid it, *non*. Delay it, yes."

"I do not follow you."

She took his hand. "Permit the betrothal, Haven, but on the conditions that Rebecca is well-behaved at the convent and that Watley earns lands sufficient to support them."

Haven ran his thumb over Gennie's knuckles. "Aye, that may serve. 'Twould point to their shared responsibility in this evening's farce and give each of them something to strive toward."

"Good. Now that Rebecca's fate is settled, Haven, let us strive toward something ourselves." Gennie leaned up and kissed him.

Haven circled her waist with his free arm. "And what would that be, wife?"

Gennie slipped from his embrace and tugged on his hand. "Let me show you." She headed toward the bed.

Just before dawn, pounding at the solar door woke Haven.

Chapter Twenty-five

His hand went to his sword, placed habitually by the bed, but he stilled when he heard Soames call out. "Sir, a messenger from the king has arrived and seeks audience."

"I will be down in a moment, Soames. See if you can rouse Rene to give the man refreshment."

"Aye, Sir Haven."

"Haven, what's amiss?" Gennie's sleepy mumble halted him in the midst of slipping from their bed.

"Nothing, sweetling. Go back to sleep." He kissed her tousled hair.

"C'est bien." She burrowed beneath the covers.

Haven pulled on his clothes and left. He trotted down the stairs, wondering what Edward's message might be. The information about the mine should have reached Edward by now. Hopefully, the king had sent orders regarding the silver.

At the sight of the blond giant seated over a meal,

with his back to the stairs, Haven leapt over the last three steps to the floor. He let out a delighted shout and ran to where the man now stood. When Haven got within two paces, he was lifted from the ground and crushed within the giant's bearlike grip. "Michael Beltour, by all that is holy. What brings you to Two Hills Keep?" Haven grunted from within the big fellow's stranglehold.

The shaggy blond released him.

Haven's feet thudded to the ground. He slapped his friend on the back. They had served Edward together for many years now, but Haven had not seen Michael since . . . since they had traveled together to find Roger Dreyford and bring him to be tried for treason. The thought sobered Haven. "Sit. Finish your meal and tell me what is so urgent that the king uses his strongest weapon as a messenger."

Michael took his seat. " 'Tis nothing urgent," he said around the piece of bread he stuffed into his mouth. "Unless you consider Edward's presence here on the morrow urgent."

"The king here? Tomorrow?"

Michael wiped his mouth and grinned. "Aye. He thought it mannerly to give notice of his arrival."

"Gennie will be frantic."

"Hoho. So the widow Dreyford is become Gennie. She must be an armful for you to keep her and call her so, especially since I hear she led Roger to treason. Still, you always had a fondness for a ripe . . . female . . . or . . ."

Michael's words trailed off in the face of Haven's cold stare.

"You were not with the king at Chester, else you would know that the former widow Dreyford is my wife.

As you love me, you will love her, for I hold her in the highest regard."

Haven watched concern chase surprise across his friend's face.

"By all means, Haven. I apologize most humbly. I meant no disrespect."

Haven nudged Michael's shoulder with his fist. "Nonsense; you meant every low word. But I forgive you, for you spoke in ignorance."

"Aye. So when do I get to meet this paragon?"

"As soon as she rises, if you do not have to return to Edward immediately."

"Nay, he commanded that I await him here." Michael finished his meal and pushed the platter away.

"Good. Let me send word to Gennie of the king's arrival. Then I will take you on a tour of the tower and bailey."

"While you are at it, tell me how you like married life. If it suits you, mayhap I will give married women another try."

"After that last disaster, I would think you had enough of cuckolding your fellow knights?" Haven smiled.

" 'Tis a bachelor's knight duty to keep his married peers on their toes, lest they grow soft." He slapped his friend's shoulders as they left the hall.

On the steps of the keep, Gennie stood next to Haven and twisted her hands nervously. She watched King Edward ride into the bailey, surrounded by his household. She had tumbled into bed late last night and risen early this morning. The keep was as ready as could be for the royal visit, given the building's half-finished state.

She couldn't help but be nervous. Edward had married her to Haven "in order to prevent more treason," according to her husband. What proof would the king expect that Haven he had achieved his aim? When asked, Haven had responded that the king only wanted to inspect the progress on the keep's construction and discuss some strategic issues that had changed since Llewellyn's retreat from Gwynedd toward Builth.

Still, Gennie couldn't help but be nervous. The last time she had seen Edward, she had expected to be hanged. She had never expected to be grateful to the man for his summary decision to wed her to Haven instead. That too had seemed a horrific fate at the time.

Most of all, she worried about all the Welshmen in the keep. It was her fault they were there. Haven assured her that the responsibility was his for allowing them to remain. Her husband was wrong. Gennie felt certain that Edward would place the blame for this defiant act squarely on her shoulders, where it belonged.

The king dismounted and climbed the keep's steps. Haven knelt. Gennie and the rest of the castle's population followed suit. Edward grasped Haven's arm, pulling him to his feet. "Well met, de Sessions."

"Welcome, sire. Come within and warm yourself. There is food and ale waiting."

Edward gestured for those who remained kneeling to rise. " 'Twould be most welcome."

Haven paused on the doorstep with the king, who continued, "Based on the description in your letters, I can see you've made great progress here."

" 'Twas the Welsh who made it possible."

Gennie locked a gasp between her lips.

"Aye, Arthur Pwyll is a most apt student of James St. George."

Relieved, Gennie breathed a sigh.

"Pwyll is an asset, liege, but I refer to these good people."

What was Haven doing? He would call Edward's wrath down on them all.

Indeed, the king's voice hardened. "I presume you have a reason for pointing out to me that you defied my express orders."

Gennie cringed.

Haven smiled.

The two men moved into the keep. Curiosity pulled Gennie at a rapid pace behind them. Haven led Edward to one of three chairs next to a table by the hearth. The room filled with the Welsh, all silent, all wanting to know their fate.

"Aye. You gave me to believe that this keep and the road it guards were vital to your strategy in defeating Llewellyn ap Gryffudd. Without the labor, freely given by the Welsh, I would have been unable to hold either keep or road."

Edward nodded. "And your point . . ."

"I thought you might wish proof of their worth before I suggest that you reconsider your policy about the Welsh."

"You've sworn to protect them, haven't you?"

"Aye."

"*Oui.*" Speaking at that same moment, Gennie came forward, slipping her hand around Haven's arm.

Edward cast Gennie a calculating glance. "Did your witch of a wife put you up to this?"

Gennie paled. What did Edward suspect?

Haven put his hand over Gennie's. "Nay, sire. When I lay ill, my wife had no herbs with which to fight my fever. She sought out a Welsh wisewoman, promising my protection should the beldam save my life." Haven motioned Gwyneth forward. He placed a hand on the crone's shoulder. "In gratitude, I swore protection for all those who would aid me in achieving the task that you set for me. I have never failed you, my liege. I would not do so now."

Throughout this speech Edward's gaze never left Gennie's face. "And you, Lady Genvieve? Would you fail me?"

Gennie thought quickly. If she had to choose between Edward's life and Haven's or Thomas's, she would cheerfully kill Edward herself. Yes, she would fail England's king. Of a certainty, that was not what Edward wanted to hear.

"Well, woman?"

"I am my husband's loyal subject in all things, sire." Gennie held her breath.

Edward's eyelids narrowed over his pupils. Then he threw his head back and gave a great roaring laugh. When he calmed, he wiped his eyes. "A very pretty answer, lady. A very pretty answer indeed. And I shall respond just as prettily to your husband's request." He looked at Haven. "I will consider your suggestion that I rethink my policy for the Welsh."

Gennie exhaled and turned to see her relief mirrored in the eyes of the watching folk. She beamed at them. "Has no one any work to do?" Nodding, the Welsh left the great hall. Quiet murmurs ushered them out.

She turned back to the king. "Husband, I shall order our people to wait until you are done discussing business with the king, before they prepare the hall for tonight's feast. Sire, if you will excuse me, I will see to it that your chamber is made comfortable."

"By all means, Lady Genvieve."

Gennie curtseyed and left, calling for Marie to take Thomas.

Moments later only Haven, Pwyll and King Edward remained in the great hall. Edward invited the two men to join him at the table.

"Liege, did my messenger reach you?"

"Aye, 'tis one of the reasons I left pursuit of Llewellyn in other hands and came south."

"Did you bring a metallurgist with you?"

Edward glanced at Pwyll.

" 'Twas Pwyll who discovered the ore."

Edward nodded. "I've already had the ore tested. But I did not tell the metallurgist how it came to me."

"Is it . . ."

". . . silver?" The king nodded once more. "Yes."

"I knew it." Pwyll's fist hit the table and startled the two older men. "It's a pastime of mine," he explained. "An engineer often becomes familiar with ores found while digging foundations and other excavations."

Edward frowned the younger man to silence. "Does anyone else know?"

Haven did not hesitate. "Gennie knows."

"You have gained much faith in your wife for such a newly married man."

"With reason, sire."

"I see."

Haven wondered if the king's noncommittal comment was cause for worry.

But Edward's next words concerned him more. "I had reason to believe that a mine existed here. That is why I insisted you take charge of Two Hills Keep."

"Why did you not tell me?"

" 'Twas only a rumor, passed on to me by the man who said that Daffydd would attack this place."

"It seems your source was reliable."

"Aye, he shall be properly rewarded, as shall you both." Edward included Pwyll in his glance.

Haven waited.

"Haven, you have need of a permanent position and lands. This keep and the title Earl of Twynn are yours and your family's from this day forth with two conditions. First, that you pay the crown half of all the silver mined here."

"The crown needs more than half, liege."

"Think you so? You must take the cost of mining and smelting the ore from the sale of the silver after you give the crown its share. What say you now?"

Haven acquiesced. "You are just as always."

"I wouldn't say always. But I thank you for your faith in me. And that is my second condition."

"That I remain faithful?"

"Not just you. So long as the de Sessions family remains perfect in troth to the king of England, they shall hold these lands."

"And I, my liege?" Pwyll asked.

Haven forestalled Edward's answer. "Sire, I see workers massing at the doors waiting for us to finish."

"Let them come in. We can conclude our business while you show me the improvements Pwyll has made. Did I mention that I brought the first of the English families with me?"

"Nay, liege. You did not." 'Tis too soon, Haven thought; we are not yet ready.

Chaos reigned in the kitchen. From the corner where she attempted to quell a battle between Rene and one Goody Brown, englishwoman, Gennie watched disaster unfold.

At the huge fireplace a couple of young boys turned several spits of meat and fowl. A number of Welshwomen stood around a large table kneading dough, filling tarts and beating other mysterious concoctions in bowls. Some young girls sat by the only door plucking and cleaning fowl, effectively blocking entrance to Goody's supporters and anyone else who felt a need to be in the kitchen. A man with a wicked-looking knife sliced loaves of bread into trenchers. The scooped-out middles of each loaf went into a copper-clad kettle used for making puddings and other sweets. Next to him, four more girls peeled and pared fruits of all varieties.

Gennie shook her head. If they had to feed the king and his minions for many days, starvation would be a certainty this winter. The few supplies they had would be gone in less than a week.

The resourceful Welsh had produced a small treasure of vegetables and fruit when they realized the king did not mean to eject them immediately. The English families, who had come with the king to populate Two Hills Keep, made their contribution too. That was what started the battle between Rene and Mistress Goody Brown.

While more than willing to accept the foods given by the English, the usually affable Rene was completely unwilling to allow any of the English into the kitchen.

"I will have no talentless beginners ruin the meal I prepare for *le roi.*"

At which point, Mistress Brown countered, "I been kneading bread and roasting quail since before your mother tupped the butcher."

This insult was not to be born. Rene dipped his ladle

into the sauce he had been stirring to cool and flung the liquid at Goody.

Goody gasped and returned fire with a fist full of dough grabbed off the nearby table.

It might have stopped there, but in drawing back her arm, Mistress Brown clipped the head of a woman who was whipping eggs to a froth. The bowl slipped from the woman's hands and tipped, spilling the bubbly yellow liquid across the table and into every item being prepared there.

The woman tried in vain to capture the bowl, thus losing her balance. She fell backward, knocking the two boys away from the fire and the spits off their handles. Sparks flew, and people jumped every which way. Platters skidded. More liquids spilled. Screeches and yelps rolled in the air.

Suddenly all was still, save the stray feathers that floated like huge dust motes in the heated air. Standing in the doorway was the very friar who had heard Gennie's confession and instructed her to wear the hair shirt. When he turned his blazing look on her, Gennie shivered.

"I see your sins have come back to roost, madame. You must have lacked dedication in your penance."

How could he know? Gennie wondered.

"Hear now, you speak proper to milady." This from Goody Brown, who eyed the begging priest with disgust. Sauce dripped from every appendage, and she looked like nothing so much as a huge, underdone apple dumpling.

"I will have respect for Lady Genvieve in my kitchen." Rene echoed the Englishwoman's sentiments, his dislike of friars being well known to Gennie and evidently superior to his mistrust of Goody Brown.

From the angry flush on the friar's face, Gennie expected a rage of sermonizing. Contrary to expectation, the friar bowed to Rene and Goody Brown and said in dulcet tones, "I apologize. I meant no offense."

"And so you should," huffed Goody.

Rene merely sniffed.

The friar made an attempt at a conciliatory smile. The rather nauseating result fascinated Gennie.

"Come, children," the holy man continued. "Let us put past mishaps aside and set to rights the bounty God has given us. My brothers and I will help."

"Non."

"Nay."

But the protests of Rene and Goody alike went unheeded. For the friar, and six more like him, waded through a fallen bucket of feathers and began to *help* restore order.

Gennie watched horrified as the friars filched as much as they put to rights. In the flurry of activity that followed the priestly entrance into the kitchen, it was difficult to keep track of who put what where.

So Gennie resigned herself to the friars' questionable assistance. She cautioned Rene not to object. "Some missing food is a small price to pay, and do we object, they will but remain longer and take more."

Gennie began to think of their quick-fingered presence as a blessing, since the friars also achieved the unintended result of accord between Rene and Goody Brown.

"Milady," Goody whispered, when the friars lingered overlong, "that one is about to lift the quail from the king's platter. Else you find some way to make them leave, the king himself will go hungry this day."

Gennie cast a glance at the shadows outside the

kitchen door. "Be at ease, Mistress Brown. The chapel bell will ring evening prayers soon. Those sticky-fingered crows will have to leave then."

True to her word, the bells rang out moments later, and like a flock of ravens set upon by hounds, the friars left.

Gennie and her cook surveyed the remaining damage. "Will you be able to feed us tonight, Rene"

"*Oui*, milady. It will not be easy, though."

"We shall pull through, milady. Just you wait and see." Goody Brown dabbed away the remnants of the sauce from her face.

Rene hitched his apron. "Go you, Lady Genvieve. Mistress Brown and I have much work to do."

Assured that peace, if not neatness, would now rule in the kitchen, Gennie took herself off to find her husband. Only he could help her solve her latest problem.

Chapter Twenty-six

With Gennie beside him, Haven sat at the king's right above the salt and surveyed the great hall with satisfaction. He knew how slim the resources were with which his wife had to work. He also knew that the English families had not adjusted well to the presence of the Welsh.

Yet Gennie accomplished the impossible. The walls were bare, but all evidence of construction was gone. Sturdy tables and benches had appeared to provide seating for both Edward's household and their own. Servants brought wine and ale in abundance. Only one thing was missing: the food.

A short time ago, Gennie had come to him with a tale of a disaster in the kitchen. She begged that he find some way to delay the meal. Haven stood, and the room grew quiet. He hoped that his solution would satisfy all.

"Sire, respected guests. Our cook has prepared a very

special repast tonight. However, to whet your appetites, we have arranged a wrestling match. When Cyril Glamorgan, one of my Welsh bowmen, questioned the fighting abilities of Englishmen in general, my squire sought the privilege of defending English honor. I granted my permission, as long as they delayed their contest until now, when all could witness the truth or falseness of Glamorgan's claim that Englishmen could not defeat an enemy without Welsh arrows to clear the way first."

At this announcement, the English in the hall rose up and hurled insults at the Welsh, who soon returned the discourtesy. Haven bellowed for silence. When both parties were again seated, he called the combatants into the room. "So that all may understand the victory conditions: These two men will fight until one or the other remains pinned at the shoulders for a count of five unless one of them should first cry mercy. Watley, Cyril, do either of you wish to concede victory to your opponent now?"

"Nay," the men chorused.

"Very well, then. Let the match begin."

Haven sat.

Edward leaned over to him. "Would you care to place a wager, Sir Haven?"

"Aye, but I cannot bet against my own squire."

"Too bad; as an Englishman, I can hardly bet on the Welsh."

"I am neither Welsh nor English, sire. If my husband will permit, I will bet on Cyril against Watley."

A cheer arose as Watley retreated before Cyril's first rush.

"Are you certain you wish to do this, wife?"

" 'Twill be easy money, Haven. Look how much larger Cyril is than Watley."

" 'Tis not always size that decides a contest, Gennie."

"I understand this."

Groans and cheers mixed together. Watley had ducked under the Welshman's longer reach. The heavy Welshman could not check in time and crashed through the scattering crowd into the wall.

"As you will, then."

Cyril shook himself and turned, rushing Watley, who once again retreated before the huge man.

"Sire, what terms do you offer?"

Edward's eyes gleamed. "Would a groat be too much, milady?"

"Seems a paltry sum to me."

"Ah, but what if a promise to be named in the future comes with the groat?"

Cyril had backed Watley to the opposite wall.

"A king's promise and a groat too. 'Tis a splendid wager. I agree. Haven, you will stand witness to the terms."

"Aye."

With a nod, Gennie joined in the shouting for Cyril to crush the squire. The king voiced equally loud encouragement to Watley. Indeed, had Watley been slower, Cyril would certainly have triumphed. But Haven had to smile when he saw Watley once again duck and Cyril once again dust the wall with his face.

The contest took some time, but that Cyril's size outmatched his brains soon became apparent. Time after time, Watley would lure the fellow to embrace the walls. The damage Cyril sustained from close and repeated impact with stone was greater than any that Watley could have delivered on his own.

Eventually, the Welshman defeated himself, crashing to the ground. Winded from the prolonged chase, Watley sat himself on Cyril's chest. Haven counted five and declared Watley the victor.

"Have you your groat ready, milady?" asked Edward.

"I can get it, sire."

"Do so. I would reward yon squire. Haven, call him forward."

Gennie went to the solar to get a groat from a pouch kept in one of the chests. While his wife left on that errand, Haven motioned Watley to come to the head table.

Watley climbed the dais, then knelt. "How may I be of service?"

"Rise, good Watley," said Edward.

Watley stood. "Sire?"

The king continued. "I would reward your victory with the sum of two groats wagered on the outcome of your contest. To that I add my hearty thanks for your courage. I also ask that you consider leaving Sir Haven's service for service in my household. If Sir Haven will free you from your oath to him."

Watley's mouth gaped.

Haven smiled.

The king laughed and lifted his cup from the table.

"But I am not yet a knight."

"That can be remedied," Haven said dryly.

Edward chuckled and slapped his arm around Watley's shoulders. "Here, lad, have a drink while you think it over."

Watley tipped the king's cup to his lips and drank deeply. He placed the empty cup on the table before him. " 'Tis little enough to think about, sire. As long as Haven is willing to let me go."

"I will not hold you back. In fact, had the king not suggested it, I would have petitioned him to give you a place in his household."

"You are all that is kind, sir."

"Nonsense. If you are determined to have Rebecca Dreyford, you must first earn lands. And there is no better opportunity for that than in service with our liege."

"Do . . . does this mean you approve our marriage?" Watley blinked and rubbed a hand across his eyes.

"I approve your betrothal as long as you gain lands and Rebecca spends the years until your marriage in a convent, learning humility and thoughtfulness."

The squire's face flushed. "With your permission, Sir Haven, sire, I shall go and tell her."

The king nodded.

"Get you gone, pup," Haven growled. He watched the young man stumble the length of the great hall.

"Love seems to have done what Cyril could not," Edward remarked.

"Aye," Haven agreed, watching his squire's unsteady gait.

Watley had just reached Rebecca's side when he doubled over.

"Watley?" Rebecca shrieked.

Haven leapt from the dais. Behind him Edward roared for silence.

Haven reached his stricken squire three strides before the king. "What's wrong?"

"Something tears at my belly," Watley gritted out. "And my sight dims."

Haven frowned and helped Watley to a bench. "Here, lad, lie down."

Watley moaned. "I am going to be sick."

Haven shifted the squire's head away from the watching crowd. Watley heaved, but nothing came up.

"Sir, where is your healer?" The king's voice came over Haven's shoulder.

"You there." Haven grabbed a nearby Welshman. "Find Gwyneth."

The man looked at him in puzzlement.

"Gwyneth. Gwyneth," Haven shouted. "Find Gwyneth."

"Aye, Gwyneth." The man nodded.

Gennie returned at that moment. "Haven, what has happened to . . . *Bon Dieu*, Watley."

"Owain, Soames, to me," Haven shouted again.

The men came at the run.

"Clear those people out of this room." He swept his arm toward the onlookers. "But keep them together within the bailey."

"Aye, sir."

The room emptied, and Watley continued to clutch his belly.

Soames and Owain returned.

The squire curled his body and moaned about stabbing pains in his stomach.

Before Gwyneth arrived he had begun to tremble. His face began to redden. Saliva dripped from his mouth, and he struggled to breathe.

When the old woman approached, Haven pulled Gennie aside, holding her by the arm.

Gwyneth examined Watley, muttering in Welsh. She paused, then nodded and continued babbling over the squire.

"Owain, what says she?" Haven ordered.

"Hot as hare. Blind as bat. Dry as bone. But not yet

red as beet. Nor mad as hen," the sergeant-at-arms translated.

"What witchery is this? Remove that crone." Edward's order nearly drowned the last of Owain's translation.

" 'Tis nightshade," Owain repeated Gwyneth's words in English.

The fearsome word whispered off the stones in the great hall.

"Nay," came Haven's protest. "By your leave, sire, this woman saved my life. Let her try to save my squire."

"Nightshade? How . . . ?" Haven heard Gennie choke on the words.

"Poison?" The king cut her off.

"How could that be?" Haven completed Gennie's thought. "He was fine during the wrestling."

"Bring a full bucket of vinegar and a ladle," Owain translated Gwyneth's orders.

"*Certainment*, Gwyneth." Gennie started to leave, but Haven held her in place.

"Soames, you go," Haven ordered.

"Aye, sir."

Haven's second-in-command returned with the requested bucket.

Gwyneth muttered and Owain interpreted. "Hold him down."

Soames and Haven bent to that task.

The king moved into place behind Gennie.

Gwyneth pinched Watley's nose. When the squire opened his mouth for breath, she poured a ladleful of vinegar into his mouth and let go of his nose. He was forced to swallow the vile stuff or suffocate.

Gwyneth repeated the procedure as soon as he swallowed the first dose. She stopped whenever Watley's stomach would rebel and cast up the vinegar it had just received. Then the pinching and ladling would begin again.

A second bucket of vinegar was brought. Gwyneth did not cease her treatment of Watley until his stomach no longer rejected the vinegar. Even then, she would force a portion down his throat if he started trembling or complained of stomach pains.

When he had gone for some time without showing symptoms of the poison, Gwyneth put down her ladle. She spoke to Soames. "She wants us to move him to his bed," said Owain.

"Soames," Haven spoke before the man did Gwyneth's bidding. "Send a few men back in, Lindel and Sutherland I think."

"Aye, Sir Haven."

Now that the crisis was past, Haven turned to the king, still standing behind Gennie. "I know what you must be thinking, sire."

"Do you?"

"Aye." Despairing, Haven looked at Gennie. "There must be another explanation."

Gennie's eyes widened. "Surely you cannot think . . ." She turned to Edward. "Sire, I assure you . . ."

But the look in Edward's eyes froze Gennie to silence. "What is it that you assure me of, Madame Dreyford?"

She didn't seem to notice the king's lapse of memory in using her widowed name. "Why, I could not, would not arrange to have Watley poisoned simply because I lost a groat to you, sire."

"A groat and a promise, remember, Madame Dreyford?"

Haven ground his teeth, knowing that Edward already condemned Gennie, and her protests did nothing to mitigate that condemnation.

"Well, *certainment.*" She twisted her hands together. "A groat and a promise. But what has that to say to anything? I would hardly poison my husband's squire over such a piece of folly. I wasn't even in the room."

"No, you would not harm Watley. I believe that, madame. But you might well seek to harm the king who executed your first husband."

Gennie's hand flew to her throat. *"Non."*

"Non, say you." Edward turned and snatched his cup from the table. "Then explain why Watley fell ill when he drank from my cup and not before. My cup, which came from the kitchens you supervise, Madame Viper."

Gennie looked from the cup to the fury in Edward's face and back. "I-I cannot."

The king put his face a palm's width from Gennie's. "Of course you cannot. To explain this, you would have to confess that you tried to murder the king of England."

"I did not."

Edward's lip curled, and he straightened to his full height. "A moment ago, madame, you lost a groat and a promise to me. I would claim that promise now."

"Oui, sire."

"Promise me that without regard to consequence you will always tell me the truth."

"Certainment, sire, but will you believe me?"

"Let us find out. Did you poison my cup?"

Gennie squared her shoulders. *"Non."*

Edward clenched his jaw and closed his eyes. "Haven, have you at Two Hills Keep a room that can be locked from the outside?"

Haven felt fear, solid and cold, in his belly. "No, my liege, but the solar has a stout door. A bar can be added, and I can place a guard."

Edward opened his eyes, holding Haven's gaze with

his. He spoke clearly, loud enough for all in the hall to hear. "Then take this lying viper from my sight, e'er I order her hanged on the spot."

"Sire, you cannot . . ." Haven objected.

"As you love me, Haven, obey me now."

"Aye, Sire."

Haven took hold of Gennie's arm. With rigid steps, he escorted her from the room.

"Haven, don't do this," she pleaded.

He refused to meet her gaze or give ear to her entreaties.

Behind them he heard Edward order, "Send for Michael. I would have my strongest knight guard my back from this evil."

The solar door shut behind Gennie. She sank onto the rug near the braiser. How could this happen? She had never in her life spoken a word of treason. Curse Roger and the long shadow of his traitor's death.

She no longer feared for Thomas. Haven would do all he could for the boy. Her husband was too good a man to cover a child with the mantel of suspicion that cloaked her.

But it was Haven's silence that hurt most. Could he believe her capable of such evil? Maybe when they had first met, but surely not now? Doubt wormed its way into her mind. If Haven did repudiate her, what would become of her and the child she carried?

Chapter Twenty-seven

Haven opened the solar door. His heart skipped when he saw the empty bed, then steadied as his gaze swept the room and found Gennie asleep on the rug. The tray of food he had sent up earlier lay untouched by her side. He closed the door and swept a hand across his face. It was nearly afternoon. He had not slept since leaving Gennie last night. He could not have done so had he tried.

He walked to where she lay and sat down beside her. He placed a gentle hand on her shoulder. "Gennie."

She started up. Sleep blinked from her eyes, replaced by hurt and accusation. "What do you here? Have you come to gloat, now that my treason is confirmed?"

"Nay." He reached to stroke her cheek.

Gennie jerked away, turning her back to him. "Do not touch me."

Concern twisted Haven's heart. She had every right to be bitter. So he fisted his hands in his lap. "Edward's accusation was unjust. Anyone could have poisoned the king's cup."

"Take greater care with your words, husband, lest you be tarred with the brush of my treason."

Losing patience, Haven grabbed her shoulders and twisted her about. Fear for her made him fierce. "Listen to me, Milady de Sessions. You have not committed treason. You are not capable of the act."

Gennie's mouth opened, then shut. Her face crumpled.

Haven found his arms filled with warm, weeping woman.

"Gennie, Gennie." He stroked her dark hair. "I convinced Edward to give me a day to discover who else could have done this. Since the king sent you here, I have talked to almost every person in the keep."

Gennie lifted her watery gaze to his. "Is Thomas safe?"

Haven looked at the woman he cherished. Of course she would think first of her son. "Aye, Thomas is safe, and I will keep him so. Just as I plan to keep you."

"Do you have hope?" she asked.

"Some. No one has been allowed to leave. The assassin has to be here, Gennie. But I need your help, if we are to find him. And we are running out of time. Half the given day is gone."

Genvieve swallowed. "What do you wish of me?"

"I want you to tell me everything that you did after the king arrived."

"I rose early . . ."

He watched his wife as she related the minutia of a day spent in preparing the best possible reception for a king she had good reason to fear. Haven's heart went out to her. He heard no trace of rancor. In Gennie's situation, others might have felt justified in hating Edward. Gennie voiced only concern for the comfort of her husband's liege and the rest of the people in the castle.

He laughed a bit when she described the battle between Goody and Rene in the kitchen. He frowned at her mention of the friars. But smiled briefly, when she told how the cook and the Englishwoman had united in the face of the friars' unwanted assistance.

She ceased speaking as she noticed his frown. "Something concerns you, Haven?"

"The friars. They have been at prayers in the chapel ever since Watley fell ill. I had not thought to talk with them."

"You cannot suspect a man of God?" Gennie uttered in a horrified whisper.

"Nay, I know not who to suspect. But the friars may have seen something that will help."

"Then you must go to them now."

"Nay, I wish you to finish first."

"Very well. After I left the kitchen, I sought you out with my request that you arrange an additional entertainment because the meal would be delayed, and I had other tasks to perform."

Haven nodded, remembering her harried expression.

Her concentration now was equally deep. "From you I went to our chamber. I ordered a bath, and while I waited, I prepared my gift for you. The bath . . ."

"Hold, Gennie." Haven picked up her hand. "You had a gift for me?"

She pressed her lips together and nodded. A becoming flush colored her cheeks.

"Where is this gift?"

"When the bath arrived, I set the gift aside by the bed."

He traced the lines on her palm, pleased at her shivered response. "Do you still wish to give it to me?" He studied her face as she answered.

"Oui," she replied. "You have the right."

Her words puzzled him, but she stood and went to the bed, so he waited.

She returned with a soft knitted coverlet rolled and tied with string. "Here." She thrust the bundle at him.

Haven took it, hesitating while she sat.

"What is this?"

"Cut the string. The gift is inside the coverlet."

Bowing his head, he did as she bid but was even more puzzled. Inside laid a tiny silver rattle of the type given to infants. Then knowledge burst upon him. He raised his eyes to hers. "Does this mean . . . are you . . . ?"

Gennie nodded, her eyes gleaming wetly.

Fatherhood! Watching Gennie grow round with his child. Holding the woman he loved as she suckled their babe. Then he remembered their circumstances. Would Gennie live to give birth?

His mouth thinned.

Gennie gripped his hand. "What will we do, Haven?"

"We will find that assassin and serve him to Edward for supper. Tell me the rest."

"Where was I?"

"Your bath."

"As I finished dressing, Therese knocked on my door with a message that Goody Brown urgently needed me. I returned to the kitchen, stopped Rene from beating a scullery lad for not properly cleaning the platters and cups for the evening meal. By the time I dried the lad's tears and soothed Rene's ruffled feathers, I had time for naught but to join you at table. You know everything from that point on."

"The scullery lad—did he handle all of the platters and cups?"

"I don't believe so. The king's steward brought the king's own dishes well before the disagreement between Goody and Rene. Rene set the things apart, so that he could put the best bits on the king's platter. I am sure the cup was with the platter."

"I talked to Rene and the rest of the kitchen staff. None of them saw anyone paying particular attention to Edward's dishes, but all claimed to be very busy and could easily have missed something."

"Wait; I recall seeing one of the friars near the king's plate. In fact, Goody Brown called it to my attention. I think she feared that the plate, which was silver, would stick to the friar's fingers."

" 'Tis now more important than ever that I talk with those friars. Gennie, is there anything else you can tell me?"

She colored. "Only that one of the friars was the same one who assigned to me the penance of the hair shirt."

"For that alone, I should hang him by his thumbs. Why did you ever listen to him?"

"He was used to visit Roger and hear our confessions, since we did not have a priest in residence."

"I must needs talk with this friar." Haven leaned over and kissed her. Then he left to seek out the friars.

His kiss lingered, and Gennie ran her fingers over her mouth. Whether Haven discovered the assassin or not, her life was full, simply knowing that he believed her innocent. She wished she could help him, but locked in this room she could do little except pray. So she knelt and did what she could.

*   *   *

Behind Gennie the door opened and shut. Before she finished her current petition to God, she heard the interior bar drop loudly into place. She spoke her amen and rose, shaking out her skirts. Her knees didn't ache, so she couldn't have been at her prayers for very long. Turning, she expected to see her husband; thus the black-robed friar who stood in front of the solar door surprised her.

"Who are you?"

Taking a step forward, the friar lowered his cowl. "Surely you know me, Lady Genvieve."

It was the blazing-eyed friar from Chester and Yorkshire. The one who had lead the others to assist in restoring the kitchen to order.

Gennie suppressed a gasp and backed away. "What are you doing here? I did not request a friar."

"Ah, child, I am here because of your great need."

"Nonsense."

"Then say your husband sent me."

Hungry for news, Gennie stepped forward. "Did he speak to you? Do you bring word? Do you have knowledge of the assassin?"

"Aye. I bring word of the assassin. But I have not spoken to Sir Haven."

"Then go immediately and tell him your news. If you tell me, none will believe you."

"Have faith, child. When I tell my tale, I will be believed." He took her hand and led her to a chair and footstool that sat by the braiser.

His hand felt dry and cold. Gennie cast a glance at the lengthening shadows in the room. "The day is almost over; you must hurry," she said.

"True, some speed is necessary, but first let us complete God's work. Sit."

Gennie was glad to let go of the friar's hand, so she sat.

"I interrupted your prayers. Will you forgive me for that, Lady Genvieve?"

"*Oui.* But why stay you here? You must tell my husband what you know."

"All in good time." The friar patted her hand. "All in good time."

"How long has it been since your last confession, child?"

Gennie sent him a puzzled look. "I do not recall. A se'ennight, perhaps. What has my confession to do with anything?"

"Confession is the first of the three steps needed for salvation. Without it, neither penance nor atonement is possible." The friar clasped his hands around hers. "Now do as you are bid and confess your sins to me."

Obviously to humor the friar was the only way to get him to leave and go to Haven. She bowed her head and made her confession. When she finished and asked forgiveness, the friar hesitated. She looked up at him and wondered at his expression. The word *beatific* leapt to mind.

With eyes alight and a soft voice, he asked, "Have you nothing else you wish to confess?"

"*Non.* Please, hurry to my husband with your news."

"But we are not yet finished, milady." A note of stress entered his voice.

"What more is there, pray?"

"You have not told me that you tried to murder the king."

"That is absurd. I did no such thing."

His hold on her hands tightened. "True, I am the one who failed to rid the world of the royal viper that would rob the pope by taxing the clergy."

Gennie tried to pull away. "Nay, you are ordained, and murder is a sin," she whispered, unwilling to believe what he told her.

"Not as great a sin as allowing Edward to continue his perfidy. If I am ever to succeed, he must believe that you poisoned his cup. Just as he believed Roger Dreyford guilty of treason."

Against his grip, Gennie struggled to her feet. "Then Roger was not guilty?" She prayed for Thomas's sake that the answer would clear his father.

"Roger Dreyford was eager for excitement. What greater adventure than to kill a king?"

"Non," Gennie moaned.

"Hush, child. It is time to do your penance." He loomed over her, let go her hands and grasped her throat beneath her chin, lifting her painfully to her toes.

"I know not what you mean." Gennie ground out the words, barely able to breath, let alone speak. "You are hurting me." She clawed at his wrist and fingers with both her hands. All to no avail; his grip remained firm.

"I have heard your confession, and I shall administer penance." His free hand fumbled in the folds of his robe. He drew out a vial.

"Non." Gennie kicked out at him, but only succeeded in tangling her feet in his robe. Still she twisted and managed to make him stagger. His grip loosened for a moment. She let out a gurgling scream and tried to breathe at the same time.

She tried once more to twist free. This time she toppled them both to the floor. Unfortunately the friar landed above her and was able to press a knee to her chest. Gennie felt her lungs slowly collapsing under the pressure. She lost strength in her arms and could only watch him kill her.

With his teeth, he pulled the cork from the vial. His free hand covered her nose. The words of extreme unction filled her ears. She tried to keep her mouth closed but couldn't. Either way, she would die.

Haven dragged his feet up the stairs to the solar. How could he tell Gennie that he had failed? The friars had told him nothing that he hadn't already heard. There was no one else to ask.

He had spoken to Edward, telling the king of Gennie's pregnancy. Edward had relented a bit. Gennie must still give her life for the attempt on his, but not until the child was born. Until then she would live cloistered in a convent of Edward's choosing. On the birth of her child she would give it to Haven's keeping and accept her execution. For the sake of an innocent soul Edward would tolerate the woman's evil that long and no longer.

Haven warned Edward that he did not know what he was doing and would one day regret his actions. But the king remained adamant, suggesting that Haven say his farewell to Lady Genvieve.

Halfway up the stair, Haven heard what sounded like a scream and a thump. A shout followed from Michael, who guarded the solar. " 'Ware. To me, to me."

Haven leapt up the remaining treads. Footsteps thundered behind him. He skidded to a stop beside Michael, where he stood beating on the solar door.

Haven pulled the man away. "What goes on here?"

" 'Tis your lady wife. I heard her yell for help. Then

came a crashing sound. I went to open the door, but 'tis barred from the inside."

"Is someone in there with her?"

"Aye, the friar you sent to hear her confession."

"I sent no friar."

At that moment, several more men arrived, with Edward in the vanguard. "What has happened?"

"My wife is in there with your assassin."

"Get axes," the king shouted. "And find that Welshwoman, Gwyneth."

More footsteps thundered. Haven, Edward and Michael slammed their shoulders against the stout oaken door. Three more times they rushed the barrier before Soames and Owain arrived, each with an axe.

The moments it took to chop the door to pieces lasted too long. Grabbing one of the axes, Haven went first through the door. At the sight of his wife crushed beneath the friar, Haven swung the axe and buried it in the man's skull.

The body dropped to the floor beside Gennie's still form. For a moment all was silent.

Someone slapped Haven's back. "Move, man. We may still save her."

Haven rushed forward. Edward and Michael lifted the friar away from Gennie. Haven pulled her to his chest. She was so pale. He bent his head to her breast. Could he hear a faint flutter?

Someone tried to move his hands away. "Nay!"

"Aye, sir, ye must let me see to her." Gwyneth's voice spoke soft in his ear as someone translated her Welsh.

"She's not dead. I will not let you take her from me." He tried to deny the collapse of his world.

"That she is not, sir. But she will be, if you do not let me see to her," the interpretation continued.

"Not dead?" He looked down at Gennie. The top of her dress bore a great damp spot and her face was wet with his tears.

"Aye, sir. But she is not breathing right, so you must let me tend her."

"Yes, of course. Please, Gwyneth?"

"Put her on the bed, and I shall do what I can."

Haven nodded. "So shall I." He turned to the prayer bench.

Epilogue

Summer 1283
Two Hills Keep, Wales

Edward Plantagenant, King of all England and Duke of Gascony, looked down at the tiny black-haired child. " 'Tis a fine godson you have given me, Lady Gennie."

" 'Tis a fine godfather you make for Haven de Sessions's first child."

"Aye, by my oath this child will never suffer want."

Gennie chuckled. "I appreciate your largesse, sire, but you will spoil him."

"That is my privilege as his king and godfather."

"And 'tis my privilege to tell you honestly that many Welsh children still suffer because of your obstinacy toward their parents."

"I have never regretted winning a wager more, Lady Genvieve, than when I won the bet that gave me your promise of constant truth."

"Aye, 'tis often that I am glad you did win."

Edward arched an eyebrow at her.

"How many other women dare speak their minds to the king of England?"

Edward tossed his head back and laughed.

"What is so funny?" With Thomas beside him, Haven de Sessions, Earl of Twynn, stepped into his son's nursery and took in the smiling faces of his wife and king.

"May I hold my brother, please?" Thomas reached for the babe without waiting.

"*Oui*, Thomas, you may carry him back to his cradle."

The boy smiled. "And then I may rock him?" Eagerness lit his face.

"Only if you do so gently," admonished Haven.

"I will, Sir Haven."

Gennie grinned, pleased with the life that had come to her first-born child. Under Haven's care the boy grew strong and honorable. She was very proud of them both.

"Now, what were you laughing at, my liege?" Haven queried again, refusing to be denied his chance to join the fun.

"Your wife dares to prick at my pride."

"She's been telling you the truth again, then," Haven said.

"Without gilt."

"Too bad, sire. The truth should always be gilded with honest loyalty."

Gennie chuckled.

Edward shrugged. " 'tis refreshing to hear your wife's truth after all the lies of court. Mayhap that is why I seek her out."

"And I thought you told me you wanted to apologize."

Haven's king frowned at him.

"You have been in here since near midday," Haven continued. " 'Tis now close on eventide, and you haven't managed the words yet?"

" 'Tis no easy thing for a king to admit he was mistaken in the character of a lone woman." Edward looked straight at Gennie. "But I was, and am, most sincerely sorry for it."

"That is most prettily said, sire, and I accept. However, I must admit, I have always wondered what I did that caused both you and my husband to suspect that I was the source of Roger's treason."

The king coughed, and Haven looked down at his own feet. " 'Twas nothing you did, Gennie," her husband confessed.

"What then?"

" 'Twas what Roger said to me on the scaffold the day he was hanged." Haven related the words his friend had uttered just before dying. How he did not trust Gennie, and that she knew the man who had convinced him to try to kill the king.

Stunned, Gennie sat on the nearest stool. "Roger did not trust me? Why?"

Haven knelt beside her. "Who can say, Gennie? He was a very different man at the end than the friend I knew."

"And you took his word, the word of a traitor, as true?"

"Gennie . . ."

Edward interrupted. "You must remember, milady, that we had known Roger Dreyford most of his life. Prior to his treason, he had been a most loyal and dutiful vassal. None of us knew you. Roger's was the only word we had."

When Edward fell silent, Haven continued. "That does not excuse our distrust, Gennie. All I can say is that I am most heartily sorry and regret the pain my belief in Roger's words has caused us all."

"As am I, Lady Genvieve," echoed the king.

Gennie sat in quiet thought for several moments. "I do understand, Haven." She stroked his cheek. "I trust you completely, as you do me." Then she looked to the king. "Sire, if you are truly sorry, you will demonstrate your sincerity and change your policy against allowing the Welsh to live near or in your castles. Not just here in Two Hills Keep, but throughout Wales

Haven beamed at her.

Edward glanced at Haven. "She is relentless. How do you tolerate it?"

Haven returned his king's glance with all innocence. "Sire, I am her most true and perfect knight. 'Tis she who must tolerate me."

The king laughed and slapped Haven on the shoulder. "Let us go and get that supper you spoke of. Admiring my godson inspires an appetite."

Gennie smiled after them. "I will be down soon, husband."

"As you will, wife. I know I am no longer first in your affections."

That night, as Haven lay with his arms wrapped about Gennie, her voice came at him in the darkness.

"You are first in my heart."

His heart sang so loudly, it filled his throat to closing. He swallowed around the lump of joy that had settled there. "I know, Gennie. I but teased you earlier. Although truly, I do sometimes envy the amount of time our son gets of you."

314

"I may know a way to soothe the beast of envy from you."

"Indeed?" He grinned, though he knew she could not see it. He felt certain that she shared his happiness as thorough as he shared hers.

Her hands stroked down his chest to his hips.

"Indeed, yes. Allow me to show you."

"As you will wife."

TO THE READER

As is the case with many novels that have their basis in history, this book contains some historical inaccuracies. Some are so significant that I feel I must mention them here. First, the dispute Edward I had with the Pope over taxation of the clergy is historical fact. However, Edward did not enact any laws on this policy until 1294, roughly twelve years after the time of Haven and Gennie's story.

Second, unwilling to fight a third Welsh war, Edward issued the repressive Statute of Rhuddlan in 1284. This statute created a series of new earldoms in the western portion of Wales (that portion not already governed by the Marcher lords). The statute modified Welsh law, bringing it closer in line with English legal code. Most important to Haven and Gennie's story, The Statute of Rhuddlan established the existence of specifically English boroughs in and around Welsh castles and forbade the Welsh people to "inhabit such boroughs or to carry arms within their walls" ("A Brief History of Wales," www.britannia.com). Once more, I have altered the sequence of history in hope of heightened narrative interest. The Statute of Rhuddlan's principles, while not yet general law in 1282, provided significant conflict between Gennie and Haven, just as Edward's taxation of the clergy provided motive for his assassination. As for that assassination attempt, it is a complete fiction. There is no historical record of any such attempt on Edward's life by any member of the clergy.

At this point, I feel it is important to mention that only three characters referred to in this book—Edward I, his secretary Bek, and his master builder St. George (whom we never truly meet)—have any basis in historical fact. I take full responsibility for any inaccuracies in my representation of their characters as I do for all the events, actions and settings herein.

I hope you have enjoyed Haven and Gennie's tale. If you would like to send me your comments, please sign my guest book at www.wordreams.org or write to me care of Dorchester Publishing.

Lynsay Sands

Bliss

If King Henry receives one more letter from either of two feuding nobles, he'll go mad. Lady Tiernay is a beauty, but whoever marries the nag will truly get a mixed blessing. And Lord Holden—can all the rumors regarding his cold heart be lies? The man certainly has sobered since the death of his first wife. If he were smart, Henry would force the two to wed, make them fatigue each other with their schemes and complaints. Yes, it is only fitting for them to share the bed they'd made—'til death do them part! Perhaps they will even find each other suitable; perhaps Lord Holden will find in his bride the sweet breath of new life. Heaven alone knows what will happen when the two foes are the last things between themselves and the passion they've never known they wanted.

___4909-0 $5.99 US/$6.99 CAN

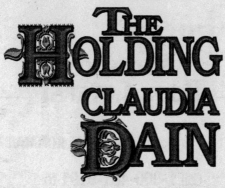

THE HOLDING

CLAUDIA DAIN

It is done. She is his wife. Wife of a knight so silent and stealthy, they call him "The Fog." Everything Lady Cathryn of Greneforde owns—castle, lands and people—is now safe in his hands. But there is one barrier yet to be breached. . . . There is a secret at Greneforde Castle, a secret embodied in its seemingly obedient mistress and silent servants. Betrayal, William fears, awaits him on his wedding night. But he has vowed to take possession of the holding his king has granted him. To do so he must know his wife completely, take her in the most elemental and intimate holding of all.

__4858-2 $5.50 US/$6.50 CAN